CU00926031

THE DARK SIDE
Doug Hornig

M
MACMILLAN
LONDON

First published in the United States of America

First published in the U.K. 1987 by
MACMILLAN LONDON LIMITED
4 Little Essex Street, London WC2R 3LF
and Basingstoke

Associated companies in Auckland, Delhi, Dublin, Gaborone,
Hamburg, Harare, Hong Kong, Johannesburg, Kuala Lumpur,
Lagos, Manzini, Melbourne, Mexico City, Nairobi, New York,
Singapore and Tokyo

ISBN: 0-333-44557-0

Typeset by Text Generation Ltd, London
Printed and bound in the U.K. by
Anchor Brendon Ltd, Essex

This one, of course,
is for Nancy.

Acknowledgements

My thanks to Chris Mendosa, for help with the technical aspects of this book, and to Pam Mendosa, for some timely suggestions.

1

She lay as if asleep, but it was the sleep most close to death.

For a month, Patricia Ryan had been in a coma. I kept asking for a prognosis and I kept getting the same reply: a shrug of the shoulders. Who could say in these matters? She'd received a terrible blow to the back of the head. It had fractured her skull and caused a fairly severe concussion.

Not a small amount of damage, and yet . . .

Brain surgery had not been necessary. The skull had knit itself back together. The effects of the concussion, as far as tests could determine, had steadily diminished. And still she slept.

Patricia's attending physician was Dr Pastreich, an intense young man with dark hair and a bristly moustache. Unlike a lot of the doctors of my experience, he was open and seemed genuinely to want to help. He couldn't help me.

'Mr Swift,' he'd told me, 'coma is one of the things we least understand. I'm sorry to have to tell you that, but it's so. A person can enter coma for any of a number of reasons, including the kind of physical trauma Patricia has suffered. We assume that in such a case the body is trying to repair itself. How long the coma continues is unpredictable.'

'But Patricia,' I said, 'she's healed, isn't she?'

'We think so. However, there may be damage that we are unable to measure.'

'And there's no way of telling . . . how long.'

'I'm afraid not. She could wake up tomorrow, or it could be . . .' He shrugged. It was a gesture I was learning to hate.

'There's nothing you can do to bring her around?'

'There's nothing we *will* do. Any action would involve unacceptable risks.'

'So we wait,' I said.

'Yes, we wait. As I've told you, I think there's an excellent chance that Patricia will come out of it before long, and with no permanent after-effects. She's a very strong woman. Her body has responded well to the injury. Better than we could have hoped for.'

I knew she was strong. In a few short months she'd managed to change my point of view about a lot of things. That'd been no easy task. She'd been dealing with someone who'd had a lot of years alone in which to set his ways.

'When she does wake up,' I said, 'what'll she be like?'

'No one can be certain,' Pastreich said. 'Most likely she'll know you, if that's what you're worried about. In general, what's lost tends to be the circumstances surrounding the injury. She may never be able to recall the day it happened. That can be for the best, of course. But there are other possibilities, and you should be prepared for them. They include everything up to and including total amnesia.'

'I think I'd even prefer that to her just lying there.'

'We all would. Then, too, there will be her physical condition. She'll be weak no matter what. Her muscles will be suffering from disuse. These are not major problems, but they will require your attention.'

'I'll be there.'

'Yes, I believe you will. I think that you care for her very much.'

'I care for her very much.'

'It's going to be hard on you. What you'll need the most of is patience.'

From most other people I would have considered it a very smug thing to say. It would have caused me to generate fantasies about rearranging the speaker's face. But from him, no.

'What else can I do?' I asked.

'Keep spending time with her,' he said. 'Talk to her. It used to be thought that those in coma were totally oblivious to the outside world. That point of view is outmoded. We now have good reason to believe that such persons are aware of a lot that's going on around them, at least at some level. I personally feel that familiar voices can be quite therapeutic.'

I'd followed his advice. I talked to her. I told her stories. I brought her friends by. I even put some of her favourite music on cassettes and played them for her.

Now, sitting by her bedside, I wondered if any of it had done the slightest bit of good. She lay inert, her auburn hair fanned out lifeless on the pillow, the clear green eyes still locked shut.

I'd been there for an hour.

'Patricia,' I said, stroking her hand, 'Patricia, I'm here.'

2

I'd run out of stories. It was time to go.

'I'll be back tomorrow,' I said.

She didn't reply.

I left the University of Virginia Medical Center. It was a warm fall day, the kind that central Virginia is good at. A day to remind you that, yes, winter was on the way but, no, it wasn't going to be as miserable as it'd be in Minneapolis or Buffalo.

I walked the streets of Charlottesville for a while. Among other things, I needed the exercise. I wasn't in the best of shape myself. The same man who had caved in Patricia's skull had left me with a broken wrist, and I was still in a semiflexible cast to my elbow. On top of that, one of his cronies had put a bullet through my thigh. I still walked with a slight limp.

Occupational hazards. I'd long since accepted that there are dangers in the private investigator trade. For the most part, though, they're overblown. Especially in a small town like Charlottesville. The night I'd been shot was the first time I'd been in serious personal jeopardy since I left Boston six years earlier. In addition, though I'd been involved with murders, I'd never had to kill.

All that had changed in a hurry. One of my cases had involved me with some characters who would have been hard even in Southie. In the end, I'd had to shoot one of them. If I hadn't, neither Patricia nor I would still be alive.

A month later I was troubled.

It had been a clear-cut case of self-defence. And the man I was firing at would have been judged unfit to live by most sane people. Yet killing is never simple.

In the early seventies I'd done a tour in Nam. It was entirely possible that I'd killed other men while I was over there. I couldn't be sure, because I'd never had to engage in hand-to-hand combat. But I'd shot at the enemy. It was likely that I'd occasionally hit what I was shooting at. Of the ones I hit, some probably died.

I carried memories of the war. From time to time I woke in the night with my heart pounding and the sweat pouring off me. But war is essentially impersonal. I barely spoke a word of the language of the men designated as my enemies. They'd been men with names and homes and families, but I couldn't have known those details. When my tour was over, I came home and tried to put the experience behind me. Most of the vets I knew had done the same.

3

I couldn't feel guilty about having been involved in something so far beyond my control.

Now, however, I'd killed someone I knew. Up close. When I shot him, the stench of his breath was in my nostrils, and his blood was on my face.

Don't let anyone tell you that it doesn't affect you. It does, no matter the circumstances. You go out and you walk the streets, and nearly all of the people you see have never taken life. It sets you apart.

I thought about that, but eventually my thoughts returned to Patricia. They always did. She was in that coma through no fault of her own. She had merely been in the way when the man had come around to kill me. He'd treated her like an insect. One small flick of his huge wrist was all it took. She went to sleep and no one could wake her.

It was my fault. I made my way in the world, doing the job that I did, and Patricia wound up taking the fall. For the past month I had felt guilt alternating with an icy, impersonal rage at the way things happened. If I'd been a believer in the traditional God, I would have tried to spit in His uncaring face.

I walked along The Corner, a stretch of University Avenue where students hang out. They looked young. I used to think that, somehow, they got younger every year. Then someone pointed out that living in a college town was like being the flip side of Dorian Gray. Every year some of the kids' faces would change, but their ages would always remain the same. Only those of us on the outside would get older.

It gave me the creeps, which is why I normally avoid The Corner. I was there this time because it's near the hospital. I glanced across the street, at the grounds of the University of Virginia. It's a pretty campus, with carefully tended lawns and the serpentine brick walls of Thomas Jefferson. In the near distance I could see the heavy dome of the Rotunda, another of Tom's designs. I thought briefly of the single semester of my youth that I'd spent at this school. Things would have been very different if I'd taken to the academic life instead of having gone on a four-month drinking binge. I might have money in the bank. I might not have one failed marriage behind me. My womanfriend would have escaped her cracked head. But I've never been that good at playing What If.

I turned down a side street and retrieved my car, which was

4

illegally parked with my Universal Life Church clergy credentials propped behind the windshield. I'm the proud owner of an orange VW, from 1972, the last year Volkswagen made the classic People's Car. I've had it since it was new and there were two incomes in my family. The sills are beginning to rust through, but otherwise it's in pretty good shape. Going uphill on a slick surface, it moves with the ease of a water bug, outperforming nearly everything on the road. Front-wheel drive may be all the rage now, but I prefer what I have. I drove home, which is in the Belmont section on the east side of town. Belmont isn't one of your more fancy addresses. Not long ago it was one of the city's high-crime neighbourhoods, and most people continue to think of it that way. This has kept rents down, which suits my pocketbook. And the area suits my style. It's a solid, working-class place, less pretentious than sections of the city closer to the university.

My apartment is in a pre-World War II frame house that's built into the side of one of Belmont's many hills. I'm around back, in the basement, sheltered from the winter winds and the tropical sun of summertime.

My landlady, Mrs Detweiler, lives upstairs. She is a world-class human being. Over eighty now, she's still a fire-eating socialist. A battle-scarred veteran of the labour wars of the thirties. She's one of the last of the breed, and she takes no crap from anyone. The previous month, Mrs D's quick thinking had saved Patricia's life, and maybe mine as well. I owed her.

It was three in the afternoon when I let myself into the apartment. I checked for any signs of unauthorized entry. Not that I was expecting any, but it's part of my routine when I've been away from home.

I'd apparently had no visitors.

I unlocked the desk drawer. My Walther automatic was in its proper place. I looked behind the couch. The loaded .38 Colt Police Positive revolver was taped to the wall, as it ought to be. I'd kept it there for four years, against the possibility of an armed burglar. The night Patricia had been injured, I'd used it. If it hadn't been there, someone else would be breathing my air.

My apartment was secure. I glanced at my watch again. Two minutes after three. That hadn't taken long. I decided it wasn't too early to pay a visit to my friend John Jameson of Bow Street, Dublin. The seal on a fresh bottle of his fine Irish cracked under my thumbnail like the shell of a beetle. I got a tumblerful of ice and

5

poured the whiskey. It went from cool on the outside to warm on the inside.

Of late, I'd been visiting Mr Jameson a lot. He helped ease the pain in my wrist and leg. More important, he helped me hide from the demons in my head.

I did realize that before long I'd have to go back to work on a regular basis. There had been no lack of jobs offered. My previous case had generated a good deal of favourable publicity. My services were in demand, an unusual state of affairs. I took the ones I could manage despite my physical condition. The easy stuff. Other days, and most nights, I spent with Ireland's bane. Time passed as gently as it could. But in the end it is simply not possible to drink for a living. If it were, I'd have done it. Willingly. Lacking that, I would have to take up something like detecting.

The first glass of whiskey had nearly disappeared when I remembered that I hadn't yet called my answering service. I use the service in lieu of the office I can't afford. It sounds better than a machine, and so far the arrangement has worked out fine. I normally get in touch first thing in the morning. Recently it had become a secondary priority.

I called.

The lady who takes my messages answered. On my better days we sometimes exchange playfully lewd suggestions. It had been a while since I'd had one of my better days. She knew it.

She ticked off a couple of mundane requests, then said, 'The last one might interest you.'

'Sure,' I said. 'Try me.'

'It came in around noon. A Mr Pethco.'

'Pethco?'

'Right. Devin Pethco. I made him spell it.' And she spelled it for me. It spelled like it sounded. I picked my little spiral notebook off the phone table and wrote it down.

'And he wants?' I asked.

'Wouldn't tell. He left a phone number and wants you to know it would be very worthwhile for you to call him.' She gave me the number and I recorded it. The number was the same area code as mine, but I didn't recognize the exchange. It wasn't local.

'He emphasized the *very*,' she said.

'Oh yeah? Where's this guy from?'

'Richmond, he said.'

'Thanks,' I said. 'That it?'

'That's it.'

I hung up and tried to think of who I knew in Richmond. Nobody. So what? Clients are always nobodies before they become clients. My brain was not working smoothly.

I dialled the number.

A female voice at the other end said, 'Fail-Safe.'

Fail-Safe? What in hell was this? I'd already had my bout with the military. I hadn't managed to break private the first time.

'This is Loren Swift,' I said. 'I've got a message to call a' — I glanced at the notebook — 'a Devin Pethco. Who is this, please?'

'My name is Barbara.'

'No, I mean, who do you represent? Is this the Air Force?'

Barbara laughed.

'Oh, no, Mr Swift,' she said. 'We're Fail-Safe Detection Systems, Inc. Just a moment and I'll connect you with Mr Pethco.'

She put me on hold. Tinny Muzak played into my ear. It was a good minute before Pethco came on the line.

'Mr Swift,' he said.

'One of them,' I said.

'The detective?'

'That one.'

'Good. I'm Devin Pethco, vice-president of Fail-Safe Detection Systems, Incorporated. To come right to the point, we would like to consider employing you.'

'How so?'

'I'd prefer not to discuss details over the phone. Could you come to my office?'

'I don't know,' I said. 'Where are you?'

He gave me an address on Broad Street in downtown Richmond.

'That's a long drive,' I said. Richmond was eighty-five miles away.

'We realize that,' Pethco said, 'and we are prepared to pay you for your time. Would five hundred dollars be adequate? Irrespective of your taking the job, of course.'

Five hundred to me is a lot. It's what I charge for two and a half days' work, and I often have to cross my fingers when I ask for it.

'Can you tell me anything more?' I said.

'I'm afraid not. Should we get someone else?'

'No. The money is, ah, suitable.'

7

'Good. Tomorrow, then?'

'Okay. Give me some time to get there, let's say ten in the morning.'

'That will be fine. We'll be expecting you, Mr Swift.'

He rang off without a goodbye. Vice-presidential types do that a lot. Maybe it's just me that it gets done to a lot.

Well, what the hell. Five hundred would more than pay my way to Richmond and back. I settled into the couch and got re-acquainted with Mr Jameson.

2

The following morning I drove to Richmond, tobacco capital of Virginia. The city always reminds me of my former cigarette habit. Every billboard, it seems, advertises one brand or another. I'm no longer tempted, though for years I was a two-pack-a-day man. Now even secondhand smoke can make me dizzy.

I located the office building without any trouble, consulted the directory in the lobby, and rode the elevator up to the sixth floor. It was the top floor, and the Southeastern Regional Headquarters of Fail-Safe Systems had the whole thing.

The elevator opened directly on to the reception area. The receptionist's name was Barbara, which I should have remembered and didn't. I crossed a dozen yards of deep wine-red carpeting and presented myself.

Barbara was one of those happy-face people. She couldn't do anything without showing a lot of teeth. They make me nervous, those people, and I was relieved when she got right to her job. She picked up the phone, punched a button, had a brief conversation, and hung up.

'Mr Pethco will be with you shortly,' she said. 'Just make yourself comfy. Would you like some coffee?' She made it sound like one of the earth's primal pleasures.

Actually, I wouldn't have minded some, but I didn't want to risk Barbara getting chatty, so I passed.

I selected the waiting chair farthest from her desk. It was leather, like the rest of them. The chairs were grouped around a marble-topped coffee table. I tried discreetly to lift a corner of the top. Nope. Real marble.

There were a number of magazines on the table. I tried a *Time*. It was as boring and uninformative as the last one I'd seen. Even though Time's articles now carry bylines, I suspect that they're all secretly written by machine. When not working, the machine drives a Volvo and sips cream liqueurs in a fern bar.

I put *Time* down and picked up a *Sports Illustrated*. It had a feature on the upcoming college basketball season. More my style. The article asked whether the premier conference in the country was going to be the ACC or the Big East. In recent years the two have traded supremacy back and forth. None of the other leagues in the country have been in the running. Not even close. In fact, things are so out of balance, it's been alleged that no one is even playing the game west of the Mississippi. Whatever, *SI* gave a slight edge to the Big East. Fightin' words to an ACC fan like myself, but probably true.

It had taken me twenty minutes of slow reading to get through the piece. I hadn't minded. At something like eight bucks a minute I could wait. I was just finishing up when Barbara's phone buzzed. The big man was ready for me.

Barbara led me through a door and down a long hall with offices on either side of it. The hall terminated at the office of Devin Pethco, Veep. It was a corner office, naturally. Barbara showed me in, then excused herself.

The office was a contrast to the reception area. The latter had been done in dark-stained wood, wine-red carpet, and brown leather. Pethco's digs were black and white and chromed steel. The modern, high-tech look, I guess it is. Such rooms give me a headache. I don't understand how otherwise levelheaded human beings can inhabit them for long stretches without turning into silicon chips.

Pethco came around his steel-and-plastic desk to shake hands.

He was an inch or two shorter than my five-ten, and wiry. Looked to be in excellent shape. Late twenties, young for a veep. His grip carried the suggestion of substantial reserve strength. Nautilus, I figured. Handball three times a week. Maybe some swimming. He'd take me three falls out of every three.

His dress was conservative. Gray three-piece suit, striped tie. Wing tips. Only with his hair did he betray his youth. It was light brown and long. Expensively razor-cut, yes, but down over his ears

9

and collar nevertheless. He was clean-shaven. You don't want to try too many things at once.

'Mr Swift,' he said. 'Thank you for coming.'

'You can call me Swift,' I said. 'People do.'

'Fine. And I'm Devin.' He had blue eyes that seemed perpetually amused. Probably at the fact that damned few of his peers had come so far so fast.

'Please,' he said, gesturing at a chrome-and-black-vinyl number that looked like a glorified captain's chair. I sat in it. It smelled like a pharmacy and was about as friendly.

Pethco's own chair looked as if it had been lifted whole from the cockpit of a space shuttle. It even had dials and switches on one of the arms. I'd seen chairs like it in catalogues from high-tech mail-order houses. The contraptions have vibrators and heating units inside. Also miniature hi-fi systems with speakers located in the upper part of the chair's wings, on a level with your ears. I don't know if the things mix drinks, but they might.

My host seemed quite comfortable. He opened one of the desk's concealed drawers, I couldn't see how. He took out a little rectangle of yellow paper and pushed it across to me. It was a cheque drawn on Virginia's biggest bank. Five big ones, made out to yours truly.

'Now how do I earn it?' I asked.

'You already have.'

'Oh. Well, in that case . . . '

He chuckled.

'Don't leave yet, Swift,' he said. 'It gets more interesting.' He raised a single eyebrow.

I wriggled around until I was as settled as I could get.

'Okay,' I said, 'I'll bite. Why me?'

'That's easy,' he said. 'You've been much in the news of late.' He gestured at my encased arm. 'You got a lot of play in the Richmond papers. We checked you out, anyway, of course. The Albemarle County Sheriff gave you a particularly good recommendation.' Sheriff Ridley Campbell. Yeah, he would. I'd iced his re-election bid for him, among other things.

'The Charlottesville City Police,' he went on, 'were less enthusiastic. You seem to have stepped on some toes there. But they grudgingly admitted that you are an honest man, at least by the measure of your trade, and that you are competent at what you do.'

'Gee, thanks, guys.'

'No matter.' He waved his hand gently. 'Your background was

thoroughly researched. You're the man we want. Let it go at that.'

'And what colour are my undies?'

'Ah, yes, we were told about the misplaced sense of humour. Look, I like you, Swift. But I'm afraid we don't have unlimited time for you. To business?'

'Okay,' I said. 'How about telling me who the "we" is that wants me?'

'Good start. "We" are Fail-Safe Detection Systems, as you already know. What we do is manufacture hazard-detection and alarm devices. A smoke detector is a simple example. Detectors such as we make are extremely sophisticated these days, and they are becoming increasingly important as the dangers in our homes and workplaces continue to multiply. We think of ourselves as providing a very necessary service to the public.

'Fail-Safe is one of the industry leaders in this field. That's not my opinion. I could show you the figures to back it, but I won't bother. We're the best, Swift. In three years we won't even have a close competitor, believe it.'

'I don't think you need me, then.'

Pethco was looking at me intently, as if I were under analysis. It's a look I associate with cops, headshrinkers, prosecuting attorneys, and psychopaths. It didn't bother me. I long ago learned to be unreadable. In my business you have to, or you get eaten alive. I'd have made a terrific poker player if I could've mastered the principles of probability.

'You wouldn't think we would,' he agreed. 'But strange things sometimes happen in the business world.' He said it like it should be news to me.

'I'm not surprised,' I said.

He nodded.

'We find ourselves in an . . . awkward situation at the moment.'

'All right, fill me in.' I was a little intrigued about what constituted awkward to someone like the youthful veep.

'Of course. But you do understand one thing. Whatever I say from now on is strictly confidential. The five hundred buys that. I've been assured that you are reliable in this way.'

'I am. If I wasn't, five hundred wouldn't buy it.'

'Right. Good. Now, the first thing you need to know is that we have a corporate affiliation.' He named one of the largest corporations in the country.

'You've heard of them, I trust?' He chuckled.

'Once or twice.'

'They're the parent. Without their backing we couldn't possibly have gotten where we are. No new company could have; we'd have been just another bunch of guys named Joe with a pretty good idea. That's one of the realities we all accept. Of course, such a relationship with the parent entails certain *responsibilities* on our part.'

'They want their money back, and then some,' I suggested.

'I suppose you could put it that way. In truth, they're equally concerned with our position in the marketplace. They want us to be numero uno. They want us to kick the competition's ass.'

He smiled in a comradely way. Yup, he could still talk with the common folk. I began to see the sweat inside the suit and to understand it. He'd hocked himself to Big Money, and something had gone wrong. He wanted badly to fix it. That was the chance you took when you played with the big boys. If you succeeded, they could take you for the longest, sweetest ride there was. But if you screwed up, they'd crush you just like they were the Mafia. Not as crudely, maybe, but just as effectively. It was a skinny line to be walking on.

Pethco no longer seemed the polished young exec. He looked more like a kid who was trying to keep from wetting his pants.

'Which is exactly what you *are* doing, isn't it?' I said.

'Yes,' he said. 'But something has come up which, ah, threatens our position.'

'Do go on.'

'All right.' He sighed. 'This is the problem.' He opened another one of those mysterious concealed drawers. To my eye, he could pass for Doug Henning. Out of the drawer he pulled a small black box, about the size of a desktop dictionary. He laid it in front of me. It was featureless except for a yellow button in the lower right-hand corner and a louvered grille in the centre. A standard electrical cord ran out the back of it. The cord terminated with an equally standard plug. I pushed the yellow button. Nothing happened.

'The Doomsday Machine,' I said. 'Peter Sellers as Strangelove. I'd recognize it anywhere.'

'It's a carbon monoxide monitor,' he said.

'My mistake. They look much alike. You make these things, I presume.'

He nodded.

'It's a good product,' he said. 'Essential anywhere there's the danger of CO poisoning.'

'I sense the punchline coming.'

'Patience, Swift.' That seemed to be the key word in my life these days. 'We have a lot of ground to cover.

'Now, you'll want to understand what this thing does. Simple. It monitors the level of carbon monoxide in the air around it. It's very accurate. When it detects a rise in the CO concentration, no matter how small, the alarm goes off. You have to remember that where CO is concerned: a little is too much. It's just that dangerous. Colourless, odourless. If you're careless, it'll kill you before you can react to it. But a man in your profession would know that. So, this device alerts you way before the toxic level is reached.'

He picked up the box and plugged it into an outlet. He pushed the yellow button. A shrill alarm sounded, loud enough to be heard on Broad Street, six floors below.

'Enough,' I said.

He released the button.

'The button tests the device,' he said. 'We recommend the user do that at least daily. He may also put batteries inside, to serve as a backup in case of power failure. And there are electrical connections so that the detector can automatically turn on exhaust fans or whatever. It's a very fine piece of equipment.'

'But?'

'Ah, yes, but. Swift, have you ever heard of Babel?'

'Famous tower. Fell down, as I recall.'

'There's a modern one. It's located in Nelson County, about thirty miles outside of Charlottesville.'

'Can't say as I have,' I said.

'I'm not surprised. They keep a pretty low profile out there. What it is, is some kind of hippie commune. An "alternative community", they call it.' I expected him to wrinkle his nose, but he didn't quite.

'They probably have to keep out of sight,' he went on. 'Rural Virginia can be pretty conservative. In any case, they bought one of our CO monitors. They needed it because they're running a gasification generator.'

'Say what?'

'You don't need the details right now. Basically it burns wood or any kind of garbage and makes electricity. It produces large amounts of carbon monoxide in the process. Hence the monitor.

'Last February, a guy was working near the generator. They found him dead of CO poisoning. The alarm didn't go off until it was too late. It failed.'

13

'Why?'

He shrugged.

'I had the thing brought in,' he said. 'We tested it and retested it and then tested it again. It was in *perfect* working order.'

'The cops look into it?'

'Of course. But what was there to find? In the absence of any evidence to the contrary, it was ruled an unfortunate accidental death. Case of a decent alarm system not working quite right.'

'But you don't believe it.'

'Not for a minute,' he said. 'The alarm went off. It was wailing when they found the body.'

'A slight problem with the sensors?' I suggested.

'No way. Its sensitivity was exact.'

'You can't be sure. There may have been something about *those* particular conditions. Something that threw it off just enough so that it was late picking up the gas. That one time.'

'Swift, I am not prepared to argue with you. I *believe* in this product. I will *not* be made a scapegoat.'

It was all suddenly very clear.

'I get it,' I said. 'Now you're being sued.'

'The detective,' he said.

'It wasn't hard. Who?'

'The dead guy's wife.'

'How much?'

He looked at me, weighed things up, made his decision. I had no clue as to whether he was telling the truth.

'Twenty million,' he said.

'Whew,' I said.

'A lot, but what's a life worth?'

'A body's a buck ninety-eight worth of chemicals, or something like that. Otherwise, no one's ever been able to say. You think she'll win?'

'It's a moot point. The suit will never go to trial. The parent is willing to settle out of court for five cents on the dollar. She'll grab it.'

'That's still a mil.'

'Small change to the parent,' he said. 'Annoying, but they'll pay it. What they can't afford is all the adverse publicity a trial would generate. They *want* this market. If you think they're going to jeopardize that for a crummy million, then you don't know what kind of potential we have.'

'I see. But *you* don't want to give in.'

'Swift, I don't blame the woman. I'd do the same myself. I'd even pay her gladly. Except . . . except, that damned alarm did *not* fail.'

That he was sure of. The glistening blue eyes were those of a true believer.

'I think this is where I come in,' I said.

'Yes.'

'You want me to prove negligence on their part.'

'If you can. Or . . . whatever.'

'What do you mean by that?' I said cautiously.

'I mean that there aren't but so many possibilities. Either the detector failed because it was faulty, which I don't believe, or it failed because of negligence on their part, or it was . . . deliberately disabled.'

'I see. You have any reason for suspecting the third?'

'I'm a thorough man, Swift. I'm trying to be thorough here. I don't think we should discount anything.'

'No, probably not.' I paused. 'You realize that February was a long time ago.'

He nodded. 'I realize that. But now is when she chose to file suit. There may be nothing that can be done. Still, I want to try. The parent has given me a month before they move to settle out of court.'

And before they move to ease you out of your cushy job, I thought.

'Will you try?' he asked. I would have said *pleaded*, but that would've been unkind.

I thought about the bills Patricia Ryan was running up. I knew what kind of insurance she had. There was a real possibility it wasn't going to be enough.

'Devin,' I said, 'I'm gonna be honest with you. I've got about one small chance in hell of bailing you out of this. So I'll give you a week of my best effort. If I don't make it, I'll cash this cheque and that'll be it. But if I succeed, if I get her to drop the suit, I want ten percent of what you would've settled for.'

He paused, scrutinized my face. I didn't give away anything.

Then he said, 'Five.'

Fifty grand. I could live with it.

'Done,' I said. 'Put it in writing.'

He called someone on the phone and gave instructions for the contract.

'Now,' he said, 'you'll need to get into the community. They

15

take visitors there, charge them a small room-and-board fee. It's mostly for people who are thinking of joining but want to check the place out first. We'll arrange for them to put you up.'

'What about a cover story?' I asked.

'I don't know. What do you think?'

'Probably best just to be more or less what I am. A hired insurance investigator. They ought to be expecting one. If they're hiding anything, it might frighten someone a little. Plus I'd likely be recognized, anyway, if they get the Charlottesville paper.'

'Fine. If there's any resistance to your coming, I'll call you. I don't anticipate a problem.'

'There is one other thing. Why me? Doesn't the parent have people of their own?'

'That's two other things,' he said. 'First of all, we wanted someone local. In that area you're it. And second, we *are* sending in one of our own people.'

'Wait a minute. I work alone.'

He shook his head.

'Not this time.'

We looked at each other. He wasn't going to budge. I thought of the possible fifty thou.

'Not this time,' I said.

'Good,' he said. 'I want you to meet her.'

He used the phone and ordered my partner the same way he'd ordered my contract. He was good with phones. Then we waited. In a couple of minutes Barbara came in. She brought the contract and laid it on the high-tech desk; they must have had it ready, waiting for the amount to be filled in. She also brought a young woman.

'Loren Swift,' Pethco said, 'Sally Hatch.'

Sally Hatch was, in a word, cute. She was in her mid-twenties, nearly a decade younger than myself, and had dark blue, almost violet eyes. Her blonde hair was in a currently popular style that I don't know what to call. It features a lot of long, loose curls that lie on the head every whichaway. The hair always looks slightly damp, as if its owner is perpetually returning from three quick games of racquetball. I associate the hairstyle with young female jocks, if that's what they're called.

From the way she moved, I guessed that Sally would qualify as an athlete. She had the grace and looks of a cheerleader, though she never would have been one. Not slender enough. You have to be like a pencil so the guy cheerleaders who throw you around don't pop a hernia every time. Sally was the requisite height, around five-three, but large-boned, round, and solid. Broad-shouldered. She was not overweight. I figured her perhaps for the swimming team.

'Pleasure,' she said, shaking my hand firmly. Her voice was husky, almost an octave lower than I would have expected. That'd drive the boys wild, if she was into boys.

'Me too,' I said awkwardly, and we all sat down. Sally looked out the window while I read the contract. It was all there. I signed it and Pethco signed it, then he tore off a copy and gave it to me.

'Should I salute now?' I said.

Sally smiled.

'That's all the time I have today,' Pethco said to me. 'I'm sure you have a lot of questions. Miss Hatch will fill you in on the ride back to Charlottesville. When you get there, she is to pick up a car that we'll be providing and proceed on to, uh, Babel. She'll be going in under cover, as a prospective member. Give her a day to get settled. We feel it would be best if you two appear not to know each other. Once you're both there, of course, you'll have to strike up an acquaintanceship so that you can work together. I'll leave the details up to you. Please arrange to report back to me as frequently as you can.' He handed me a card. 'That's my home phone on the back. Anything else?'

'I don't think so,' I said.

'Good.' He got up and we shook hands. 'You know I wish you good luck,' he said.

3

We were on Interstate 64, headed back to Charlottesville.

'You don't like me,' Sally Hatch said. Her tone was neutral, suggesting that she merely wanted to talk about it, not that she felt hurt.

'Okay,' I said. 'I prefer to work alone. It has nothing to do with you.'

'No problem, then. I'm good. And I'm used to a team approach. It'll be a positive learning experience for you.'

I started to take offence at her presumption, then I looked over and saw that she was grinning at me. She had a little Sally Struthers dimple on her chin. It made for a winning smile. I'm a sucker for those, but hers would have charmed even Jeane Kirkpatrick. The contrast of the dark blue eyes with white, even teeth was irresistible.

'I'll try to think of it that way,' I said.

'Great,' she said. 'Now, what do you want to know?'

'Let's start with the decedent's name.'

'Temple Ballard.'

'And his wife?'

'Mary Beth Jackman.'

'Ex-wife?'

'No,' she said. 'Never changed her name. One of those modern marriages. You know.'

I nodded. I suppose my failed marriage had been a 'modern' one. It had put me off the institution entirely.

'Kids?' I asked.

'None together. Mary Beth has one son by an earlier relationship. Not a marriage, we don't think. Boy's seventeen. Named Spock. Gross. Can you imagine, naming your kid after a TV character?'

Or a peace-activist baby doctor, I thought, but I didn't say so. She might not know him.

'Born in San Francisco, right?' I tried.

'How'd you know *that*?'

I laughed.

'I didn't,' I said. 'Lucky guess. Summer of Love. A lot of kids with funny names were conceived in California around then. I missed all the good times myself. Wrong coast.'

'Too bad.'

'I'll survive. These people aren't young, then?'

'Nope. Mary Beth's thirty-seven. Hubby was four years older when he crossed over.'

'Crossed over?'

'Died. Sorry, just an expression I use.'

'Okay. Was he carrying insurance when he crossed over?' I asked. First question in the trade: Who profits? 'Big bank accounts, that kind of thing.'

'Uh-uh. He didn't believe in insurance, apparently. The widow didn't inherit much, near as we can tell. Maybe that's why she's suing.'

Well, that took care of that. Nobody profited. Not yet, anyway.

'So,' I said, 'tell me. What do we know for sure about our Mr Ballard?'

'Right,' she said. 'Temple Ballard. Only child. Old New England family. No longer as wealthy as they once were but still very snobbish. No substitute for good breeding, and all that. Went to MIT. Aerospace engineering after he graduated. The family probably wanted a lawyer, but that's what they got. Temp worked for NASA during the race to the moon. Whiz kid. Lived in Houston. Went into private industry after a while.' She named a major aerospace corporation. 'Then, in the late seventies, something happened. He dropped out. We don't know what he was doing. Looking for the meaning of life, along those lines. He surfaced in Virginia two years ago, with Mary Beth and Spock. Did some consulting work for a while. Then, early last year, he joined Babel. This February he had the accident. That's about it.'

'Interesting,' I said. 'And her?'

'Not much to tell. From California. A free spirit, I guess you'd say. Raising a kid on her own and all. She's got a master's in social work. Don't know how she met Ballard, or when, or why they got married. I doubt that it's important. In fact, I'm not sure any of this is. All we need to find out is why the damned alarm didn't work, isn't it?'

'Yeah, that's it. But you have to consider all the possibilities. Including that someone deliberately disabled it, knowing full well what would happen.'

'Premeditated murder,' she said.

'It's the least likely, but it could be.'

'Devin and I hardly discussed that. I guess we didn't . . . want to. You know, you figure that if it had happened, the police would have found out about it.'

I shrugged. 'The cops occasionally make mistakes. Pethco's been having lots of second thoughts.'

'So have I. But, well, I've never investigated a murder before.'

'It's different,' I said. 'You do security work full-time?'

She nodded.

'What do you get mostly, industrial espionage?'

'Yeah. It's a competitive field, and the technology changes fast.

19

Knowing what the other guy's up to can be critical. We also get a fair amount of software piracy, our own employees ripping off stuff for their benefit. That's popular these days. Damned hard to uncover too.'

'How'd you get into this?'

'I don't know. Just drifted, I guess. I majored in math, didn't want to go to grad school. It was the most interesting job offer I got. What about you?'

'Me? Another drifter. I worked for an insurance company up north when I got out of the army. After I learned the ropes I went out on my own. To make a long story short, I've been poor ever since.'

'You married?' she asked.

'Divorced.'

'I'm sorry.'

'Don't be. My ex thought she could run my life better than I could. I thought I could convince her otherwise. We were both wrong. No sob stories.'

'You one of those tough-guy private eyes?'

'You know it, sweetheart. Hard as they come.' A Bogart sneer. She might not even know who he was. But she smiled, anyway.

'And soft on the inside?' she said.

'Yeah, soft on the inside.'

The VW tracked straight across Virginia's Piedmont, gently rolling terrain with the elevation steadily increasing. Historically, it was the site of some of the bloodiest of Civil War battles, but today it's quiet country. A lot of small farms. And woodlands, the pine forests of the east becoming gradually mixed with and then dominated by stands of hardwoods. Along each creek is a winding line of sycamores. From the Interstate, side roads lead you to places like Short Pump and Gum Spring, Fork Union and Zion Crossroads.

The Piedmont was passing. Soon it would give way to the foothills of the Blue Ridge, in which lay Charlottesville, city of Jeffersonian light.

'You think I'm a dyke?' Sally asked.

'I don't discuss sexual preference on the first date.'

She laughed.

'I deserved that,' she said. 'It's just that a lot of people do. Because of my voice. My build and all.'

20

'I try not to stereotype,' I said.

'Would it matter to you if I was?'

'Nope.'

She seemed content to let it go at that. The question had come from pretty high off the wall, and it would have thrown me if I didn't have a stock answer in my joke bag. But in actuality it really didn't matter. She could do it with anyone she pleased, so long as she was a good detective.

And the old occasionally reliable sixth sense was saying that she just might be.

'How much do you know about this Babel place?' I asked after a decent interval.

'What'd Devin tell you, it was a hippie commune?'

'Yeah.'

'He would. He's a nice guy, but there's a lot he doesn't understand at all. He's got some set ideas.'

'It's not a hippie commune,' I said.

'Nah. It's an intentional community. They do experiments with alternative energy sources and stuff like that.'

'Solar, wind generators?'

'Uh-huh.'

'And this gasification thing Pethco told me about,' I said.

'Right. That's what killed Ballard.'

'Funny, you'd think an engineer like him would've been more careful around dangerous machinery.'

'Who knows?' she said. 'Maybe he was an absentminded scientist. Or . . . ' She paused. 'You know, there's another possibility you didn't mention.'

'What?'

'Suicide.'

It hit me like a stone. The thought hadn't even occurred to me. Hatch was sharp.

'You mean, disabled the alarm himself.'

'Yeah.'

'That would leave us with a very large question.'

'Two,' she said, 'the way I see it. Who reactivated the device? And why? Still, we need to consider all the alternatives, don't we?'

'You're right. We do. Add suicide to the list.'

We rode in silence for a while, mulling possibilities. If Ballard had committed suicide, there was only one person who had an

21

obvious logical reason to cover up the fact. The grieving widow. But then, there might be other people with motives equally logical, if less obvious. Not to mention the illogical.

Speculation was idle, so I said, 'I wonder why I never heard of Babel before.'

'I understand they don't want publicity. The idea is to become self-sufficient, I think. Get away from the outside world.'

'Still, they're near Charlottesville. I've been living there almost six years, and no one's ever mentioned it. How long have they been around?'

'Since seventy-seven.'

'Not bad,' I said. 'As these things go. Who's the leader of the outfit?'

'They don't have one,' she said.

'No fabled founder? No guru? Nothing?'

'Nope.'

'That's odd. Usually the ones without strong leadership don't survive.'

'Well, here's an exception to your rule. They don't believe in authority figures. Feel pretty strongly about it, apparently.'

'Who handles administrative details?'

'Ah yes,' she said, 'the inevitable paperwork. They have committees that change each year. Every member has to serve from time to time. The books get kept.'

'And someone has to enforce the rules, don't they?'

'They have a small private police force.'

'I knew it. You never — ' And then I glanced over at her and saw that she was putting me on. She let out the laugh she'd been suppressing.

'Thanks a lot, Hatch,' I said.

'No offence,' she said, 'but I couldn't resist. It's just that Devin's got his preconceptions, and I figured you'd have yours.'

I couldn't help smiling. It looked like Ms Hatch was going to be okay. She reminded me, in her own offbeat way, of the first rule of investigative work: Never theorize in advance of the facts.

'Yeah, maybe,' I said, 'but I'm still gonna pay you back for that.'

'If you can.'

'Don't be a wiseass, young lady. No one likes a wiseass.'

'Sorry, sir. It's only, I was so afraid.'

I chuckled. That'd be the day.

22

'So,' I said, 'what's the layout of this place? Everybody live together?'

'Some do,' she said. 'There's a couple of group houses. The singles mostly live there. The families tend to have their own homes. And you've got a core house. It's the biggest one on the land. They keep an office in it, hold community meetings and parties there. New members who don't have anyplace to stay can live in the core house until they either build or move in with someone. And there're rooms for visitors. It's where you and I will be staying.

'Naturally, the core house is the first thing you come to when you enter the land. It's visible from the road. Most of the rest of the houses you can't see right away. They're clustered here and there, back in the woods.

'Then there's the Ark.'

'Aha,' I said. 'I knew we'd find religion in there somewhere.'

'Good guess, Swift. But wrong. The Ark is one of their experiments. They borrowed the name from some other community up north. It does refer to Noah's boat, but in a different sense. That one carried its own food supply; this one *produces* same. The theory is that Babel's Ark can sustain the community's people through any sort of upheaval. Short of global nuclear war, I suppose. Anyway, it's basically an oversize greenhouse. You'll see it from the road. It's where — '

'Temple Ballard expired.'

'Right. Such a team we are. Finish each other's sentences just like Bo and John Derek. Anything else you'd like to know while I'm at it?'

'Let me see, Bo. . . . Yeah, how many people live out there?'

'It varies. They come and they go, y'know? Right now, maybe thirty adults. I don't know how many kids.'

A fair-sized group. That could be good and it could be bad. On the one hand, we could find ourselves going in too many directions at once. On the other, it meant a certain freedom of movement. No single person could keep track of what we were doing. And it would be easy to isolate people who seemed to know something.

But then, if there *was* anything to know, there was always the possibility that the person or persons who knew it had long since left the community.

'We've got some hard work ahead, Sally Hatch,' I said.

23

'Yeah,' she said. 'You up to it?'

I shrugged.

'I'll tell you something, though,' I said. 'Strangely enough, I'm looking forward to it.'

'Me too.' She paused. 'I guess.'

We found the beat-up old Chevy in the parking lot where it was supposed to be. It looked about as much like an investigator's car as mine does. I dropped Sally off.

Before we split up, we decided on a course of action. She was to continue on to Babel and I'd follow the next day. We'd meet there as if by chance. We would then pretend to be smitten with one another. This would give us the opportunity to spend time alone to exchange information. She would stay under cover; I'd be the only one to report back to Devin Pethco.

Her story was to be that she'd finished college as a math major, gone to grad school, but dropped out because she didn't like it. This stuck pretty close to the truth and was unlikely to trip her up. Since then, she'd taken odd jobs. She was bored, at loose ends, looking for something meaningful to do with her life, when she heard about Babel. She thought that the community might be the answer for her. She was visiting in order to find out. I saw no reason why the story shouldn't hold.

My reason for being there would be simple too. I'd play myself. Loren Swift, famous local investigator, hired by an insurance company to look into the death of Temple Ballard. I had the right to ask a few questions. They wouldn't be thrilled to have me around, but if I was nice about it, maybe they wouldn't throw me off their land.

'How much land do they have, anyway?' I asked Sally.

'About four hundred acres,' she said.

'Tidy.'

'Them's some *rich* hippies down there.' She laughed.

'They call 'em yuppies these days. Now, I'll need to know how to get there,' I said.

She gave me directions and we parted.

I called Ridley Campbell, the sheriff of Albemarle County. Babel was over in Nelson, which lies south and west of Albemarle. Rid doesn't have any jurisdiction there, of course, but he'd have the proper connections.

Campbell had been sheriff of Albemarle as long as I'd lived in

Charlottesville. He was very popular. When the county converted to a police force, as it looked like it was going to, he'd be the first chief. He and I have a relationship that has been at times adversarial, at others cooperative. At the moment he was in my debt and could be counted on to do me some small favours.

I asked for one. I wanted to know if there was anything unusual in the autopsy report on Temple Ballard. He told me no problem, he'd have the information by evening. I also asked if there was a way to check whether any of the community members had run afoul of the local law. 'Possibly,' was the answer. But it'd be a lot of work without their names. I told him not to bother, that I'd get back to him if there was someone I was specifically interested in. Hell, Mary Beth and Spock Jackman were the only ones I knew by name so far. Except for the deceased.

Campbell asked what I was working on. I told him, more or less; there was no reason not to. I left out my employer's name and didn't mention Sally. He grunted. It was pretty dull stuff, more than six months gone and buried. But he wished me luck and offered whatever assistance he could give. I thanked him, hoping our camaraderie would outlast the next time I crossed him.

I went to see Patricia Ryan.

She was the same. I willed her to wake up, but she didn't. So I talked to her, apologized that I wouldn't be able to visit her daily for a while, and explained that I was working to make some money to help with the medical bills. Then I left.

Back home, I fixed myself some supper. Baked fish again. Scrod topped with mushrooms and sliced onions, grated cheese added at the last minute. For the better part of my life I'd been pretty much a steak-and-potatoes man, though I acquired a lasting taste for seafood in Boston. Lately that had changed. It happened when I sat with Patricia, the blood pooling under her head, waiting on the ambulance for five minutes that seemed like a hundred. Since then, I had not been able to eat red meat. The sight and smell of it nauseated me. I wasn't a full-fledged vegetarian yet, but I had eaten a lot of fish and chicken. The doctors all told me that was a lot healthier, anyway. I was still adjusting, trying to figure out how to get some variety into my diet.

I drank a Stroh's with dinner and a couple more afterward. I had a slight buzz by the time I called my friend Jonesy. He's my contact at the Charlottesville *Daily Press*. If anyone would know the hot gossip about Babel, he would.

No luck. He was familiar with the place but didn't know any more about it than I did. It had never made news, to the best of his memory.

Sheriff Campbell called a little later. The autopsy had been cut-and-dried. Temple Ballard had died of oxygen starvation brought on by carbon monoxide poisoning. Period.

Well, one thing was becoming quite clear. I was going into this one dead-cold. I popped the top on a nightcap beer.

4

The next day was a Saturday. It was a rerun in terms of the weather. Warm and sunny with clean, dry air. I dawdled until noon, to let Sally get situated, then I drove to Babel.

The drive took me south and west, into the upper midsection of Nelson County. It was a beautiful area, made even more so by the first turning of the leaves. At its centre lay the Rockfish Valley and the river of the same name, which drained it. All around were the foothills of the Blue Ridge. On the western edge was the Blue Ridge itself, rising from about nine hundred feet to over three thousand.

Nelson County's physical beauty stands in mute contrast to its economic poverty. Though it abuts Albemarle, one of the wealthiest counties in the nation, it is one of the state's poorest. It is, I suppose, typical of a rural area that has come wandering into the late twentieth century with a topography unsuited to industry. Its small farms no longer produce enough to meet the costs of running them. Its young people, bred to boredom by technology, drift away. Honeysuckle and kudzu claim its once productive apple and peach orchards.

One would expect the population of Nelson to be on the decline. It's not; in fact, it's growing steadily. There are three main reasons for this. First, the county is just close enough to Charlottesville for commuting, and Charlottesville is a large employment market. Second, Nelson has begun to exploit its primary resource, the mountains. A ski resort has been built and, around it, a substantial vacation and retirement community. And third, there has been a major influx of transplants, as they're called locally. Most are from the urban centres of the East Coast. They come for the clean air and water, the cheap land and the low taxes. Some don't make it and move on. The rest settle in, start small businesses, begin to raise families.

A number of the area's new residents are members of intentional communities. Some of these are spiritual in nature. Both Eastern religions and Christian sects are represented. Others of them are completely secular, organized around the principles of the land trust.

One of them, whatever it might be, was called Babel.

My directions were good. They landed me, without any wrong turns, at the foot of a hard-packed gravel driveway. There was a wooden sign imprinted with the community's name. Beneath the name was a small face with its mouth open wide. Babbling, presumably.

I got out of Clementine, my VW, and looked around. I was at the southern end of the Rockfish Valley. From what I could see, the Babelonians had got themselves a fine piece of property. They fronted on a state road, beside which ran one of the major tributaries of the Rockfish River. You crossed a small bridge to get on to their land. It was good bottom land, forty or fifty acres' worth. They grew hay and corn, at the least.

From the river bottom, the land sloped gently upward to a long, straight ridge a quarter mile away. Beyond that, there was evidently a hollow, and then another ridge. In the distance there was a small cone-shaped mountain. A few cows and horses grazed in one of the open fields along the river.

I could see the core house that Sally had described. It was a large, two-storey structure with board-and-batten siding. The roof was peaked and shingled with cedar shakes. Some of the windows were odd shapes; some had stained glass in them. Parts of the place looked as though they'd been afterthoughts. It was the kind of thing you see in books like *Handmade Houses*. For Nelson County it was pretty funny-looking. I could imagine what the longtime county residents thought of it. They'd have agreed with Devin Pethco.

Beyond the core house was a good-sized barn. And beyond that, dug into the south-facing ridge, was what had to be the Ark. It was a long, low building with a shed roof. The front of it was some translucent material. It seemed to shimmer in the afternoon sun. Higher up, near the Ark, was a windmill. A modern one.

I let the peacefulness of the scene soak into me. It's much too seldom that I get out into the countryside surrounding the city in which I live. Whenever I do, I invariably feel revitalized in some way. I wondered that I could truly be here to investigate a mysterious death. All but the natural death of the seasons seemed inappropriate.

Eventually I got back into my car, crossed the river, and made my way up the gravel drive. I parked next to the five other vehicles in front of the core house. There was a battered American sedan, Sally's Chevy, a blue pickup, and two older Volvos. Changing times. Ten years ago the Volvos would have been beetles like mine. The sixties generation has moved upscale. A blonde woman in her mid-twenties was walking toward one of the Volvos.

'Hi,' I said.

'Hi.' She looked at me with an expression that appeared devoid of expectation.

'I'm Loren Swift.'

'Pleased to meet you.' She made to get into the car.

'Wait a minute,' I said. 'Do you know who I am?'

'Sure. You're a guy who drives an orange VW, you've got a nice smile, but if it's the car you're selling, I don't think I trust you enough to buy it. Other than that, you're anybody.'

So much for having a winning smile.

'I'm trustworthy,' I said.

'Good, Loren Swift. See you later.'

'Hold on. I'm expected.'

'Not by me,' she said.

'Well, who's in charge here, then?'

That cracked her up. She laughed heartily as she climbed into the Volvo. It hadn't seemed all that funny to me.

'Who's in charge?' she said to herself, and laughed some more. 'The Lord, I suppose.' Also to herself. And then to me, 'Check the office.' She gestured vaguely at the core house and took off.

I went through the door closest to the driveway. I found myself in a small room. There were a couple of couches. Along one wall was a bulletin board with dozens of messages tacked to it. Along another were several rows of wooden boxes with names written next to them. The mail was apparently delivered to a single address and then sorted here.

I moved along, into a narrow corridor that ran at right angles to the message centre. The first door on my left was open. I looked in. It was a tiny office. Just enough room for a couple of four-drawer

28

filing cabinets, a desk, and a computer station. A small man sat before the computer, his back to me. The CRT glowed green, like the eyes of the last cat left alive.

I knocked discreetly.

The computer operator swiveled in his chair. He was brown-skinned, an Indian or possibly a Bengali. About thirty, at a guess. His features were symetrically arranged in a small, perfectly round face. He resembled the gingerbread man of some badly remembered childhood. His hair was black, and he was wearing khaki slacks and a blue knit sport shirt, complete with the little alligator. His look was friendly in a detached sort of way.

'Hi,' I said. 'I'm Loren Swift.' I didn't know what else to add, so I didn't say anything.

'Yes,' he said, and turned back to the machine.

I waited a few moments, then cleared my throat.

'Is someone expecting me?' I asked.

'I am,' he said to the screen.

'Oh.'

There was apparently a time for all things at Babel, and this wasn't mine. I wandered back out to the front room. I passed some time checking out the bulletin board. It was interesting. There were notifications of committee meetings: Finance Committee, Outreach Committee, Livestock Committee. There was a letter from a Delaware woman explaining why the community wasn't right for her. There was a petition for 'provisional membership'. It set forth the petitioner's goals at some length. There were slots for twelve signatures beneath the argument. Seven of them were filled.

Then there were personal notes. John was publicly apologizing to Mary for something he'd done. Someone was missing a pair of eyeglasses. Stuff like that. And I found the following note, almost obscured by the surrounding scraps of paper: 'An insurance investigator will be visiting in the near future. Please give him your full cooperation. Thanks.' It was signed 'MBJ'.

Welcome to Babel, old man. You're expected.

I crossed the room and examined the names on the mailboxes. They were all first names. It was an average assortment, not particularly informative. I located Mary Beth and Spock. Temple was there, too, but someone had drawn a line through it and written Randy above. The slot was empty of mail. Idly I ran my finger along its lower edge.

As I did, I became aware that someone had come up behind me. I turned. The gingerbread man was standing there. I felt slightly embarrassed, as if I'd been caught at something.

'Just looking,' I said lamely. 'It appears that Mr Ballard has been replaced.'

'Oh?' he said.

'Someone has taken his mailbox, I mean.'

'To my knowledge, no one has felt comfortable taking Temple's box.'

I pointed at it. 'Randy,' I said.

'Ah,' he said, 'of course. But that's not a name. It's a comment. It was made before he died.'

'A comment. I see, about Ballard.'

'Yes.' He extended his hand. 'My name is Raghu Chaudri. I am to greet you. You have not been inconvenienced?'

'Swift,' I said. 'No. This is all quite . . . fascinating.'

'You do not have experience of intentional communities.'

'I'm afraid not.'

'Good. Then you will learn. Most of the members call me Rags. You may if you wish.'

'Rags,' I said. 'And you don't mind?'

'No. It is most unwise to confuse the name with what is being named, is it not?'

I nodded. Rags had the knack of looking guileless no matter what he was saying. It was too soon to tell whether it was a pose.

'May I show you your room?' he asked.

'Sure.'

I got my bag from the car, and Rags led me to my digs. We went down the narrow corridor past the office, a couple of bathrooms and a kitchen. The corridor, and the kitchen as well, gave on to a large room that was open to the roof. It had the feel of a meeting hall and was probably used as such. There was a cast-iron wood stove in one corner, several furniture groupings to define more intimate spaces, and a big plank table with benches, for group meals.

Beyond the meeting hall was the sleeping wing. There were small bedrooms off a central corridor, three on each side. Assuming the second floor was similarly set up, twelve in all. Mine was first floor, left middle.

The room was tiny. Mattress on a platform, end table, dresser, one chair. A little alcove with a bar to hang things on. That was it.

'This will be sufficient?' Rags asked.

'Sure,' I said. 'Fine.'

'They aren't meant for permanent residence, of course.'

'I could tell. How many people live here, anyway?'

'In this house?' I nodded. 'At present, only five. There are two guests; yourself and a young woman who arrived yesterday. In addition, two provisional members and one permanent member who is not yet landed.'

'Who cooks?'

'One or another of the members. You may be asked to help.'

He seemed to be waiting for something.

'Okay,' I said. 'Do you have some time to show me around this afternoon?'

'I am at your disposal, yes,' he said.

'All right, I'd like to see a few things.'

'Whatever you like. You may find me in the office.' He gave a slight bow and left.

5

Chaudri was in the office, as promised. He was playing with the computer again. This time I didn't interrupt him. When he'd finished, he printed something, then shut the machine down.

'Now, how may I assist?' he asked me.

Where to begin? I thought. At the beginning, of course, if possible. Lacking that, begin at the end.

'I'd like to see where Temple Ballard died,' I said.

'Certainly,' he said.

We went outside. We stood on the gravel drive, facing north. Three or four idle bicycles leaned against the side of the house.

'This is Babel,' Rags said, gesturing in a 180-degree arc. 'The northern boundary is Cobb's Knob.' He pointed at the cone-shaped mountain. 'The state road to the south, of course. Actually the river, to be perfectly accurate. This way' — the west — 'it doesn't extend that far. Two hundred yards or so.' It was a dense scrub-pine thicket that came to the edge of the drive. 'And our cropland.' To the east. The lush, level bottomland along the river. 'The hay goes to the milk cows and we sell what is left. In a good year we'll get three cuttings. It's not a lot of money, but it helps.

We use every bit of the corn, to generate energy and for fish food.'

'Fish food?'

'Yes. You will see when we get to the Ark.' He pointed. 'You are familiar with it?'

'Sort of,' I said. 'It's a greenhouse, right?'

Two hawks drifted by, high overhead. They appeared to be circling lazily. But each seeming circle was part of a spiral. A long, gentle spiral that carried them inexorably south along their autumnal migratory path. Rags was looking at me with what I might take to be amusement if I knew him better.

'In a way,' he said.

We headed down the gravel drive. Just beyond the barn, it forked. The left fork went into a patch of woods, beyond which I could see a large field lying along the ridge's flank. I assumed one of the housing clusters was back there, in the farther woods. The right fork branched at the base of the woods. One branch went up past the Ark and over the ridge; the other stayed at its base and proceeded along the edge of the extensive lower hay- and corn-fields. Eventually the road was lost to sight, though I thought I might be seeing its continuation ascending the ridge, in the far distance.

A boy was coming down the left-hand fork. At least I ended up deciding that it was a boy. At first I couldn't tell. He was wearing torn, faded jeans and a loose-fitting olive-drab army jacket with HAVERMAN stenciled over the pocket. The kid was not Haverman. For one thing, he wasn't old enough to be in the army. And even if he'd lied about his age, there were still the faded slogans burned into the fabric. Slogans like 'Gook Bait' and 'Born to Die' above a grinning death's-head. I'd seen thousands of such jackets. But that was half a world away, in a war so far distant in time that people were beginning to forget its lessons.

The jacket's present owner had added some stencils of his own. 'Dead Kennedys', I read. And 'The Clash', and 'Free Amerika'. 'Question Authority' was lettered down one pant leg, while on one hip was a thick black swastika. An ugly MP's nightstick that hung from his belt slapped against the swastika as he walked. The jacket was also adorned with short lengths of silver chain, oversize safety pins, and a myriad of buttons. As he got closer I could make out some of them: a marijuana plant; the haunted face of Jim Morrison next to a smiling Ronald Reagan inside a red circle with a thick red line diagonally across it. Others made no sense to me.

But what had caused the gender confusion was his hair. On top it was long and fluffy, teased upward and held in place by one of the new mousse dressings. It was bright yellow. The sides of his head were shaved. In the back there was a long, wispy thing that would've been called a ponytail if it were thicker. It was pink. There was something on the boy's lips that made them seem slightly deeper in colour than they would normally have been, and there was a circle of rouge on either cheek. From his right ear dangled twisted strands of silver enclosing a single hawk's feather.

I was aware of the punk phenomenon, but I'd never seen anything like him, not on the streets of Charlottesville. He gave Rags a cursory nod. Me, he looked over with something of a sneer on his face. He continued on his way without a word.

'*What* was *that*?' I said.

Chaudri smiled as though it were a question he'd been asked many times before.

'It is expected that the following generation rebel against the previous,' he said, 'is it not?'

'I suppose,' I said.

'It is. But it is a *duty* to make one's protest against the values of the middle class, for they are the values that threaten the earth. The young, lacking weapons and an experienced voice, resort most naturally to symbols. In our day it was the shaggy hair and the colourful clothes, yes?'

'I don't know,' I muttered. 'I kind of missed all that. The army.'

'Precisely. The young man must fight too. Only that which he opposes is the greater force. Unchecked, it will cause the planet to explode, or perhaps to slowly choke itself to death.'

'You believe he's thinking about all that?'

'Of course. Although he would put it rather differently, I imagine. We are all of us here aware of the peril. It is why Babel exists.'

'I don't follow you,' I said.

'We seek to practice conscious alternatives. You will understand better when you see the Ark.'

He led me to it. We passed no more strange people along the way. As we neared the building two women emerged from its farther end and headed down the road along the hayfield, their backs to us.

'Who are they?' I asked casually.

'The dark one is Nancy,' Rags said. 'She is a member. The blonde lady is our other visitor. She is called Sally, I believe. She

33

will probably be receiving her orientation tour.'

'She's cute, the blonde,' I said.

Rags shrugged. He gave the impression that it was something of no concern to him. Now that I thought about it, I realized that he had struck me as being oddly asexual from the beginning. It's a dangerous assumption to make about someone you don't know. Yet Chaudri appeared to inhabit some interior world where the body was looked on as merely a clumsy vehicle to move the mind from here to there. I'd known a few men like that, no women. The years invariably left them as dry and stiff as untanned leather. My guide, however, might prove to be an exception.

'And this is the Ark,' I said.

He nodded.

It was an impressive structure. Made of wood. Maybe fifty feet long, I guessed. Half as deep. Sixteen feet from floor to ceiling. Attached to it, on the left, was a small enclosed wooden shed.

Adjacent to the shed was an open area containing a large metal cylinder. It was about eight feet high and two feet in diameter, and it resembled an inverted silo. There was a minimal roof over the cylinder, just enough to keep the rain off. Standing next to it, on a raised platform under the same roof, was something that looked like an automobile radiator.

The section of ridge directly behind the cylinder/radiator arrangement had been bulldozed and a wide earthen shelf constructed. Access to the shelf was via a gently graded earth ramp that rose from our level to the top of the cylinder. The ramp was wide enough to accommodate a moderate-sized vehicle.

I examined the setup without much comprehension.

'And this is?' I said.

'This is a gasifier,' he said. 'I will show you how it works.'

He motioned to me and I followed him up the earth ramp. The top of the gasifier was fitted with a cover that reminded me of the lid on the old metal trash cans, except that the handles were on the side. There were clamps to hold it firmly in place.

'The gasifier is used to produce both heat and electricity,' Rags explained. 'It's loaded at the top. We can back a small truck up here and shovel in whatever we've got. Anything combustible of the right size and shape will do. This time of year we use corncobs that have been dried after shucking. You remove the top and just stuff them in. A full load will burn for about four hours.'

We went back down the ramp. 'At the bottom here' — he

pointed to the large steel box on which the inverted silo rested — 'is the combustion chamber. Once the fuel is in place, it's ignited by a flare. The combustion rate is then carefully controlled by limiting air intake. Unlike with most fires, you want inefficient combustion. You want the organic material heated by the fire below it, just enough to drive off the volatile gases. Do you follow this?'

'I guess so,' I said.

'Good. Now, the gases we are interested in are carbon monoxide, hydrogen, and methane. Primarily carbon monoxide. They are withdrawn here.' He pointed to a pipe that exited high up on the gasifier. The pipe then descended and entered the radiator thing, emerged from the other side, and passed through the wall of the adjacent shed.

'Carbon monoxide,' I said. 'I think this is the part I'm interested in.'

'Yes. Now, the gases that are driven off in the first step are very impure. They're mixed with water vapour, creosote, particulate matter. This device' — he pointed to the radiator — 'is a condenser. It removes anything that can be reduced to a liquid. What's left goes inside.'

We walked around to the entrance to the shed. It was a low door. Above it was a series of half a dozen slats. They were closed. We went inside.

It was a small room, filled with equipment of various kinds. I located the pipe from the condenser. It entered a square metal box about a foot on each side. The pipe coming out the other side of the box fed an automobile engine. The other relevant item was mounted on the Ark wall. It was a carbon monoxide detector identical to the one I'd seen in Devin Pethco's office.

'This is where it happened?' I asked.

'Mr Ballard's death, yes,' Rags said. 'The gasifier itself can remain out in the open, as can the condenser. But this equipment must be protected from the weather. Being enclosed, the shed is the most . . . dangerous place.'

His voice had caught, just for a moment, and his eyes were seeing something that wasn't in this little room with us. I had no inkling what it might mean, but I filed the incident anyway. Almost immediately Chaudri's face reassumed that expressionless expression of his. I was beginning to wonder if it represented a gentle mockery of everything around him.

He pointed to the square metal box. 'Inside this is a series of

35

filters to get rid of any remaining particles. What comes out the other side is the relatively pure mixture of flammable gases we talked about earlier.'

'Like carbon monoxide,' I said.

'Yes, like carbon monoxide. After the gases are purified, then they're ready to be burned. The engine is from an old Chevrolet, actually. The engine turns this generator, giving us electricity. In addition, we capture the heat from the engine coolant and that from the exhaust. I'll show you what we do with it later.'

'I assume there must have been a leak in here,' I said.

'There are many places where a leak could develop; that is why we had the defective detector.' He said the word *defective* with what seemed, for him, excessive bitterness. He led me to the filter box. 'Here is where it did.'

He pointed to the place where the last section of pipe exited the filter box. It was enclosed by a heavy rubber gasket.

'The vibration from the engine, over a period of time, had caused this gasket to loosen,' he went on. 'Eventually, it loosened enough that carbon monoxide was able to escape into the room. The gasifier had been running for three hours when Temple entered the shed. This space was filled with the gas. The alarm should have gone off. In addition, the alarm is keyed into that exhaust fan.'

A fan was mounted over the shed door. When it was operating, the slats I'd seen outside would be forced open. The fan looked large enough that, with the door open, it'd be able to quickly replace the air in the room. Rags slipped a switch on the wall. The fan came on. It was noisy. He switched it off.

'It should have come on automatically as soon as the CO concentration began to rise,' he said. 'It didn't. Temple never . . . had a chance.' His voice hitched again. Ballard's death, though it had occurred six months earlier, was obviously still a painful subject for him.

'I'm sorry,' I said. 'Were you close friends?'

'We were all close to Temple,' he said. The emotion was gone. 'He was a person of consequence. He was responsible for the transformation of Babel.'

'How do you mean?'

'I will show you when we get to the Ark. Do you wish to know more about the accident?'

'Actually, I do. How often is the system inspected?'

36

'Each day it's sight-checked. Once a week, on Saturday morning, we clean the filters. At that time we take the detector down and pass it slowly along the line to see if it picks up anything, because a small leak would not be easily spotted. The detector is plugged in now, but it operates just as well off the batteries. Ironically, Temple died on a Saturday night. That means the gasket sprung loose sometime that day. A few hours earlier and . . . we would have found it.'

'That's an odd coincidence,' I said.

'Yes,' he said. 'It happened all the same.'

Did he say it a little defensively? I couldn't be sure. One thing I was sure of, though, was that over the years I'd been driven to believe less and less in coincidence. I let it go for the moment.

'All right,' I said. 'Who's responsible for the daily inspection?'

'We rotate. One person is responsible each day for firing the gasifier in the morning. That's when most people check out the lines. The same person then has the job of refueling the gasifier as the corncobs or whatever are consumed. It needs to be done about three times in an average day.'

'And Ballard was on duty that night?'

'No, it was Freddie. You will wish to speak with him.'

'Then what was Ballard doing here?'

Chaudri pointed to some standard one-inch galvanized pipe that came up through the shed floor, turned ninety degrees, and headed into the Ark.

'That's a water pipe,' he said. 'The windmill brings the water up. It's stored in a cistern under the floor here and pumped from there to the Ark as needed. This elbow joint had developed a leak. It was getting worse. Temple came here to fix it. He's . . . he was our best plumber.'

'I guess maybe that answers my next question,' I said. 'I was going to ask why he didn't notice the first signs of CO poisoning and get himself out of the room. But I suppose if he was intent on something like replacing an elbow joint he might not have realized what was happening until it was too late.

'Yes,' he said. 'He noticed, but the carbon monoxide level in the shed must have been very high. In such circumstances, time is short. He died here.'

He gestured to a spot on the floor. Ballard had failed to make the door to fresh air by about three feet. I stared at the spot as if a chalk outline of the body might suddenly appear there. I tried my best to

37

sense what Ballard's last moments had been like. All I got were some chest pains and a vague feeling of abandonment. His spirit must have long since quit the place.

Still, there was something in the air, some voice whispering that resolution in this matter had not yet come. What voice? That of my own occasionally reliable sixth sense? Or Chaudri's, perhaps? I looked at him, and he gazed impassively back. I felt strongly that I would never be able to read him but that, given the right moment, he would talk to me. And what would he say?

'Does it feel as if someone died in here?' he asked.

'Yes,' I said, 'it does.'

'It is said that the imprint of the departing soul requires a year in which to dissolve.'

The image of Patricia, lying in her hospital bed, levered its way into my mind. I fought it away from me, forced myself to walk over to the Ark wall. I looked up at the CO detector. It was suspended from a hook, well up on the wall. Beneath it was a small stool. I stood on the stool. That put the detector within easy reach. I detached it from its hook and lowered it. It was plugged into an outlet that lay directly behind it, so I pulled the plug to free up the cord. I turned the thing around in my hands. An innocuous black box, just like the one I'd seen in Richmond. Part of the back of it was a little door you could pop open. I looked inside. Two D batteries were in place. I closed it up, reconnected the cord, and hung the device back on its hook. I hit the yellow button; the alarm shrilled until I released it. I got down off the stool.

'It is not the same one,' Rags said.

'Yeah, I know,' I said. 'This one works.'

We went through the door into the Ark. It was like stepping into the jungle. Hot, humid. The October light was streaming in through the translucent front of the building. I rapped on the material.

'Don't they make greenhouses out of glass anymore?' I asked.

'Seldom,' he said. 'Too expensive. And it breaks. This is a fibreglass-based product. Good light transmission. Tough. The only thing we don't know is how long it will last. There is a certain amount of deterioration involved.'

I looked around me. The Ark was a single huge room. It had an earthen floor that had been built up and graded so that there were several levels. On some of the levels were large, shallow tanks of water. They had catfish swimming in them. On the levels between the pools were standard greenhouse arrays of growing vegetables and flowers.

'Here is where it's all put to use,' he said. 'The electricity from the generator runs the circulating pumps, the oxygenerators, and the fans, which regulate the temperature in here, among other things. The heat we reclaim from the engine's radiator is used to warm air, which is blown into the Ark, helping to heat it. The heat from the engine's exhaust is transferred to water which is then pumped back into the pools.

'The Ark, as you see it, was Temple Ballard's great contribution. Before he came, it was a passive solar structure. The fish were grown in tanks like those.' At the back of the Ark were several cylinders made of the same material as its front. 'The water in them, like the Ark, was heated by the sun. This system worked well enough. We were meeting our own food needs and we were recycling things efficiently. We grew the corn to feed the fish; their waste was used to fertilize the soil here in the Ark; and the excess fish could be ground up and used to fertilize field crops. But this is an expensive structure. A lot of people put a lot of time and money into it. The return on that investment has not been great.

'Temple realized that right away. He showed us that in order to be truly efficient, as well as to survive in the modern world, we needed the Ark to start generating profit. It couldn't do that if it depended solely on the sun, so it was redesigned. We added the gasifier and its peripheral equipment. We replaced the small cylindrical tanks with the big pools. We installed some sophisticated monitoring devices. The aquatic environment is now warmer, purer, and more highly oxygenated. As a result, the fish grow faster and we can turn them over more rapidly. Plus, of course, the larger pools hold many more of them. We sell them to a processing plant over in the Shenandoah Valley, which grinds them into cat food. The Ark is operating solidly in the black now.'

'Impressive,' I said. 'And you still waste nothing.'

'We waste even less than we did. Temple was a man of vision.'

'And all of this runs off corncobs. You know something, Rags, I'd never heard of a gasifier before. It seems so practical. How come every farm doesn't have one?'

'Many of them did,' he said. 'During the Second War, when gasoline was scarce. It has been our collective misfortune to have oil so cheap for so long. We are too dependent on it. But you may trust that the gasifier will once again become popular. There will be the need to exploit renewable resources. No government, no giant corporations will be able to alter that.'

I walked through the Ark, peering at the interlocking life support systems. Like everyone else, I was aware that the natural resources of the country, and the world, were being depleted at an alarming rate. Did something like the Ark represent a partial solution to that problem? I wondered if I was looking at the shape of the future, or just another idealistic hope about to die.

6

'Sooner or later,' Chaudri said, 'you will be wanting to talk to these people. We have decided that it would be advantageous for it to be sooner.'

The table in the core house had been set for nine, and the group had begun to gather. I'd already made the acquaintance of Lisa Berlinger, who was doing the cooking. Lisa was a slender, ethereal, pale blonde woman. The last time I'd seen her she'd been climbing into a Volvo, laughing at my question about who was in charge. She was the one permanent community member still living in the core house. I'd wandered into the kitchen and met her over the tomato sauce.

'Spaghetti?' I asked.

'Yup.' She grinned. 'My other speciality.'

'Other than what?'

She just kept grinning. She had a right mouthful of teeth in there.

'There is one thing,' I said. 'I haven't been able to . . . eat beef, or like that lately. Were you going to put any in?'

'I never do. Not to worry. You're safe here.' She smiled at the word *safe*. She had one of those smiles that strikes you at first as completely ingenuous and at second glance as totally lascivious.

'Do you use chicken or fish?' I asked. 'I'm a little worried about my protein intake.'

She pointed at a block of rubbery white stuff that stood on the cutting board next to the chopped scallions.

'Tofu,' she said. She pronounced it 'doè-foo'.

'Who foo?'

'More protein than beef,' she said. 'Not to worry. It's very good for you. The Chinese have been eating it for years, and look how many of them there are.' And she grinned the lascivious grin again.

I beat a hasty retreat before I saw what else was going into the sauce.

Sally Hatch had also shown up early. She sat on the sofa, leafing through a magazine. It was a good opportunity for me to put the moves on her. I went over.

'Hi,' I said, and we introduced ourselves. 'I guess we're kind of the outsiders here.'

We chatted on like that, exchanging basic information. We laughed at each other's jokes. To anyone listening, it would appear that we were two single strangers who were discovering that they enjoyed each other's company. If the grapevine here worked adequately, it would be common knowledge within twenty-four hours.

After Rags arrived, Sally and I split up and he began to fill me in on what was planned.

'As I said this afternoon,' he explained, 'there are just the five living here. Lisa you've met?' I glanced at the kitchen. She was still in there, now making garlic bread. I nodded. 'And Ms Hatch?' I nodded again. 'They're the only ones who would normally be eating here with you, other than the two provisional members. But they won't be with us this evening. Anne still has a male friend in town, and she's with him. Jeff's in town too. He has a job waiting tables on Friday and Saturday nights.'

'Who fills out our table for nine?' I asked.

'Ms Jackman, of course. Her son Spock. Freddie Evans. He's the one who discovered Temple's body. His wife Nancy. And Thomas Bender. He was one of the founders of Babel.'

'The Supreme Court,' I said.

'Excuse, please?'

'The Nine. Supreme Court, so to speak.'

'Oh, yes. In any case, there were six of them, originally, the founders. Thomas and Nancy and Freddie are the only ones left. This is Thomas now.'

A squat, blocky man entered the room. He was about forty, with a wide, cheerful face. The top of his head was nearly bald, and he'd trimmed the sides close. He was clean-shaven. Incredibly, he was the spitting image of the young Dwight Eisenhower. I must have done a double take.

'Call me Ike,' he said, laughing. 'Everyone does.'

That'd take some getting used to for me. When I think of Ike, I more often have in mind a skinny black man who was married to Tina Turner.

'Glad to meet you, Ike,' I said. He shook my hand vigorously. There was about him an air of controlled energy. Not repressed, but capable of being directed. I felt that I would have been able to pinpoint him as a founder type.

Bender went into the kitchen and put his arms around Lisa from behind. He kissed her on the neck. When she saw who it was, she shook her head and casually pushed him away. They began to have what appeared to be an unserious conversation.

'The Evanses,' Chaudri said.

Though I might have been able to select Bender from a lineup of possible founders, I never would have picked Freddie Evans. He was in his late thirties, short and thin, with a homely face full of freckles, and hair that was as carroty as it must have been when he was eight years old. He was a high-energy person, too, but it was all nervous energy — one of those people who seem to be moving even when they're standing still.

Nancy Evans was dark and of medium height, which made her taller than her husband. She was about the same age as he, and as plump as he was wiry. Her face was unremarkable, but it dimpled nicely when she smiled. The effect was winsome. She seemed placid, especially next to old Fred. She shook my hand warmly, Freddie perfunctorily. Then they went over to talk to Sally.

'Well, what do you think so far?' Freddie said to her.

'Gee,' Sally said, 'I don't know. There's just so much. It's hard to take it all in at once. It's almost like being back in school.'

Freddie laughed. It was a shrill, rather unpleasant sound. He sat down next to Sally on the couch and put his arm around her shoulders. They were an affectionate bunch, these folks. I found myself feeling a little annoyed with him, then berated myself for a stupid chauvinistic response. Sally could well take care of things. If she didn't want his attention, she'd let him know.

Nancy sat down on her other side. She coaxed Sally to talk about her past. Sally obliged. A careful mixture of truth and lies emerged, as smooth and seamless as the surface of an egg. Ms

42

Hatch was good at this. I turned back to Chaudri, so as not to betray my admiration.

'Our final guests may be a little late,' he said.

'Spock and Ms Jackman,' I said.

'Yes. Mary Beth is a person who believes strongly that every action should be purposeful.'

'Meaning she's always fashionably late?'

'I wouldn't put it quite so crudely. Life has complexities that tend to become obscured in the modern tendency to abbreviate them. For Mary Beth it is important to do something at as nearly *correct* a moment as possible. The moment to arrive at a dinner party is just before the food is served. She would prefer to fill time such as we are now sharing with more important matters.'

'Such as?'

'The investigator in you is often uppermost, is it not, Mr Swift? The important matters to Mary Beth are, of course, for her to tell you.'

'Of course,' I said. 'No offence. But I am supposed to be working here.'

'I do understand that. I hope that it will not interfere with your coming to know us personally. Nor that it prevent an appreciation of what we are attempting to do.'

'I'll try not to let it.' He gave me another of his little bows.

Chaudri was correct. The slippery mound of spaghetti lay steaming in a pottery bowl on the table when Mary Beth Jackman made her entrance. I could see why she liked it that way. She was a striking woman. Sally had told me she was thirty-seven, and she looked that old, primarily because of her hair. There was a thick mass of it, curling down to shoulder level. At one time it had all been black and glossy, but now it was liberally flecked with grey, which seemed only to add to her aura. She was about five-two but compactly build, like a sleekly muscled cat. She walked with a self-assurance that commanded your attention. Her eyes, too, were powerful. They were a deep brown and shone like polished agate. I would have chosen her as one of the founders, had I not known she and Ballard were latecomers.

Spock trailed her into the room, like some mistreated domestic animal. He was as sullen as he'd been earlier in the day, when I'd seen him walking down the gravel drive. The bright pink-and-yellow hair contrasted nicely with his mother's.

43

The meal was delicious. Plenty of spaghetti, garlic bread, salad, red wine, and a tangy tomato sauce that somehow didn't seem too strange with the white cubes of tofu floating in it. A dinner to please my half Italian ancestral soul.

During it they treated me like a guest.

'So, Mr Swift, this is your first experience of community?' Ike asked.

'Unless you count the army,' I said.

He laughed. 'It would be difficult to find a group less like the military.'

'Except for Zero,' Lisa said, and everyone but me laughed.

'And foot soldier Spock,' Freddie said, shooting the lad a sly look.

'Leave me outta this,' Spock growled.

'Who's Zero?' I asked.

'Commander Zero is our resident Survivalist,' Ike said, 'with a capital S. He truly believes that the apocalypse is around the corner. Perhaps you will meet him, perhaps not. He doesn't come out of the forest that often.'

'You have a survivalist living in your woods?'

'Yes,' Chaudri said. 'We do not place judgments upon those who wish to join us. There is ample room for diversity.'

'Hence Babel,' I said.

'Very good,' Ike said. 'It is, of course, our desire that our many voices be as one.'

'Yet y'all have no leader.'

'We have no need of one.'

'Leaders represent the insecure side of one's own self,' Chaudri said. 'One creates them in order to externalize those insecurities. Of necessity, they must reinstill the same insecurity back in the people.'

Mary Beth said, 'As usual, Rags is taking a little extra time to say that power corrupts.'

That got her a chilly look from the Indian, to which she smiled and nodded politely.

'So what do you have here?' I asked. 'Anarchy?'

'Quite the contrary,' Ike said. 'We have true democracy. When there is a decision to be made, the entire membership votes on it. The majority rules. Naturally, we try to resolve problems without voting on them, since voting is essentially a process of polarization.

44

You'd be surprised how many conflicts can be worked out with a little third-party mediation and some compromise.'

'I believe I *would* be surprised.'

'That's because,' Nancy said, 'you're a product of an aggressive, competitive culture. There won't be a better way of doing things until the people have an expectation that it can happen.'

'Look at me,' Sally chipped in. 'That's why *I'm* here.'

People nodded their approval. I didn't doubt that she had already won a lot of them over.

'I don't know,' I said. 'It doesn't seem to me that people are basically very cooperative.'

'Well, that's no surprise,' Lisa said. 'Look at the business you're in.'

That got some laughs.

'Yeah,' Freddie said. 'You ever consider changing jobs?'

'At times.'

'You might should. It could change your whole outlook.'

'I'm not sure there's anything *wrong* with my outlook.'

'You enjoy sticking your nose in other people's business?' Mary Beth asked.

'I enjoy investigating things. That's not quite the same.'

'Big-deal private eye,' Spock said.

'Really, Mr Swift,' Ike said, 'understand us, if you will. We're all aware that you're working, that you wouldn't be here if you weren't being paid to be. Which makes you quite different from anyone else at this table. Nevertheless, we represent an alternative to life as you now know it. Please feel free to take advantage of the opportunity to learn about us. We don't resent your presence. Our fondest hope would be that you like what you find here and eventually become one of us. Be open to the possibility.'

'Wait a minute. Speak for yourself, Ike,' Freddie said.

'Yeah. I ain't signing his petition,' Spock said.

'It looks as if your membership application will be . . . a stormy one,' Mary Beth said. She regarded me coolly. She seemed enormously self-centred, and she probably didn't like me very much, but there was no denying that she was a magnetic person. At one time in my life I would have fallen very hard for her.

There followed a chaotic debate on the merits and shortcomings of Babel's present admissions policy. It was apparently a well-worn controversy. Ike, Nancy and Lisa favoured a real open-door

45

approach. Freddie was as strongly of the opinion that the community should be extremely selective. He was joined, oddly, by Chaudri, who argued softly that hasty decisions were all too often intemperate.

I thought at one point that the disagreement was going to degenerate into a food fight, but it didn't.

Mary Beth, who'd remained aloof through it all, said to me, 'Welcome to Babel.'

'What about you?' I asked her. 'You don't care?'

'I don't care. After I get my money' — she pointedly held my eye when she said it — 'the place can go to hell. Now, if you'll excuse me . . .'

She left. Lisa followed her into the hall. They talked for a few moments before Lisa returned. Shortly afterward Spock got up, poured a nearly full glass of wine down his throat, and shuffled off without saying anything to anybody.

'Is it my breath?' I said.

'Perhaps when I said that we welcome your presence here,' Ike said, 'I shouldn't have included the Jackmans.'

He smiled and all, but something in the way he said it made me feel that he wasn't too thrilled to have me, either. It was the first time I'd felt that from him, and the feeling was strong.

'Understandable,' I said. 'Well, maybe now would be a good time to talk about Temple Ballard.'

There was a silence. It felt strained.

'What would you like to know?' Ike asked finally.

'I don't know. General things. What sort of man he was. What people thought of him. I've been told that he wasn't one of the founders.'

'True,' Ike said. 'Only the Evanses and myself remain from the original group.'

'But Babel is as much Temple as any of us,' Freddie said. 'He was brilliant. He challenged us to make our community viable in the modern world, and he had the expertise to bring that about. Losing him was a . . . blow.'

'You see,' Nancy explained, 'when we founded Babel, our idea was to create a self-sustaining entity. To shut ourselves away from a world we'd grown to hate. Only it didn't work. No matter how independent we became, we were still a product of that world. You can't close yourself off from yourself. We're tied to the society, and it's tied to us. Not to mention that as the years went by we became

46

progressively poorer. We needed to acknowledge our relationship with outside, to accept those things that are not so bad and to merge them with our own values. We also desperately needed a project that would bring some money in. Temple pointed the way out of our dilemma.'

'When you began, you were survivalists of a kind,' I said.

'You bet,' Freddie said. 'Live off the land, all that. We did it too. Ike and I designed the Ark, after a similar one that had already been built up north. With that as a base we could have done it. If we'd had the money.'

'Don't be misled,' Ike said. 'We're not totally selfish people.'

'We intended to share what we learned,' Nancy said. 'By following our example, others could take charge of their own lives. We believe that the only hope for the world is a voluntary return to a simpler life-style.'

'But then you went broke,' I said.

'Not broke, exactly,' Ike said. 'We did come up against some economic realities that we hadn't reckoned with, however.'

'So' — I nodded at Rags — 'you decided to take up commercial fish farming.'

'Yes,' Rags said. 'As I explained, that was one of Temple's great contributions. He not only showed us how it might be done, he put in more physical labour than anyone. In addition, he convinced us that we shouldn't spurn help from outside. There are a number of government grants set aside for projects not much different from this one. He instructed us in how to apply for them. We are now very close to receiving our first.'

'Temple expanded our consciousness,' Lisa said.

'A real oddball,' Freddie said.

'He was,' Nancy said. 'On the one hand, an aerospace engineer, if you can imagine. NASA. But not like those guys who all they know is their own little field. Temple knew a lot about a lot of things. Plus a tremendous awareness of world problems and this burning desire to help.'

'And funny,' Lisa said. 'He made us laugh.'

'All this and randy too,' I said.

Silence. I laughed nervously.

'Just kidding, folks,' I said. 'It's what somebody wrote beside the name on his mailbox.'

'This is my fault,' Chaudri said to the group. And then to me, 'Perhaps I have misled you. That someone chooses to comment on

47

another does not thereby give the comment validity.'

'It's a joke, then?'

'Temple was a normally sexual male, if you call that randy,' Nancy said rather coolly. The others maintained the uneasy silence.

I wasn't surprised that the tone of the conversation had chilled. It's been my experience that when you put a group of people in close contact, it isn't long before you have a hotbed of sexual intrigue. The Peyton Place syndrome. I didn't see why Babel should be any different simply because they thought of themselves as alternative. In any case, Temple Ballard's sex life might have relevance to what I was doing, and it might not. There was time to look into it. Later.

'So no one disliked him,' I said.

They looked around at each other. Finally Ike shrugged.

'We were really fortunate to have him,' he said. 'He was a hard person to dislike when he'd done so much for us.'

They all nodded. I decided not to point out that the question remained basically unanswered.

'All right,' I said. 'How did he seem just before he died? What was his mood?'

'Super,' Freddie said. 'The project was going great. He was excited.'

'I'd never seen him looking better,' Ike said.

'With Temple,' Rags said, 'there was not the artificial division between internal and external. He wore his joy on the surface.'

There was another round of nodded agreement.

'Okay, one more thing,' I said. 'Could y'all tell me what happened the night Ballard died?' I looked at Freddie. 'I understand that you found him.'

'Yes,' he said. 'It was my day to tend the generator.' He seemed more nervous than normal, now that we were getting down to it. If there were something to be found out, I suspected that he would be the one to find it out from. 'Also, weekly maintenance,' he went on. 'I checked out the system in the morning. No sign of any leak then. I cleaned the filters. And I fired it up. I made two trips out there during the day, to refuel. Temple went up, I think it was about seven-thirty or eight. There was a leaky pipe in the shed and he was going to fix it. He did stuff like that. I was down here at the core house. I happened to be outside, getting some wood for the stove, when I heard the alarm go off. It was some time later. I hurried up there because, you know, you get a lot of gas leaking and there can be a fire. I was worried for the Ark. I didn't even think of Temple, not immediately.

'First thing I did when I got there was to cut off the air supply to the gasifier. Then I closed down the gas line into the shed and vented it so that whatever else came through would just escape into the open. Then I looked in the shed and found Temple. He was . . . dead.' He paused. 'Then Rags arrived. He'd come down from his house to see what was going on.'

I looked at Chaudri, and he gave a little bow, agreeing that that was the way it had been.

'We left the shed door open,' Freddie continued, 'to let the air clear. The big fan was going, so it didn't take long. Then Rags went in to look at Temple. I went into the Ark and used the phone to call Ike and Nancy. They came down right away. It was Ike who called Mary Beth.

'When we were all together, we tried to decide what to do. We didn't know what had happened to Temple, of course. He might have had a heart attack or anything. We ended up calling the local doctor. He recommended that we have someone from the sheriff's office come out, too, which we did.

'It wasn't until the autopsy that we finally learned Temple had died of carbon monoxide poisoning, which meant that the alarm system had failed. It's supposed to go off as soon as the CO level starts to rise. If it'd done what it should have, Temple would have gotten out of there. And he wouldn't have fooled around about it. He knew the danger.

'That's the extent of it, Mr Swift. If you think you're gonna find anything more mysterious, you're wrong.'

He tried to add a note of defiance to his voice, but it didn't work. If anything, the effect was opposite to what he intended. Up to that point I had been willing to believe that Devin Pethco was grasping at straws in order to keep his own gig running. But what Freddie said — more important, the way he said it — pushed me the other way. I became strongly suspicious that there was more that Freddie Evans could tell about the untimely death of Temple Ballard.

'I don't think anything,' I said neutrally.

'Whew,' Sally said, 'this is all too heavy for me. I reckon I'll do the dishes.'

'I'll help,' I said. 'One minute. Could everyone let me know where they live?'

'There is a map,' Rags said, 'with all the houses on it. They're in

49

clusters, so you shouldn't have trouble finding any of them. The map also has our telephone numbers on it. I'll get you one from the office.'

'Thanks.'

The dinner party broke up. I got the map and put it in my room. Then I helped Hatch with the dishes. We joked and carried on and threw soapsuds at each other. I hoped that it seemed like the natural behaviour of two people becoming increasingly chummy.

Afterward we went out on to the deck at the back of the core house. It was a clear night, cool but comfortable. The stars glittered. We sat out there with Lisa and Rags, who'd stayed behind. We drank hot tea and chatted amiably.

I learned that Raghu Chaudri was from Washington, DC, the son of an Indian diplomat. He'd gone to engineering school in Charlottesville. His original intention was to learn something useful and then go back to his native country. He still intended to go back, but somewhere along the line he'd decided that engineering skills weren't what was most needed. He'd come to Babel to learn what was. He thought intensive fish-farming methods might be it.

I didn't want to be cynical about it, so I didn't say anything, but I'd met a couple of guys like Rags during my single semester at the university. When they're twenty, they're full of the desire to take the wonders of America back to the Third World. Only trouble is, they've grown up here, they're accustomed to a certain level of comfort. You can see it in their life-styles. You can hear all the implicit assumptions in the way they talk. You can't imagine them settling for less. In the end, you can't help but believe that ten years down the road they'll be just like their parents. The last place they'll want to go is 'home'.

Lisa turned out to be from Connecticut. She'd attended the University of Virginia but, like me, had dropped out. Unlike me, she had done so by choice. She wanted to be a dancer and had discovered a top-flight teacher in town. College was no longer relevant. Though she didn't go into it, her bearing and manner of speech strongly suggested an upper-class background. Taken together with her interests, that made Babel seem an odd choice for her. I asked her casually what had brought her here. She said that she found the environment very friendly to what she was doing and let it go at that.

Sally told some childhood stories that had us all laughing help-

50

lessly. Then I recounted a couple of the more unusual cases from my files. I kept it light. It wasn't a night to talk of the naked evil I'd sometimes encountered.

Eventually, we all tottered off to separate beds. As far as I knew.

7

In the morning I volunteered to help Lisa split some wood for the core house's airtight cast-iron stove.

There was a big pyramidal stack of logs out back, in a cleared area beyond the deck. I recognized oak, locust, hickory, and poplar. The logs had already been sawed to stove length. All that needed to be done was to split the bigger pieces down to a comfortable size. There was a splitting block next to the pile for that purpose. Around it the ground was littered with wood chips and mounds of sawdust.

Nearby was one of those prefabricated metal sheds. Lisa sent me to it to get the splitting maul. I wasn't real clear about what one was, but I didn't want to show my ignorance. I figured the maul would be obvious.

It wasn't.

The shed was full of tools. Piles of tools on the floor. Tools in chests and on shelves. Tools hanging from hooks. Gardening tools, woodworking tools, auto repair tools, plumbing tools. Some were familiar to me and some were not. If there was order in disorder, you probably had to be a lifetime member of Babel to know where it was. I looked around, feeling like an alien. I finally settled on a nice, long-handled axe. It seemed to be one of the newer tools. I tested the edge with my thumb. Sharp. I congratulated myself on my choice and stepped outside to split some wood.

Lisa laughed. 'Don't know much about country living, do you?' she said.

'City boy,' I mumbled. 'Why, what's wrong?'

'Oh, nothing. Let's try this one, okay?' She pointed to a locust log a little bigger around than my thigh. 'Set it up for me, please.'

I placed it on the chopping block. It was a little awkward, what with my cast, but I managed. I wanted to feel useful. She swung the ax behind her, whipped it up over her head, and struck the log a decent blow. The ax blade bit in a couple of inches and stuck. She had to rock the wood back and forth to get it out. She struck again. The blade went in a little bit farther. This time we had to set the log on the ground and stand on it before we were able to extract the ax. And she still had a ways to go to split the bastard.

'Enough,' she said.

'Sorry I can't help,' I said. 'But my wrist was broken last month. I doubt that the doctor would think it was therapeutic.'

She looked at me critically. 'It's not a matter of physical strength,' she said. 'It's a matter of finding the right tool for the job. I just wanted to demonstrate. C'mon.'

She led me back into the shed. The ax was replaced on its pegs. She picked up an evil-looking orange thing off the floor. It had a big wedge-shaped head attached to a long, hollow steel handle.

'This,' she said, 'is a splitting maul,' and she handed it to me. My arm dropped. The thing was *heavy*. 'It's a fifteen-pounder. Not for wimps. Now, let's go out and I'll give you Berlinger's quickie course in wood splitting.'

Outside, she asked me to set the locust log on the block. I did, without thinking about what I was doing.

'First thing,' she said, 'you've got the log upside down. It's a little less wide at this end than it is at the other, right? So what you did, you rested it on the wider end. Ninety-nine out of a hundred people would do the same. It seems more stable that way. But it's wrong. If you can tell which is which, you always put the smaller end down. Why?'

I thought about it, but nothing came. 'Beats me,' I said.

'Because the log tapers in the direction the tree grew. The smaller end was higher up, you see? So you place that end down. Then, when you go to split, you're splitting *with* the growth pattern of the tree, instead of *against* it.' She raised an eyebrow to see if I was getting the point.

'Logical,' I admitted. It was the sort of thing you ought to think of but seldom do. I repositioned the log.

'Now then,' she said. 'The use of the maul. It's a little heavy to swing like an axe. Probably tear your arms out of the shoulder sockets if you tried. So we'll do it the easy way.'

She raised the maul above her head, so that it was perpendicular to the ground. Then she brought it down on the locust log, guiding it with her arms rather than swinging it. She bent her knees to carry the force through the log. The wood split cleanly with the first stroke. The twin locust halves toppled over.

'Simple,' she said.

'If you say so,' I said.

We worked together smoothly. She set up the logs and split them. Rounds into halves. Halves into quarters. Quarters for the stove. I carried the splits to a roofed area adjacent to the house and stacked them up under cover. There was a small door in the house wall through which the wood could be passed into a bin inside. The bin was close to the stove. The setup made heating with wood a lot less messy.

It felt good to be out in the clean air and sunshine, working my muscles. I hadn't exercised much in the previous month. Though the temperature was only about sixty, I'd soon worked up a healthy sweat. I'd also worked my wounded leg until it ached. Lisa seemed to know.

'Had about enough?' she asked.

'You should see me on my better days,' I said. 'I can split oak with the edge of my hand.'

'You've had enough.'

We went inside, and Lisa quickly put together some pancake batter. Sally was back from the store with the Sunday *Washington Post*. Jeff, the provisional member, had just gotten up. He wore a small silver cross around his neck. Babel was nothing if not diverse.

I called Mary Beth Jackman and arranged for a visit to her house after breakfast.

Over the hotcakes I asked Lisa why, since she was a permanent community member, she was still living in the core house.

'There needs to be someone here,' she said. 'Look after the place, keep the pipes from freezing in the winter. Before Jeff and Anne came, there was only me. I kind of got used to it. Besides, I'm not really into building my own place right now.'

'You don't have an S.O. here?' Sally said.

Lisa smiled. 'I see you're beginning to pick up the jargon already,' she said.

'I got a little crash course from Nancy yesterday.'

'What the hell's an "S.O."?' I said.

'Significant Other,' Sally said. 'It's what they call each other's relationships here. Among themselves, they're not comfortable

53

with the old terms, like boyfriend and girlfriend, husband and wife. Too much stereotyping attached to those words. S.O. is more neutral. Right?'

Sally turned her midnight blues on Lisa. Something passed between them, I didn't know what. Lisa lowered her eyes demurely. Her expression was the flip side of the lascivious grin.

'Right,' she said.

'No S.O.?' Sally said.

'Well, none worth moving out of the core house for,' Lisa said, as if it were a challenge.

'Dancing before men, I'll bet,' I said. For something to say.

'Dancing is the most important . . . thing in my life currently,' Lisa said.

'There are more important things,' Jeff said.

Lisa shot him a look that made him return his attention to his food. Apparently they had been over this territory a time or two, though the issue was unclear. Might have been sex, or it might have been Jesus.

'Me, I wish I *did* have something more important than relationships,' Sally said, stretching her arms over her head. It was a rather sexy gesture. 'Maybe then I'd do better at avoiding the bad ones.'

Lisa laughed, I laughed, Jeff poked at his pancakes like there was no way they could be transmuted into *his* flesh. Abruptly he got up and left.

'What'd I say now?' Sally asked.

'It's nothing,' Lisa said. 'Jeff's a strange one. He doesn't really belong here. There's no way enough people are *ever* going to vote for him for permanent membership. He keeps trying, though.'

'Maybe he sees it as missionary work,' I said.

'He trying to make you or convert you?' Sally asked.

'Both.' Lisa laughed.

'Must make for some long, lonely nights,' Sally said.

'It does. Anything else I can get you two? I've gotta get moving here.'

Sally shook her head.

'Thanks, Lisa,' I said. 'I'm fine. Go ahead. We'll clean up.'

'Okay, see ya.' She winked at Sally. 'And play nicely, y'hear?'

It appeared that Ms Hatch and I were becoming an item. Good.

We kept it casual while we finished the Sunday paper. Then I asked her if she wanted to walk with me as I made my way to the

Jackmans' house. She said sure, she was going that way too. When we were out on the gravel drive, we felt like we could talk some business.

'She's gay,' Sally said.

'Huh? Who is?'

'Lisa.'

'How in the hell do you know that?'

'C'mon, Swift. There are things that someone like me knows, okay? Trust me. You kind of stuck your foot in it when you made that crack about dancing before men. I nearly broke up. She handled it nicely, though, I thought.'

Now I understood the odd looks that had passed between Sally and Lisa. But Ms Hatch, she remained an enigma.

'Well, what did you *expect* her to say?' I asked. I was feeling defensive, the way I always do when conversations I've been involved in have actually been taking place on more levels than I was aware of at the time.

'Don't be a jerk,' she said. 'The people — '

'Watch it, Hatch! Just because you — '

She just smiled and put her arm on my shoulder. Her fingers kneaded the back of my neck. They were good, strong fingers. I suppose I should have shrugged her arm off and continued to sulk, but I couldn't. It suddenly seemed childish. Besides, she was a talented masseuse.

'You know, you're right cute when you're angry,' she said. 'But anyway, what I was going to say was that the people here are different from the ones you probably know. You're gonna have to tune in to that or we won't get anywhere. Now, what Lisa *might* have done was challenge you for laying your personal expectations on someone you didn't know much about. I don't think people here shy away from that kind of thing. But she ended up being rather gentle with you. Maybe she thinks you're cute too.'

'Don't get smart. So what are you saying, that this is a gay community?'

'Actually, I don't believe it's specifically one way or the other. What I'm saying is that it's not going to be the *issue* here that it is in other places. The issue they respond to is more likely to be people's prejudices.'

'You seem to have picked up a lot in two days,' I said.

'It's what I do, remember?'

'Yeah, I remember.' My partner was proving to be as sharp as I thought she would. I should have been pleased. Damn it, I *was* pleased.

We ambled up the gravel drive, stopping to gawk at the horses in the field, the chickens in their wire compound, the livestock in the barn. We admired every view. Just two regular folks falling for each other. The mini neck massage probably looked particularly good. I wondered whether she had considered that or whether it was spontaneous. I opted for the latter. Why not?

'So do you think all this has anything to do with Ballard's death?' I asked her.

'Search me,' she said. 'But we have to understand who these people are before we can draw any conclusions about that.'

'You're right. You pick up anything else I ought to know about? Or are you through showing me up for the time being?'

'Well, now that you mention it . . . ' I groaned. She grinned like a kid and took my arm. 'It's nothing specific,' she went on. 'The woman I've gotten closest to so far is Nancy. She's been sort of my guide. I like her. She told me about Ballard, what he'd done for Babel. She mentioned his death, too, but I got the impression that it's not something she likes to talk about, and that she brought it up only because you were coming out here and would be asking everyone a lot of questions, anyway. They all seem a little apprehensive about you, but then, that's probably natural.

'When Nancy showed me the Ark, I made like I thought it was pretty scary, with all the carbon monoxide and stuff. I had her show me where he'd died. I asked her how the leak had happened. The question seemed to throw her, just for an instant. She looked confused. Then she pointed out where the seal had come loose. It was only a tiny hesitation, but it could mean something. I'll try to follow it up as Nancy and I become better friends.'

'Good,' I said. 'What do you think of her hubby?'

'He's a nervous little guy, ain't he?'

'Yeah. If something strange *did* happen, he's probably the one to go after.'

'My take is that he's a better bet for you than me. He doesn't seem like a woman's man.'

'I agree. Anything else?'

'I'd say the first step is to untangle these people's interrelationships. And we should probably concentrate on those who were at dinner last night. They may not believe in leaders here, but those folks come close.'

'All right,' I said. 'I'll see what I can find out from Ms Jackman this morning. What're your plans?'

'Unfortunately, I've got to act like a prospective member. I'm off to meet some of the lesser lights. I'll keep my eyes open, but don't expect much.'

We'd reached the first fork in the road, and it was time to part company. Mary Beth's house was off to the left, down the side road where I'd first seen Spock. I now knew from the map that there was a housing cluster back there, in the woods to the west that surrounded the open field. Mary Beth lived in the cluster, as did Chaudri.

So I was going left, while Sally was continuing along up over the ridge. For the first time I became aware that there was a man standing a short ways down from the crest of that ridge. He was staring at us and nothing else. He didn't move. I told Sally to say something to me.

'What do you mean?' she said.

I started laughing like it was the funniest joke I'd ever heard. I put my arm around her. She was puzzled, but she joined in wholeheartedly.

Under cover of all this, I said, 'There's a man I don't recognize up there. He's been staring at us for a while now.'

He was a strange-looking man. Tall and lanky, with thick, matted black hair that came down to his shoulders. He had a full beard that seemed to cover most of his face. And he was dressed in an army camouflage outfit. It was difficult at this distance to tell his age, but I guessed not much over thirty.

'You see him?' I asked.

'Yeah. He does appear to be interested in us.'

'You know who he is?'

'I think it's Commander Zero, unless they have more than one guy around here who fits that particular description.'

'Ah, our resident survivalist. You seem to be headed his way. Think you can handle it?'

She gave me a look like I had tofu for brains. 'Give me a break,' she said, and headed on up the ridge.

8

The Jackmans' house, like others I had passed on my way, was small. It was made of wood, as they all were. The siding was shiplapped boards, unpainted, slowly greying in the rain and the sun. There was a nice-sized woodpile outside, the logs split and stacked. A ceramic thimble emerged from the house halfway up one wall. Within it was a shiny black stovepipe. The pipe turned ninety degrees, rose above the roofline, and terminated in a conical rain cap. There were guy wires to keep it from blowing over. Everyone here, it seemed, heated with wood or solar energy, or some combination of the two.

Inside the house there were four rooms, built two over two. The front door opened into a living room/kitchen. It was the only room I was invited to see. The door to the other downstairs room remained closed. Access to the second floor was by a black, wrought-iron, circular staircase, selected probably because it was a more efficient use of space than conventional stairs. When I closed the front door behind me, it thunked solidly. The house felt tightly constructed and well insulated. That was what I would have expected if Temple Ballard had had a hand in building it.

The living area was sparsely furnished. Just a couple of chairs and one of those futon couches that converts quickly into a guest bed. I chose a nice bentwood rocker, and Mary Beth sat on the couch. She was wearing a dark sweater and jeans. If she wanted to try out for the part of the mysterious Lady in Black, she'd get it.

Ms Jackman was regarding me with no love at all. But I still felt that if I wasn't careful, I'd find myself falling right into those eyes.

'I am, of course, a hostile witness,' she said by way of openers.

'You needn't be,' I said.

'You're here to try to deny me money that's rightfully mine.'

'If it's rightfully yours, you'll get it. If it's not, then I'm sorry, you won't.'

'And there is absolutely no reason why I have to talk to you.'

'No, there isn't. But the sheriff's office is aware of my investigation,' I lied. 'If people refuse to cooperate with me, then he just might be persuaded that there's something funny going on.'

'I see.' She took a deep breath and exhaled audibly. 'Well, Mr Swift, I have nothing to hide. We have nothing to hide. There has been a tragic accident here that never should have happened. That's what you will find. My husband's gone, and nothing will bring him back. The company at fault should be made to face their responsibility in his death. It's as simple as that.

'Now you may ask me anything you like. I'll answer whatever questions I choose to answer. If something's none of your business, I'll tell you so. And if I don't like your attitude, I'm going to throw you out of here.'

Her look defied me to make something of it. This wasn't going to work. Unless I was able to thaw her a little, it would be a very short interview. I decided to take a large chance.

'Mary Beth . . . ' I said. 'Ah, may I?'

She nodded.

'Please call me Loren.' Normally, I prefer that people call me Swift, but it didn't quite feel right. 'Mary Beth, I know that you are looking at me as the enemy. And I can understand that. I don't blame you. You don't want me to 'succeed', if that's the word, and you never will. All right. What I would hope is that you do not develop personal feelings of hostility toward me. I am not, personally, your enemy. I wish you no ill will in the world. If you can make that distinction, I would like it very much.'

I paused for a moment, then continued, 'Inside, I am a person, just like you. Sometimes I'm happy, sometimes I hurt, sometimes I don't give a damn. Right now I'm hurting for you, because you lost someone you loved. But I'm hurting for the person I love too. She is a nice person, someone you would like, and she needs my help just now. I can help her by working. This is the kind of work that I do. If this particular job is against your interests, then I'm sorry. But I still have to do it, you see?'

It had worked. I'd judged that she might be responsive to the truth, and she was. She had softened noticeably. After I finished, she offered to make some coffee and I took her up on it. The break gave me a chance to gather my thoughts, and it helped reinforce the idea that I was a guest and not an intruder.

When we were again seated across from one another, she said, 'All right, Mr . . . Loren. I'm sorry. Please ask your questions. But I do think you're wasting my time.'

'Perhaps, but thank you,' I said. 'I guess what I'd like to know is what Temple was like, from your point of view. You knew him best.'

'After last night you probably think he was a god.'

I smiled. 'That would appear to be the consensus.'

She smiled too. 'Well,' she said, 'in some ways he was. Tall, dark, and very handsome. The ladies swooned with some regularity. Plus he was brilliant. Brilliant in his own field, of course. But in general, as well. He knew an awful lot about a lot of different things. Not just science; the arts too. And he was a gifted problem solver. He had the knack. If he couldn't logically think his way through something, he'd find the answer intuitively, and he'd almost always be right. On top of it all, he was physically strong, worked hard, and had tremendous natural energy. That about your idea of a god?'

'It comes close, Mary Beth. I understand he was originally in aerospace. NASA, right?'

'Right. He was hired right out of college, back in sixty-two. There's one thing you have to understand about my husband, Loren. He hated school. He was one of those people who are only held back by organized classwork. Temple wanted to be *doing* things. That's how he learned.

'As soon as he graduated, he moved to Houston. That's where the action was in those days. From what he told me, they were incredibly exciting days. We were racing to beat the Russians to the moon, and he was an important figure in the program. It was the happiest time of his life.

'But then we won.'

'That must have made him happy too,' I said.

'Oh, it did. But it also meant the game was *over*, do you see? Once we got to the moon, everyone suddenly realized that there hadn't been any reason to get there before the Russians, after all. A lot of people in the aerospace field felt very let down.'

'Among them your husband.'

'Yes,' she said. 'The moon became a place for men to go so they could hit a golf ball farther than they ever had. Can you imagine? I understood Temple's disappointment.'

'And that's why he quit NASA?'

'It's one reason. There were other changes too. When we were trying to *get* to the moon, no one cared who you were as long as you could help. Those were the years of the whiz kids. After we'd mastered the mechanics of it the bureaucracy slowly began to settle in. People's credentials became more important. Temple didn't even have a master's, let alone a Ph.D. That was suddenly noticed. What he could *do* began to matter less. Other people, less talented people, started getting the good jobs ahead of him, simply because of those little letters after their names.'

'He could have gone back. For the degree.'

'He *could* have, but he never would have. He was beyond being able to tolerate instructors who knew less than he did.'

'After he left NASA,' I said, 'he stayed in aerospace, didn't he?'

'Yeah. He tried private industry. I don't think he ever expected it to be different, and it wasn't. He lasted a couple more years at it, then he dropped out for good.'

'What'd he do?'

She shrugged. 'What does any disillusioned idealist do? He became a drunk.'

I knew what she meant. There have been times for me when I thought my best friend lived inside that green Jameson bottle. For perhaps not dissimilar reasons.

'How did he live?' I asked.

'He had substantial savings. When they were gone, he did odd jobs. He could fix anything. He drifted. A lot of people did in the years after Watergate and the war and all that.'

'Yeah, including me, I guess. Somehow I ended up here.'

'Temple wound up in San Francisco. I met him at a party. He was a miserable excuse for a god, but there was still something about him. You could see it if you looked real hard.'

'You helped him back?'

She nodded. 'It was a long climb. Getting the drinking under control was the worst part. I'm still amazed that we were able to do it at all.'

'When was all this?'

'I met him about five years ago. It was a couple more years before he was really back on his feet.'

'And somewhere in there you got married?'

'Yeah. In Golden Gate Park. Isn't that corny?'

I laughed. 'I'm not sure,' I said. 'I've never been to Golden Gate Park. When we passed through Oakland on our way west, they never let us off the base. They never knew who'd skip town if they did.'

'Take my word for it, then. It's corny.'

'Okay. So why'd you leave California?'

'I don't know,' she said. 'A new beginning, I suppose. Temple was feeling good about himself again. And both of us had had enough of city living. Something died in San Francisco when Moscone and Harvey Milk were assassinated and they let that Twinkie-head creep off the hook.'

'Why here?'

'Temple and Ike are old friends from MIT.'

'Oh?'

'Uh-huh. Ike's another used-to-be engineer. Only, when he dropped out, he had something else in mind.'

'Babel.'

'Right. He was able to hold on to his idealism and make it into something new. Anyway, Temple had the address from when Ike first moved here, so he wrote him to ask about the area. Ike sent us a rave review of central Virginia. One thing led to another, and we finally asked ourselves: Why not? We lived in Charlottesville for a while. Temple got a small consulting job. But he became increasingly interested in Babel. We both did. Finally, we joined, and Temple threw himself into the projects you've heard about. He was reborn at last. The year and a half before his death, he was the happiest he'd been since the early days in Houston. The accident was a tragedy, Loren, it really was.'

I had no reason to doubt her. She looked wistful but not as if she were about to cry. It was well in the past now. We drank some coffee in silence.

Then I said, 'And what about you? Do you have a tale of broken dreams too?'

She chuckled. 'I'm afraid I never had time for my dreamy phase,' she said. 'Too busy. My folks sent me to Radcliffe after high school. They still thought of college as essentially a finishing school, and there was a lot of snobbery involved. None of the California schools were thought to be "good enough" for me. So I got trucked clear across the country. My freshman year, I committed an, ah, indiscretion. I got pregnant. Abortions were a bit hard to come by in those days, and I didn't really fancy one, anyway. I went back to California. My folks were surprisingly sympathetic. I moved to San Francisco and they helped me financially. After Spock was old enough for day care, I enrolled at San Francisco State. I worked straight through to my M.S.W. I was doing social work when I met Temple. A break for him. He was in no worse shape than most of the people I was seeing every day.'

'Ballard your first husband?' I asked.

'Uh-huh. I was kind of turned off to men for a while there. Most of them aren't into a woman with a kid, anyway. Not when they're in their twenties.'

'Speaking of kids, how did Spock get along with his step-father?'

'Oh, the usual friction, you know. Basically, pretty well.' I noted that she'd said it a little too quickly. 'Of course, adolescence is always a difficult time, isn't it?'

'You mean the punk thing?'

'Spock's not a real punk,' she said. 'But life out here is difficult for him. It's too quiet for a teenager. He has to express his individuality some way, and that's how he does it. I mean, he doesn't go out and get into fights or anything. He's a good kid. Don't let his appearance put you off.'

'He's how old?'

'Eighteen in November.'

'Not still in school.'

'No, he's through high school. I told him he could continue to live here until he decided if he wanted to go to college. He's deciding. But I don't expect this is of any real interest to you, is it?'

'I don't know,' I said. 'Probably not.'

I took that as my cue. Ms Jackman had been courteous and most cooperative up to this point. I didn't want to risk overstaying my welcome.

'Well, thank you very much, Mary Beth,' I said. 'I can't think of anything else. In fact, hopefully I won't have to bother you again.'

'Thanks for not making it too awful,' she said.

We made our goodbyes like the most civilized of friends, and I walked back down to the core house.

9

Sally returned there for lunch. We were joined by Anne, the other provisional member, who was back from her boyfriend's. She was thin and rather studious-looking, an effect that was heightened by her steel-rimmed glasses and the way she wore her straight brown hair tied tightly back. We all munched on cheese sandwiches and salad.

'Fresh tomatoes,' Anne said.

'From the Ark, right?' I said.

'Right. We can grow them year-round. That's one of the advantages of living here.'

'It *was* Commander Zero,' Sally said.

'Oh, yeah?' I said. 'So you met him.'

'Uh-huh. He seemed to be interested in me. He wants me to come out to his place.'

'I wouldn't do that,' Anne said.

'Why not?'

'I don't know. Zero gives me the creeps. Living by himself out there. With all those guns and everything. If he asked me, I believe I'd say, "Thanks, but no thanks." '

'Guns?' I said.

'Oh, sure. It's a fortress, you know.'

'No, I don't know. And I don't think Sally does, either.' Sally shook her head. 'Why don't you fill us in?'

'Well,' she said, 'I don't know him, you understand. And I've never been out to his place. But they say he built it like a concrete bunker in the woods and covered it over with dirt. Supposedly, he keeps a real arsenal in there. He believes that there's going to be a war, maybe a nuclear war, or at least that there's going to be a big catastrophe in this country. He thinks that the only people who will survive are the ones who have staked out their spot and are prepared to defend it. He even took his name from some guerrilla fighter.'

'He doesn't sound like much of a community person,' Sally said.

'He's not. He doesn't participate in anything. The only thing he does is pay his monthly dues. He gets interest from a trust fund someplace.'

'How come he's still here?' I asked.

'He likes it. He's found his spot.'

'No,' I said, 'I mean, how come he's *allowed* to be here?'

Anne shrugged. 'He's a member.'

'Isn't there some way to get rid of people who aren't really contributing?'

'Nope. We try to do our weeding during the provisional period, and that doesn't always work. Zero was much different when he first came here, they tell me. If he'd been like he is now, he wouldn't have made it. But once you're in, you're in.'

'That's strange,' Sally said.

'Maybe,' Anne said. 'But it was one of the founding principles of

Babel. The founders wanted to make sure that no person or group would ever have the power to get rid of another person or group. That way, the power could never be abused. They wrote it all into the charter of the community.'

'That's pretty optimistic,' I said. 'The assumption is that there aren't any really rotten apples out there.'

'Not quite,' Anne said. 'The assumption is that living here would transform any of the rotten apples who made it in. Babel is an attempt to do things differently, Mr Swift. Different means *different*.'

'But he still gives you the creeps,' Sally said.

Anne blushed. 'I didn't say I wouldn't be happy to see Commander Zero disaffiliate.'

We all laughed.

'You don't think I should go up there?' Sally said.

'I don't know,' Anne said. 'Everyone says he's harmless. And it's true that he's never bothered anybody that I know of. 'Course, I've only been around six months. But still, maybe it's just me.'

'I don't much care for people who stockpile weapons,' Sally said.

'Tell you what,' I said to Sally. 'I'll go see Commander Zero with you. How's that?'

'Oh, my hero,' Sally gushed, clasping her hands together.

Anne laughed. 'Nice,' she said admiringly.

'You know,' I said, 'the hell with Commander Zero.' I jerked my thumb at Sally. 'I think *this* is the one I'd better be careful of.'

'Ah, come on, Swifty,' Sally said, patting my cheek, 'don't get all bent out of shape. I'm not afraid of the man, but if you feel better walking up there with me, that's fine.'

She gave me an affectionate little smile. Anne looked from one to the other of us and grinned like she understood perfectly what was going on.

Just as we were leaving, Jeff came out of his room. We headed up the gravel drive. So did he. He walked with us without saying anything. It was okay by me.

'You're not really mad at me, are you?' Sally asked me.

'No, of course not,' I said. 'But you know why I'm here, you know what I do for a living. I'm probably a little more comfortable around guns than you are.'

'Last state target-shooting championship, I placed third.'

'My mistake,' I said with a small bow. 'Odd hobby for a

mathematician,' I added for Jeff's benefit.

'Family pastime.'

'I see. So . . . the lady just keeps getting more interesting.'

'Don't mind if I do,' she said.

'Are you going to come to this place?' Jeff asked suddenly.

'Who?' I said.

'Not you, detective. You, Sally Hatch. Are you going to come to this place?'

'I'm already here. I think.'

'Do you wish to join Babel?'

'I don't know. I'm still trying to learn about it. It's fascinating, isn't it?'

'It's wicked.'

'Huh?'

'They fornicate here, the sexes with their own kind, contrary to God's law.'

'Don't you think that's their own business?' I said.

'It's God's business,' he said firmly. 'It's all God's business.'

'Well,' Sally said, 'if it's wicked, then what are *you* doing here?'

'I am called. Jesus was not afraid to go out among the sinners. Nor am I. I will show those who lie down with their own kind that it is not the way. The one Way is to follow the example of Jesus Christ. He alone can help them.'

'Good luck,' I said.

'I have no need of luck. I have the Lord.'

The whole time he'd been staring intently at the ground, as if hunting for something he'd dropped the last time through. We came to the fork in the road. He was going left, while we were continuing on over the ridge.

He looked Sally in the eye for the first time. 'This is not for you,' he said. Then he turned and left us.

'Whew,' Sally said.

'Yeah, he's an intense young man.'

'I mean, I don't begrudge anyone their religious beliefs, but when they get like that one, inquisitions and stuff come to mind.'

'I'm with you. Sometimes it seems like *gay* is just the latest word for *witch*.'

'So . . . did you find out anything of interest this A.M.?' she asked.

'Hard to say. A lot of background on Temple Ballard. Did you know that he and Ike Bender were old college buddies?'

'No,' she said.

'It's true. Ike's the reason Temple and Mary Beth came to Babel. It also means that we've got a relationship between Ballard and Bender that goes back twenty years or so. Who knows what there might be in that? Ike and I will have to talk sometime soon.'

'Good idea.'

'And then we got into her marriage,' I went on. 'How they got together and all that. I like her. She doesn't seem to be the kind of person who'd kill her husband in order to make some money out of the deal.'

'A little smitten with her, are you?'

'Now, that would be most unprofessional, my dear. Besides, you know I only have eyes for you.'

Still, I must have looked a little embarrassed, because she said, 'I thought so. Look, Swift, be careful, will you? There's a lot about her that you don't know.'

'And I suppose that you do, as usual?'

She stopped and looked up at me. The dark blue eyes were hot.

'Let's stop this,' she said. 'Right now. I am working *with* you. I am not trying to beat you out of something. So no more jokes about it, no more little put-downs, okay?'

I found I had to clear my throat. 'Okay,' I said. And I meant it.

'Good,' she said, as though she trusted me. 'Now, what *I* found out during an otherwise very boring morning of meeting new people was who Lisa Berlinger's lover is.'

'I'll bite. Wh— ' Then, of course, I knew.

'Mary Beth Jackman,' she said.

I was standing in the middle of the road looking foolish. Sally just smiled, took my arm, and started me walking again.

'How in the hell did you find that out?' I asked.

'I told you, Swift. The people here don't think it's all that big a deal. They're not uptight about who's sleeping with whom. I showed a little casual interest in Lisa, and I got warned off. It was easy.'

'Did you find out how long it's been going on?'

'A while.'

'Since before Ballard— '

'Since before.'

'That does complicate things,' I said. 'Doesn't it?'

'Uh-huh.'

'And for your information, she's not my type, anyway.'

67

Sally laughed.

We paused at the ridge top. From there you could see it all. Below us, the Ark. To the right, some woods, the field along the side of the ridge, and the cluster where the Jackmans lived. To the left, the extensive lower fields by the river. And standing sentry, its blades towering above us, the windmill.

We crossed over the top of the ridge. On the other side was a hollow with a small stream running through it. Three houses were built along the high side of the road. On the low side was an extensive garden area. It was a peaceful scene, like something out of a nearly forgotten past. Sally echoed my thoughts.

'My ancestors came to this country three hundred years ago,' she said. 'Sometimes, places like this, I feel like I can see them still walking around.'

'Half of mine were shooting each other in the hills of Calabria,' I said. 'Even fifty years ago.'

I felt like giving her a little hug, so I did.

It was a long hike to Commander Zero's digs. The cluster of houses in the hollow was the last outpost of Babelonian civilization. After that, the road died and we followed a path through the forest. It wound up the side of another ridge, then down, then up again. I asked Sally if she was sure of the directions, and she said he'd told her to just keep following the path, always branching left. We stuck with it.

About a half hour out, we were walking single file, with me in front. I heard Sally stumble behind me, curse, and then give a little yelp. I turned. She was standing there, looking back the way we'd come. Ten feet from her was Commander Zero. He was wearing his camouflage outfit and, in the enclosing woods, looked even taller than he had on the ridge.

I hadn't heard him. He was good.

'Hi,' I said.

'Who're you?'

'This is my friend, Loren Swift,' Sally said. 'Loren, Commander Zero.'

I held out my hand. He took it unenthusiastically, then seemed to think of something.

'Loren Swift,' he said. 'Loren Swift. I know you. Brown's Cove, right?' He gripped my hand more firmly before he let it go. He was

68

referring to one of my earlier cases, which had resulted in a bloody shootout outside of Brown's Cove.

'Right,' I said.

He gave a slight nod. I'd obviously just been elevated in his estimation.

'Hell of an operation,' he said. 'Wish I could have been there.'

I didn't care much for people who liked the idea of firing guns at other people, so I just shrugged.

There was a moment of suspended animation. I looked into Commander Zero's eyes. They were hazel and . . . what? Suddenly I knew where I'd seen him before. Not him, personally. But I'd seen those eyes. Eyes that were sharp as a hawk's, flicking here and there, missing nothing, yet which held within them a kind of logical madness that no one else could ever fathom.

I'd seen those eyes in Vietnam. They were the eyes of a LURP, someone who volunteered for long-range recon patrols behind enemy lines. LURPs would go in, alone, usually at night, and stay for days, sometimes for weeks, living right in the belly of the enemy. You had to be a little crazy to volunteer for such a thing in the first place. And a couple of trips into the jungle made you even more so. As did the drugs. Among LURPs, the drug of choice was speed. Their life expectancy was short, the probability of complete madness very high.

With my recognition came curiosity and, somewhere deep inside, the first faint stirring of fear.

'What was your outfit?' I asked.

'What?'

'During the war. What outfit were you in?'

Commander Zero laughed. Actually, *guffawed* would be more like it. I noticed that he had several missing teeth. The ones that were left didn't look all that healthy.

'What's so funny?' I said.

The guffaw subsided into a chuckle.

'Swift,' he said, 'I like your sense of humour. But I don't fight *other people's* wars.' He said it as though I were one of God's chosen fools to have done so. 'How about we let it go at that?'

'Just thought I'd ask.' I couldn't always be right.

'I wanted to see your place,' Sally said. 'Swift came along for the ride. Is that okay?'

'A vet, eh?' he said. I nodded. 'Sure, come on, soldier brother.'

69

He laughed again and started down the trail. I looked at Sally. She shrugged. Might as well finish the trip.

Zero led us well back into nowhere. The trail branched twice, and we took the left fork both times. Eventually we came to a small clearing. There was a little grass-covered hummock at the back of the clearing. Behind it, a rock wall rose sharply.

From the front the grassy knoll was featureless. The entrance was in the rear, down a narrow incline between mounds of earth. The outer bulkhead was covered with sod a foot thick. You had to heave it up to get in. Off to the side were a couple of densely tangled bushes. That was where the vents would be concealed. I also noticed a cleft in the cliff face that wasn't visible except from up close. It provided an emergency exit to somewhere, I assumed. The Commander had chosen his site carefully.

The place was, as we had been warned, a bunker. Small but not tiny. Massive concrete walls. It could have been transplanted to a World War II Pacific island except that it lacked slits for the machine guns. Those are useless, anyway, unless the men inside are anxious to die for the cause. Someone will always get close enough to send home a grenade. In Zero's case the best thing to do would be to defend from outside, moving around, using his superior knowledge of the terrain. The bunker's sole function would be to provide a space beyond the reach of radioactive fallout.

There were two rooms. The front was for living. A bed, a chair, a table. A sink and stove. Electronic equipment of various kinds. The back room was storage. From what I could see, primarily it was sealed ten-gallon cans, stacked from floor to ceiling. The bunker was dank and somewhat musty, but that would be part of the deal.

'Impressive,' I said. 'You build it yourself?'

'Of course,' Commander Zero said.

'How'd you get the concrete in here?'

'I carried it.'

He said it contemptuously. I pursed my lips and nodded. Building the place had been an act of dedicated labour such as I couldn't even imagine. It was the work of a True Believer.

'This is the answer,' he said to Sally. 'In here I could survive for nearly three years. Or two people for eighteen months. No matter what was going on outside. It would be enough. After that, it would be a new world. Ready to be repopulated.'

'What about water?' she asked him.

70

'An underground spring,' he said. 'Good filtration. I tried to contaminate it and couldn't. It pipes right to the sink. Gravity feed. Not much pressure, but then, who needs it?'

She gestured to the back room. 'That's the food supply, of course.'

'Beans, grains, powdered milk, freeze-dried fruit and vegetables, vitamins and minerals, everything. Nitrogen-packed. Indefinite shelf life. Got to be on the safe side, though. I eat out of them and rotate. Supplement the wild stuff.'

'Waste?' she asked.

'Chemically treated. Down the drain.'

'You're going to need power, it looks like. She glanced at all the electronics.

'Ah.' His eyes brightened. 'Yes. The lights, radio, monitoring equipment. Very important. I'm wired all around. Heat sensors, vibration sensors. I need to know when someone's coming. So . . . my masterpiece. Twelve-volt system, of course. Battery storage. Entirely solar-powered! Part of the hill folds back to expose the collectors, when they're needed. Motor-driven. We're fully charged right now. Lots of sun lately.'

'You get a string of cloudy days in a row — ' I said.

' — and I live in the dark for a while. Worse things, eh? Better than storing a lot of kerosene. No risk of carbon monoxide poisoning, either.'

He grinned and looked right at me. He had to be referring to Ballard's death. But his eyes were merry. Merry, or as mad as a hatter. Though Anne had said he was regarded as harmless and all, I was beginning to think it wouldn't be a great idea to be stuck in this rabbit hole with this guy for too long.

'One of the other members told us you keep some guns here,' I said cautiously.

'Guns, yes. Fishing gear, too. You don't have to screw, but you've got to eat.'

'Deer?'

'Yuh. Rabbits, groundhogs. There's a pond over thataway.' He gestured vaguely. 'Nice bass.'

There was a little .22 varmint rifle hanging over the bed.

'That your arsenal?' I asked.

He gave me an amused look.

'I'm sort of interested in weapons,' I said. 'I'm in the business.'

'Ah, yes. Loren Swift, private eye, hero of Brown's Cove. And

71

what'll *you* do when the war comes?'

I shrugged. 'Charlottesville's targeted, I imagine. I'll probably turn into vapour like everyone else.'

'Everyone but me. And whoever else . . . sees. What're you doing here, private cop?'

'Insurance investigation.'

'Insurance, eh?' He laughed, went over to the bed, reached under, and pulled out a footlocker. 'You want insurance? *This* is the only kind of insurance worth buying.'

He unlocked and opened the locker. Inside was his arsenal. I nearly choked. I'm no expert on guns, but I know quality when I see it. He had a trunkful.

'That's quite a collection,' Sally said.

'I don't see your M16,' I said.

He snorted. 'Automatic weapons are a waste,' he said, 'unless you've got military support. You should know that. They only encourage you to use up your ammunition. Suicide, yes?'

'That one on top looks close,' I said.

He picked it up. 'Beautiful, isn't it?' He beamed like a kid with a winning science fair exhibit and handed me the rifle. I hefted it and pretended to admire the workmanship. If I'd been a gun nut, I wouldn't have had to pretend.

'It is,' I said, and gave it back. He passed it to Sally for her inspection.

'Heckler and Koch HK91 heavy assault rifle,' he said. 'The best. They try to jam it, they fail. If you can't defend yourself with that . . . you can't defend yourself.'

Sally was giving the HK91 a close scrutiny. I peered into the locker.

'Shotgun, of course,' I said.

'Naturally,' he said. 'Remington 870 twelve-gauge. Puts more lead into the air faster than anything else, even your beloved M16.'

He was right. The Remington was massive firepower. It had been fitted with an eight-shot magazine extender, which meant that it could launch a couple hundred pellets of buckshot in three or four seconds. The gun had further combat modifications too. It featured a folding stock, adjustable sights, pistol grip, and sling.

'That it does,' I said.

'You recognize the pistol, I presume,' he said.

Sally put the HK91 back in the trunk and took out the Colt Commander .45 automatic. She handled it professionally.

72

'Mm-hmm,' she said. 'Nice. Throated and ramped?'

Commander Zero's eyes lit up like Christmas was happening inside his head.

'You know guns,' he said to her.

'A little,' she said. Then added, 'My daddy.'

'Oh . . . but that's wonderful,' he said.

They bent over the Colt together, admiring how he'd configured it. Neoprene grips, long trigger, flat mainspring housing, oversize slide release and safety levers. I checked the trunk further. There was another pistol, a snub-nosed .38 revolver. There were cans of ammo and magazines for the pistol and rifle. On the underside of its lid were a number of belts and loops holding accessories and whatnot: stripper clips and clip guides, scopes, revolver speed-loaders, spare parts. The man was serious.

'Would you like to shoot it?' he was saying to Sally.

'Yeah, I would,' she said, handing the pistol back to him. 'But not today. We have to get back.'

'Tomorrow, then.'

'I don't know. We'll see. I'm going to be around for a while. I like it here. So there's no hurry.'

'I think we have a lot to talk about.'

'C'mon, Swifty,' she said. 'I got a bunch more new people to meet this afternoon.' Then to Commander Zero, 'Thanks for the tour of the place. It's quite . . . something. I'll be back again.'

'Yes,' he said. 'I know you will.'

He looked like a happy man. We left him in the bunker, standing there among the kind of toys we've had to develop in order to cope with our vision of the future.

10

Freddie and Nancy Evans lived in the hollow on the other side of the ridge from the Ark, so I stopped off on my way back through, to clarify a couple of things with him. Sally went on about her prospective member's routine.

I found Freddie out behind his house, working on his woodpile. With the balmy Indian summer weather, it was difficult to imagine that the cold months were just around the corner, but they were. It was time for prudent people who heated with wood to be out cutting, splitting, making ready.

Freddie had on jeans and a plaid flannel lumberjack shirt that had seen a good deal of hard usage. He was also wearing a hard hat with integral protective face mask and the kind of noise-suppressing earmuffs you see a lot of at airports. The curly carrot hair managed to poke out here and there amid the equipment. The effect was comical, especially considering the skinny body beneath it all. He looked like a kid, trying to dress up as some space invader, who couldn't get his costume quite right.

Despite his seeming physical frailty, Freddie handled the big Stihl 031 with aplomb. He set the logs carefully and guided the saw's sixteen-inch bar quickly down through them. The chain was sharp, but it was still a demanding task. I reminded myself that people like Freddie often have a wiry strength that can be easily underestimated.

I made my way slowly out to where he could see me. You don't want to come up suddenly behind someone who's operating a chain saw. When he spotted me, he finished off the log he was working on. Then he shut down the saw, flipped up the face mask, and dropped the earmuffs down around his neck.

'Hi,' I said.

He nodded. He wasn't thrilled to see me.

'A couple of things occurred to me,' I said. 'You mind a few questions?'

'Yeah, I mind,' he said. 'But that's not going to stop you, is it?'

'I guess not.'

'You know, Swift, there are some people here who are trying to get over what happened. It was a shock, hard as it may be for you to understand. There are those of us who don't take kindly to what you're doing here. You follow what I'm saying?'

'Freddie,' I said, 'I am trying to intrude in your lives as little as possible. But there have been serious questions raised. All I'm trying to do is be sure of what happened to Temple Ballard. Wouldn't you like the same?'

'I already am sure.' He was properly defiant, but the pose was just a little off-centre. Freddie Evans wasn't entirely comfortable with himself.

'Then you shouldn't mind talking to me for five minutes.'

He sighed exaggeratedly. 'What do you want to know?' he said.

74

'Thank you,' I said. 'I appreciate it. I want to know if on the morning of the day Ballard died you tested the carbon-monoxide detector.'

'Of course,' he said wearily.

'Could you describe your routine?'

'I go into the shed.' He spoke like a robot. 'I get the stool. I stand on it. I push the test button. The alarm goes off. I reach behind and pull out the plug. I push the test button again, to make sure the battery backup is working. The alarm goes off again. I plug the detector back in. End of test. It was working fine at that time.'

'You mean the alarm was working fine.'

'That's what I said.'

'No, you said the detector was working fine. But all that your tests did was check the alarm, which was working. Nothing you did would test whether the detector itself was functioning properly.'

'Whatever,' he said.

'It's an important distinction. Was the detector's ability to monitor CO ever checked?'

'I ran it along the line too. Like I was supposed to,' he said defensively.

'That still wouldn't do it. If it wasn't working, it wouldn't go off. And it didn't that morning, right?'

'Yeah. It didn't.'

'So is there anything else you do?' I asked.

'Um, there is. Once a month. We fire up the gasifier and open the bleeder vent. Hold the alarm over it. See if it goes off.'

'And it always did?'

'Yeah.'

'Good,' I said. 'But that still doesn't really test it. That only shows that the device is sensitive to a blast of CO hitting it. It doesn't mean the thing would work under conditions of slow buildup, which was what actually happened, does it?'

'Wait a minute here,' he said suspiciously. 'Are you trying to say the detector was defective? Whose side are you on, anyway?'

'I'm not on anybody's *side*. I'm attempting to find out if y'all perform any regular tests that would show whether the device was absolutely doing what it's supposed to do.'

'Well . . . I guess maybe not, if you put it that way.'

They were questions I'd had to ask, at the risk of making him feel more guilty than he already felt, if he did already feel guilty. Now it looked as if he might be headed in that direction. I didn't want it to happen, so I changed the subject.

'All right,' I said. 'How long had you had the detector?'

'You mean, before . . . ?'

'Right.'

'Let me see. Since the gasifier was installed. About a year.'

'And did it ever go off? Other than in testing. Was there ever a leak sufficient to activate it?'

'There . . . was. Once. When we . . . first had the gasifier running. Someone . . . replaced the top to the filter unit improperly. Enough gas . . . leaked out to trigger the alarm.'

'This was also in the shed,' I said.

'Yes.'

'And was anyone working in there at the time?'

'No, I don't think so.'

'That was the only incident in a year?'

'As far as I know.'

'Okay,' I said. 'So all that we can say is that the detector did work at one time. But we don't know for sure whether it ever picked up small changes in CO concentration, like it's supposed to.'

'I guess.'

'Now, just one more thing. Who knew that Ballard was going to be working in the shed that night?'

'I don't know. I did. Nancy did.'

'You can't speak for anyone else?'

'No. Probably most people knew, though. It wasn't a big secret. Everyone knew about the leaky water pipe.'

'So it wasn't something he did suddenly?'

'No,' he said, 'not if you mean he went up there five minutes after deciding the pipe needed attention. We'd been after him to look at it for a couple of days. He told me that that night would be the first chance to do it. If he told me, he might have told anyone.'

'Is there anyone who *wasn't* here that night?'

'You mean in the whole community? Hell, I don't know that.'

'How about among those who were at dinner last night?'

'Let me see. Ike and Rags were here, of course. Me and Nancy. Lisa was. Mary Beth and Spock. No, we were all on the land. Except for that visitor, Sally Hatch.'

'How about the provisional members?' I asked.

'Anne's too new. She came out here for the first time last

76

summer. Jeff, ah . . . Yeah, he might have been here. He's been provisional for nine months, I think. I can't tell you if he was physically here.'

'Doesn't he work Saturday nights?'

'He didn't always. That's fairly recent.'

'He's a strange one,' I said.

'Yeah. He won't be here for much longer.'

'He seems intent on staying.'

'He is, but you can only be provisional for a year. After that, you have to be voted permanent, or you don't get in. And he doesn't have the votes to make it. Even those who most thought he'd change are losing interest. Look, are you about through now?' He gestured at his woodpile.

'Just about,' I said. 'What do you think of Commander Zero?'

'He's a case.' Freddie chuckled. 'I think he's basically harmless.'

'When did he build that bunker out in the woods?'

'Oh, a while ago. Three, four years.'

'He come down here much?'

'Not a lot. Only once a month for certain. That's when he gets his cheque in the mail. Cashes it, pays his dues, buys supplies at the local store. Then you might not see him until the next month. That doesn't mean he's not around, though. He's very good at moving quietly. Sometimes I think he can make himself invisible.'

'I've noticed,' I said. 'So you think he roams the land a lot?'

'Yeah. I've seen him out of the corner of my eye a few times.'

'What did he think of Temple Ballard?'

'He didn't like him.'

'Oh?'

'Temple wanted to develop Babel as a model for the efficient use of modern technology. He wanted people outside to know what we were doing here. Zero hates publicity, of course. He's a little . . . paranoid.'

'A little?'

Freddie shrugged. 'I've got to get back to work,' he said. 'I believe you were finished.'

'Sure. Thanks, Freddie. I'll try not to bother you again.'

He just nodded. Then he flipped down the face mask, fixed the earmuffs back over his ears. He pulled the Stihl's starter cord. The saw caught the first time.

I wandered down to the Ark. I stood there and stared at it for a while. No brilliant ideas came to me, so I went into the shed. The

Chevy engine was running, generating electricity, helping the fishes to grow. I looked and listened, trying to tune myself to the proper frequency. If, as Rags had said, Temple Ballard's spirit still haunted this place, maybe it could tell me something. I allowed myself to slip into a state of no thought, open to whatever chose to enter my mind. I waited.

Nothing came to me. Sometimes the magic works and sometimes it doesn't.

I walked around the shed, looking closely at the setup, following the pipes that carried the carbon monoxide about its business. They were all blank-faced, neutral pieces of machinery. Nowhere did I sense the imminent presence of death. It was about as innocuous as the pump room at a municipal swimming pool.

Yet a man had died here. Why?

I went over to the CO detector. It hung on its hook, silent but presumably vigilant, making sure that I didn't follow Temple Ballard into endless rest. I pulled the stool over and stood on it. I examined the detector from every angle. It was black and featureless, like it had always been. The cord that plugged it in was invisible behind its body. I removed it from the hook, set it on the floor, and looked closely at the wall it was suspended in front of. An ordinary wall, fitted with a brown grounded outlet like any other. I ran my hand over the wall. It was relatively smooth. Smooth, except . . . I felt again. Something ticked against my fingers, something that wasn't an irregularity in the surface. I picked at it with my fingernail until it peeled off the wall, being careful not to drop it, then transferred it to my palm. I poked at it. It was old and only slightly tacky now. It had yellowed and gone somewhat brittle. But it was unmistakably Scotch tape. One corner from the end of a strip.

Maybe it meant nothing. There were a hundred and one reasons why it might have been there, all of them good ones. Yet I suddenly found the shed intolerably damp and chilly. I put the detector back and went out into the sunshine.

Yes, I thought, that's how I'd have done it. If I knew there was a leak in the line. Remove the batteries, then unplug the detector. But I couldn't just leave the cord dangling, because normally it was out of sight. Someone entering the room might notice it and realize right away that something was wrong. So I'd tape the cord to the wall. Then the detector would look okay to all but the closest

78

scrutiny. Since it already would have been checked earlier in the day, there would be no reason for anyone to be suspicious.

Then, after someone had entered the shed and a reasonable time had passed . . . I took a deep breath. I went back into the shed, pantomimed replacing the batteries, untaping the cord and plugging it in, replacing the detector on its hook. I hurried out of the room and exhaled. No problem. I'd easily done it all on one held breath. I'd committed a nearly perfect murder.

The only question was: Who was I?

11

Dinner that night was a lot more modest. Just Sally and I, Jeff, Anne and Lisa. Anne cooked. She made a mushroom quiche, which is something I normally like even if that does reflect adversely on my manhood. Hers was passable.

At one point Lisa asked me with mock seriousness, 'So, Mr Swift, have you unearthed any deep, dark secrets yet?'

'Oh, yes,' I said, 'quite a few. Drug smuggling, kiddie porn, counterfeit money. A couple of others.'

The three Babelonians stared at me blankly. Sally covered her smile with a discreet cough.

'C'mon, folks,' I said. 'Only kidding. Joke.'

'Bad joke,' Lisa said. 'You see, around here we have to take things like that seriously. We're outsiders living in what is basically a very conservative part of the country. Our values are . . . different from those of our neighbours. Naturally, they're suspicious of us. Chances are a lot of them think we really *do* smuggle drugs and make pornographic movies here. Ingrained prejudices are hard to break down.'

'Sorry,' I said.

'You're forgiven.' The lascivious grin spread across her face. 'Doesn't mean we don't have our secrets, though.'

'Some of them not so secret,' Jeff said sullenly.

'How so?' I asked.

'We believe in being open with one another about our feelings and what we do,' Lisa said. 'I'm afraid Jeff doesn't entirely agree with that philosophy.'

'It's not my decision,' Jeff said. 'It's the Lord's.'

'Jeff,' Anne said, 'if you weren't worrying about the Lord all the time, you might be able to understand a little better what was going on around you. There are people here who want that.'

'I do not worry about the Lord. That would be much too prideful of me.'

'What is the Lord to you?' Sally asked politely. 'How do you conceive of Him?'

'The Lord is beyond our feeble imaginings. He is present at all places and all times.' The tone was decidedly condescending. Sally appeared not to notice.

'Then He must be here with us,' Lisa said.

'Of course He is.'

'And He must know our secrets,' Anne said. 'But He doesn't seem to be judging us. I don't feel judged. Perhaps our secrets don't displease Him at all. Perhaps it's only y—' She stopped suddenly, as if realizing she'd been saying the wrong thing.

He waved his fork at her like it was a weapon in the holy war.

'You are foolish,' he said. 'You are *all* foolish. The ultimate judgment is yet to come. But do not think that you are not being judged from day to day. The Lord watches and He judges. His retribution is swift and it is terrible. Temple Ballard was a warning to us all.'

Everyone froze. Jeff sat there with something like a little smirk on his face.

'Jeff,' Lisa said. It was a clear warning.

'You know it,' he said sternly. 'Temple Ballard was punished for his evil—'

'Jeff!' Lisa shouted. She rose.

'You can't bury the truth beneath—'

'Jeff, that's enough,' she growled. 'Come with me. Now.'

He hesitated, looking from Sally to Anne. Sally returned the look; Anne stared at her place.

'I said *now*!' Lisa insisted.

He got up.

'Come on,' she said more gently.

He came around the table. She turned, and he followed her. There was a strong temptation to see him as a dog trotting after its master, but I knew there had to be a lot more to it than that. They went out the door to the deck, into the night.

'Wow,' Sally said.

We looked at Anne.

'He . . . gets like that,' she said nervously. 'He has some real conflicts with his religious beliefs. It's my fault for setting him up. I wasn't thinking.'

'Don't blame yourself,' I said.

'When he gets like that, Lisa's the only one who can handle him. He's in love with her.'

'And hates himself for it,' Sally said.

'I guess. But he'll do what she tells him. She'll calm him down. Sometimes I wonder if a lot of it isn't for her benefit in the first place.'

'I can't believe he's still here after nine months,' I said.

'Some of the members think that Babel can change anyone,' Anne said. 'Given enough time and free exposure to our ideas. It's a nice thought, but it hasn't worked with Jeff. Still, people want to give him the benefit of the doubt, give him the full year before they vote him out.'

'What was it that he was raving about?' Sally asked casually. Bless her.

'Oh, he's kind of fixated on that Ballard guy. Apparently, Ballard was bisexual. Jeff found out about it shortly after he came here. It wasn't a big secret or anything. Jeff was outraged. He started a personal campaign to save Ballard from eternal damnation. I guess Ballard treated him like a fool, which only angered him more. When Ballard died in the accident, Jeff felt vindicated. Ballard became this symbol of what happens to sinners. But it's scary, too, you see. Because now Jeff has direct evidence of how the Lord intervenes in our affairs. Which means that *he'd* better watch *his* step. The same fate might be waiting for him if he isn't pure.'

'If he lusts in his heart for Lisa,' Sally said, 'that must drive him half crazy.'

'I think it does. That plus the obsession with Temple Ballard . . . well, every once in a while he gets into a state like you just saw. Actually, you only saw the beginning. It gets a lot worse. Lisa's learned to see it coming. She kind of takes responsibility for him, which we appreciate. She'll walk him around for a while to bring him back to earth. Funny thing is, it hasn't really happened in a while. Not like this. Something must have set him off.'

Sally crossed her arms in front of her and hugged her shoulders. She shivered. 'It gives me the creeps,' she said. 'Does he ever get physically violent?'

Damn but she was good.

'I don't know for sure,' Anne said. 'I don't think so. It's against his religion.' She chuckled inadvertently. 'Excuse me, I don't really think it's funny. . . . He did get in a fight once, though.'

'Oh?' I said.

'It was before my day. Right after Temple Ballard died, I believe. Jeff was just getting into his feelings about it. He made the mistake of laying them on Freddie Evans one night, and Freddie went after him. Ike and Nancy had to jump in the middle of things to get them apart. I don't think Jeff and Freddie speak to this day.'

'That's heavy,' Sally said. 'But you folks ought to fit right in around here. They've got some feuds back in the mountains that've endured since Jefferson was carrying on with his slaves.'

Anne laughed. 'It's not *that* bad,' she said. 'Most people here get along real well.'

'I don't know,' Sally said. 'It's beginning to sound like a hotbed of intrigue to me.'

'It's not. Really. There are some bad feelings here and there, of course. Jealousies. The usual. But no more than you'd find any-place else.'

At that point Lisa returned, alone.

'I'm sorry,' she said to us. 'Shall I serve dessert?' We all nodded enthusiastically.

Over the peach cobbler I said to Lisa, 'Anne was telling us that you have to do that from time to time.'

'I'm afraid so,' Lisa said. 'But don't worry. He's cooling off. He'll probably be out walking for another couple of hours. I feel sorry for the kid, so I try to help him. I don't think it does much good, though. Inside, he's at war. One minute he's trying to save my soul, the next he's trying to get me in bed with him.'

'I couldn't handle it,' Sally said.

'I can cope,' Lisa said. 'But I won't weep when he finally leaves.'

'You're never worried?' Sally asked. 'You don't think he could turn on you when he realizes that he's not gonna bring you to the light *or* get in your pants?'

'Nah. He wouldn't hurt me. He wouldn't hurt . . . anyone.'

We finished our desserts.

'Delicious,' I said. 'I'll do the dishes if nobody minds.' Nobody

82

minded. 'Let me just ask you one more thing, Lisa.'

'Sure.'

'The people who were here last night, are any of them around during the week? Do they have outside jobs or what?'

'Well,' she said, 'I won't be here much tomorrow. Freddie's supervising a building job off the land, so he'll be gone too. The others all work here. Rags does freelance computer programming. Nancy has a dried flower business, and Ike oversees the fish-farming project. Mary Beth quit her job in town a few months ago, and Spock just sort of is. I can't testify to anyone's particular plans, but that's the general rundown.'

'You dancing tomorrow?' I asked.

'Among other things.'

'Well, don't forget to smile.'

She groaned. 'God, if you only knew.'

After the dishes I called Ike and asked to see him in the morning. He said fine. Then Sally and I retreated to our spot on the deck again. We made small talk and did affectionate things with each other. Anne joined us for a while. Chaudri stopped by. It was a subdued social evening, unmarked by any further revelations. Speaking of which, we never saw Jeff again.

It began to cool off. Sally asked shyly if I wanted to go in and get warm. 'My place or yours?' I asked. We went to my room. Some-one had turned the core house stereo on. Rock and Roll. It was loud enough that we felt comfortable talking.

'This place is weird,' I said.

'No shit, Sherlock,' Sally said, and we both had a good laugh about it.

'I like your technique,' I said.

'You haven't even seen my technique yet,' she said, batting her eyelashes.

'Come on, I mean the way you handled the conversation at dinner. Very deft.'

She bowed. 'Are you beginning not to regret our partnership?'

'I'm beginning to like it very much.'

It was a slightly awkward moment. So far our intimacy had been out on the stage, for the benefit of whoever was looking, to establish credibility. Now we were alone, and I realized that it hadn't been such an act, after all. I was genuinely fond of this woman. I cleared my throat.

'Well,' I said, 'What major scoops do you have for me this

evening?' I sat on the edge of the bed. She took the single straight-backed chair the room came with.

'None, really. But I may be getting close.' She was enthusiastic.

'Nancy?'

'Uh-huh. I spent some more time with her this afternoon. She's real nice, but there's something troubling her, I can tell. We're not good enough friends yet for her to confide in me. We're getting there, though.'

'You think what's troubling her is relevant.'

'Yeah, I do. Whenever I talk about Ballard or the accident, she changes. The subject makes her nervous, and she's not ordinarily like that at all. Something was going on between the three of them, she and Freddie and Ballard, I can feel it. Give me another day or two.'

'Okay. I'll stay clear of Nancy. It might even work better that way. If she thinks I'm not interested in her, it might make her more likely to open up to you. I won't bother Freddie, either. I talked to him this afternoon. I'm pretty sure he has something to tell us, but I'd like to be a little clearer on what it is. He's going to be off the land during the week, anyway.'

'Fine. And how about you? Find out anything today?'

'As a matter of fact, I did.' I told her about my conversation with Freddie and about my subsequent visit to the Ark. I told her what I had found there and what I thought it might mean. I asked her what she thought of the scenario.

'Could be,' she said.

'I don't like to theorize in the absence of facts,' I said. 'But in this instance I'm afraid we're going to have to. From what Freddie said, there's no way we'll ever know for sure if the detector was working properly. I don't see how they could have mishandled it to cause it to fail temporarily. And Temple Ballard did not kill himself and then trip the alarm. That leaves us with someone having done it for him. The piece of Scotch tape tends to support that theory. As does Pethco's lab report on the detector.'

'You're right. And I've got that funny feeling too. Any suspects in mind?'

I grinned. 'Only a handful so far. I'm sure we can turn up a few more.'

'What's next?'

'Ike Bender for me. How about you?'

'I volunteered to help Nancy with some dried flower arrangements. We shall see.'

'Well, that should do it for tonight,' I said.

She sat there, resting her chin on her hands, looking at me. The midnight-blue eyes zapped me. I felt my mouth go dry. Where had she been ten years ago when I really needed her? No, I knew where she had been. She'd been in high school. Breaking pimply hearts. She came over and sat next to me on the bed, turned so she could face me. She laced her fingers around the back of my neck.

'I like you, Swifty,' she said.

'I like you too,' I said.

'And you really are kind of cute. We can sleep together if you want.'

I chuckled. 'And here I thought you were gay.'

'Ah, that's just a word.' She smiled. 'Help you put people in little boxes. I like men just fine. Life is a lot more interesting if you don't categorize other folks.'

'Isn't it?' I said, and we kissed. She was a very good kisser. It went on a lot longer than I had expected it to.

When we broke for air, I said, 'Look, Sally . . . '

She put her index finger on my lips. 'Don't,' she said. 'It's okay. It only is what it is for us here and now.' She leaned over to kiss me again.

She radiated heat. I wanted her. God knows, I wanted her. It had been an awfully long time. I was aching with the want, and she was a soft, lovely, desirable woman whom I liked and respected as well. She offered only the pleasure of the moment. It would have been the easiest, most natural thing in the world. But I couldn't. I put my hands on her shoulders and stopped her.

'Sally,' I said gently, 'I mean it. I have to tell you something.'

The question was there in her eyes, the same dumb question we immediately ask ourselves: What's wrong with me?

'It isn't you,' I said. 'It's me.'

She relaxed, and then I told her. I told her everything, from the day I'd met Patricia until the night a madman had caved in the back of her skull because of me. It was the first time I'd really talked to anyone since it had happened. Some part of the burden fell away from me.

'It feels good to tell someone,' I said. 'Maybe not as good as sex would have felt, but . . . '

We laughed and hugged each other.

'Thank you for telling me,' she said. 'She sounds like a great lady.'

'She is. You'd like her.'

'I don't doubt it.'

'You don't feel rejected, I hope.'

'No, of course not.'

She hugged me again. As she did, I looked across the room at the window. I saw movement. It wasn't much, the echo of a shadow. The room was bright, the night dark. Looking outside at someone, motion was all you might expect to see.

I froze. Sally picked it up right away.

'What is it?' she whispered.

'Someone's been watching.'

I got up and went to the window. There was nothing to see.

'Who?' she said.

'I don't know. Stay here for a minute.'

I went outside. The fields lay silent around the core house. Little wisps of mist were visible in the starlight. The barn was a large blank shape in the near distance. Beyond it, the ridge loomed, slightly darker than its background. The Ark could not be seen.

I circled the house slowly, setting my feet with care. It was no use. Whoever had been there was gone. When I reached the window to my room, I tapped on it. It was double-glazed, but I had to check. Sally came to the window.

'Go over to the chair and start talking in a normal voice,' I said loudly through the glass. 'There's no one here.'

She did it. As I'd suspected, the words were muffled by the glass, blended up with the rock and roll. Only here and there did something stand out. Whoever had been out here wouldn't have learned Sally's and my true relationship. He or she would have seen two people talking, then kissing, then talking some more, then hugging. For all practical purposes we would have looked like we were about to become lovers. Good.

I tapped on the window again. She came over, and I gave her a thumb-and-forefinger circle.

'I'm coming back in,' I said.

I walked more quickly this time, my thoughts elsewhere. There was a large boxwood . . . and then Sally was shaking me.

'Huh?' I said. 'What?'

'Swift,' she was saying, 'come on.' She was kneeling over me,

86

shaking my shoulders, gently slapping my face.

'Huh?' I said.

'Come on, wake up. What are you doing?'

'What am I doing?'

'What *happened*?'

Cold. The ground was cold. The ground? Why was she shaking me? It was still dark. It wasn't time to get up yet.

I was outside, on the ground. Not in bed.

'I must have fainted,' I said.

'Jesus Christ,' she said. 'Come on.' She slid a hand under my shoulders and started to pry me up.

'Ouch,' I said.

'What's the matter?'

Gingerly, I felt the side of my neck. It was as sore as hell. I suddenly remembered having been at the window, then why I'd been there.

'How long have I been out here?' I asked.

'I don't know. Two minutes, three. You were coming back in, then you didn't show up. I came looking for you. It hasn't been long.'

'Somebody knocked me out.'

'What?' She dropped me.

'Ow,' I said.

'Oh, Jesus, I'm sorry. I didn't mean to do that.'

'It's okay.' I levered myself back up, then on to my feet. She only helped a little.

'What do you mean somebody knocked you out?'

'A tiny love tap on the side of the neck. Just enough to stun me for a few minutes. I'm fine now.'

We went back to my room and I sat down. I rolled my head. The neck was sore, and it would be sorer, but I was all right.

'Swift,' Sally said, 'what the hell is going on?'

I shrugged. As I did, I became aware of something in my shirt pocket. It was a folded piece of paper. I took it out and opened it up. Sally came and looked over my shoulder. There were only two words on the paper, printed in the kind of block letters that wouldn't betray the handwriting. The words were: LEAVE BABEL.

'Well, at least he gets right to the point,' I said.

'I don't like this.'

'You should see it from where I am.'

'Don't joke about it. What are we going to do?'

'You're not going to do anything,' I said. 'You're not the one who got sapped. Me, I think I want to take a couple of aspirin and sleep on it.'

'Okay. I'll stay with you. It'll look better that way, anyway. Think you can keep your hands off me?'

'If you can keep yours off me.'

'I'll try,' she said stoically.

We laughed. Sally went to the bathroom for aspirin while I got into bed, after pulling the curtains across the window. When she came back, she had a nightdress on. She climbed in beside me. I had a moment of weakness, but it passed.

The music shut off for the night a little later. The house was silent for a while, then there was sound. Soft at first, then building to a climax, then ebbing. The unmistakable cries of people making love. I marvelled at how silly it looks and sounds to everyone but those actually involved, and how serious it is for them. I chuckled to myself. Beside me, Sally began to giggle too. Then she turned over and snuggled into my back. Lord, give me strength, I thought. But we fell asleep that way.

I never wondered who the lovers might have been.

12

When we woke up, our bodies were still pressed together. It was a strange moment. I'd never before slept like that with a woman who wasn't my lover. I felt shy and about half my age.

'Sleep well?' Sally asked.

'Yeah. Surprisingly enough.'

'How do you feel?'

'I'm sore, but I think the prognosis is good. Listen, thanks for . . . being there. Whatever.'

'Aw, shucks,' she said. She gave me a little kiss and hopped out of bed. She went to her room, got dressed, and came back.

'Anyone stirring?' I asked.

'I didn't see anyone.' She pitched her voice low. We were both still feeling wary. 'What do we want to do today?'

'Why don't you follow through with Nancy as planned?'

'Okay.'

'And I think I'll go get acquainted with the Nelson County Sheriff.'

'Is it time for that?'

'I think so,' I said. 'He probably won't want to get involved, but I at least want him to be aware that there's someone here who doesn't like me poking around.'

'I guess it can't hurt.'

'And who knows, there's always the chance he'll think we've found enough for him to reopen the case. I've never met the man. He may be the model of a modern law-enforcement officer.'

'Don't count on it.'

We had breakfast. Sally and Anne and I. Afterward, I called Ike Bender and rescheduled our chat for the afternoon. Then I drove to Lovingston.

Lovingston is the county seat of Nelson County. It's a pleasant little village of a few hundred souls that sits next to US 29 about thirty-five miles south of Charlottesville. It snugs up against a sheer cliff face, giving it the look of a town whose location was chosen for defensive purposes. I doubt that that was actually the case.

The administration of local government is Lovingston's function in life. The relevant buildings are clustered on the east side of town. They're an unimpressive lot. Nelson County is thinly populated and it's poor. There is neither the desire nor the need to impress with fancy modern architecture.

The sheriff's offices are in the basement of a white-painted cinder-block building, hidden away like the unwanted step-child of the Health Department that sits above them. I made my way down the access ramp and through the outer door. It was a tiny anteroom with an unshaded bulb in the ceiling and wanted posters on the wall. There was a waist-high divider with a uniformed man sitting behind it, speed-puffing unfiltered cigarettes. The air was thick with smoke.

'What can we do for you?' the guy asked.

'I'd like to see Sheriff Jakes.'

'Who're you?'

I gave him one of my cards. He stared at it, then flipped it over, looking for something on the back. I realized that all it had on it was SWIFT INVESTIGATIONS and my phone number, and that that might not be enough.

'I'm a private investigator,' I said. 'From Charlottesville.'

He eyed me disdainfully. 'What'd you want to see Faber about?' Puff puff.

I'm working on a case down here. I'd like him to know what I'm doing. Courtesy call.' I put on my most winsome smile.

He looked utterly unconvinced, but he punched a button on his phone and spoke to the boss.

'He'll see you,' he said.

The sheriff's office was modest but clean and functional. The man himself was medium height, wiry, with brush-cut black-and-gray hair. He had cool, flat eyes behind wire-rimmed spectacles, and he never blinked. His lips were thin and bloodless. I couldn't help but be reminded of the stereotyped Gestapo interrogation officer in any number of Hollywood B movies. I was used to dealing with Sheriff Ridley Campbell, Albemarle County's tough but genial NFL linebacker type. This dude was about as opposite as you could get.

We introduced ourselves.

'And what brings you to Nelson County, Mr Swift?' he asked.

'Babel,' I said.

'I see.' He kept the poker face. I would have bet that he always did. 'Go on.'

'Last February there was an accidental death out there. Carbon monoxide poisoning.' He nodded. 'My client wants me to make sure that it really was accidental.'

'And your client is?'

'Sorry.'

'Of course,' he said. 'You are like a . . . priest, aren't you? I'm afraid I don't meet many men in your . . . profession down here. Do you think that we mishandled the investigation?'

'I don't think anything at this point. But I would very much like to have your opinions on the subject.'

He shrugged. 'I doubt there's that much to it. No evidence of foul play, as I'm sure you know. Mr Ballard went to that whatever they call it of his own free will. There was a leak in the line. The place filled up with carbon monoxide. The alarm didn't go off in time, so it killed him. Accident.'

'The alarm was tested. There wasn't anything wrong with it.'

'Don't mean nothing. I got a radio at home; sometimes it works, sometimes it don't.'

90

'You don't think it's odd that the alarm didn't go off until Ballard was dead?'

'Sure, it's odd,' he said. 'But it happened, didn't it? I imagine maybe the thing was set wrong, so it didn't pick up the carbon monoxide until the room was loaded with it. Then it finally spread the news. That's the most logical explanation.'

I saw that it would be fruitless to try to convince him of the significance of a piece of Scotch tape, so I told him instead that I'd uncovered evidence that a number of people at Babel may have had reason to dislike the deceased. He told me that was interesting, but he didn't really think so.

'Then last night,' I said, 'somebody knocked me out from behind and stuffed a note in my pocket telling me to get lost.'

'Now that's better,' he said. 'You want to file a complaint?'

I thought about it. If the sheriff and his men came out to investigate a case of alleged assault, what would that accomplish? Nothing. They'd never find out who'd done it. All that would happen was that the person involved would be a lot more careful until the troops lost interest. Most likely, it would hinder what Sally and I were trying to do.

'No,' I said. 'I doubt there's much point to it.'

'I agree. You got to consider, too, that there's a lot of reasons you might have been hit over the head.'

'What're you saying, that it's unrelated to what I'm investigating?'

'Could be.'

'Oh, come on, Sheriff. I don't have any enemies there. Other than those who don't want me to find out what they're trying to hide.'

He shrugged. 'Suit yourself,' he said. 'Me, I wouldn't jump to conclusions.'

'Okay. Thanks for your time, Sheriff.' I got up. 'Just wanted you to know I was around, really.'

''Preciate it. You come across anything more specific, you let me know, y'hear?'

'You got it,' I said. 'And anything happens to me, don't let the bastards get away with it.'

He nodded. I'd done all there was for me to do. I went back out through the smoky anteroom. A black man was in there, complaining that he hadn't been speeding but had been the victim of a

91

deputy who had it in for him. He sounded sincere, but he was still going to pay.

The road back to Charlottesville is divided highway, through the mountains. It's a pleasant drive, and it was another pleasant day. Along the way I did some thinking.

Obviously, someone at Babel was getting nervous about my questions. He or she had thought the case was closed, and now here I came along, stirring the thing up again. If I could be gotten rid of, maybe it would all die down. The main problem I was having was with the crudity of the warning. Wouldn't the person realize that a physical attack would only make me more suspicious? Of course. The only explanation was that I was expected to scare easily, to decide that it wasn't worth the risk to my skin, to run off and file a report stating my opinion that it was an accident, after all. Possible. And if I didn't scare? Maybe I was supposed to think that the next warning wouldn't be so gentle. Maybe the next warning was going to be more than just a warning. I didn't like that idea.

I turned my thoughts to who my unknown assailant might have been. The possibles made a depressingly lengthy list, even though the actual person might not even be on it.

First in line was Mary Beth. She had the best reason for wanting me gone, but I liked her least as a suspect. Her interests were best served by having me investigate unimpeded and coming up empty. She wouldn't want to hand me proof that there was something there. Besides, I didn't think what had happened was at all her style. And besides that, she was small. It would have been very difficult for her to pull it off. Of course, she could have had her son do it. If he was into punk, he might be no stranger to violence.

Next was Freddie Evans. He'd openly expressed his hostility to me, and he'd been in at least one fight that I knew of. I felt that he was hiding something, and Sally felt that his wife was too. On the other hand, I had a hard time imagining Freddie moving quietly enough to set me up like that. And he, too, was short, making it awkward to strike the blow correctly.

Then there was Jeff. He was the only one that I knew for sure had been out there in the night somewhere. I had no trouble picturing him at the window, spying on Sally and me as we wallowed in sin. He'd been in an agitated state as well. Anne had said that something must have set him off. Maybe it was my investigation. That could have brought a lot of his ill feeling about Ballard to the surface. He might resent me for the pain I was causing and want to

92

get rid of me. Not to mention that there was the remote chance he'd been God's agent in the dispatching of Ballard. It wasn't a bad scenario. I put him in the pile with people more likely than others.

Finally, there was Commander Zero. At this point I liked him for it the most. He was tall, and he moved about like he was invisible. He'd know where and how hard to hit you. I'd been told that he was paranoid about the public attention Ballard intended to bring down on Babel. He had to be a prime suspect, for both Ballard's death and the attack on me. But of them all, I most hoped it wasn't him. He was well armed and he was dangerous. If I got any closer to him, well, without a lot of help it was much too likely that they'd find my own hide hanging out on the line.

When I got to Charlottesville, I stopped off at the hospital. Patricia still looked like she was going to wake up any minute, and she still hadn't. I whispered to her that I was hornier than hell but that I was saving myself for her, against horrendous odds. She smiled in her sleep. Or maybe I imagined it.

Before I left, I went by Dr Pastreich's office and dropped off the phone number of the core house at Babel. Then I drove to my apartment. It looked no different from when I'd last been there, what seemed like weeks ago. I poured myself a little Jameson over ice — for medicinal purposes, of course. I went through my collection of 1960s rhythm-and-blues records, selected Aretha Franklin's *R-E-S-P-E-C-T* album, and lay down on my couch to listen. The music relaxed me. I managed to forget for a time that there are a lot of people wandering the nighttimes of the world, waiting for the opportunity to do violence.

When Aretha was through soothing my soul, I got down to business. First I called Devin Pethco.

'We're making progress,' I told him.

'You think it wasn't an accident?' he said. He couldn't contain his excitement.

'Don't run to the parent yet, but yeah, I don't think it was an accident.'

'What do you think?'

'I think it was murder.'

I don't like the idea of someone being made happy by news of a murder. But Pethco was going to be, and I couldn't do a thing about it. To spare myself, I abbreviated the description of what Sally and I had found so far. I omitted mentioning the state of my neck. That might encourage him to become more involved, and his involvement I didn't want.

'It's nothing concrete,' I said, 'but it's a lot more than zero.'

'Good, good,' he said. 'How are you and Miss Hatch getting along?'

'Fine. She's very professional.'

'I was sure. She's one of our top young talents. Still, if you need more help, just let me know.'

'Don't worry, we can handle it. I hope to have more for you in the next couple of days. It'll take some time. The situation down there is more complex than I would have thought it could be.'

'Okay,' he said. 'Keep me posted. You're doing great. We really appreciate it. I've got a meeting now. Gotta run.'

After Pethco, I called my pal Jonesy at the *Daily Press*. I asked him if he could check his files for some weather information. I gave him the date of the night Ballard died. It might not be important, but it might. He checked. The night had been clear and cold, but not bitter. Temperature in the middle thirties. No snow had fallen. Phase of the moon? Three-quarters full. Enough for decent visibility. Any snow on the ground? None in any of the photos in the paper.

I asked him how the book was coming. He was doing a book on the case that had left me with the broken wrist and the game leg. He said it was nearly done and that he had a buyer based on an outline and the first three chapters. I told him to go for it. Jonesy loved the story. He was certain it was going to make us rich. And perhaps finally get him a job offer from the *Washington Post*, which he coveted more than all of mankind's gold.

Lastly I called Ridley Campbell, the Albemarle County Sheriff and a sort of friend. I explained to him what I was doing.

'That's nice, but it ain't my jurisdiction, Swift,' he informed me. 'I got enough problems right here to home.'

'I know,' I said. 'I just wanted your opinion. What's your feel for Faber Jakes?'

'I don't criticize fellow members of the constabulary.' He chuckled. 'You know that.'

'But?'

'But he's a hard case.'

'Honest?'

'Yeah, he's honest. He don't do more'n he has to, though.'

'I got the impression I don't want to cross him,' I said.

94

'The man has been known to carry a grudge.'

'How much will it take to move him?'

'A whole hell of a lot.'

'Look, Rid, there's dude down there with more fancy guns than you need for a little weekend target practice. Your word carry any weight with Jakes if I get in a jam?'

'Nope.'

'You're not making this easy.'

'Swift,' he said, 'you'd best consider that you're on your own. You want some advice?'

'Yeah, okay.'

'If you don't like what's happening, drop the case. Let the woman have her money.'

'I can't,' I said.

'Why not?'

'Personal reasons.'

'All right, I don't want to know.' He sighed. 'You get in trouble, call me. I'll see what I can do for you. No promises, you understand.'

'Thanks, Rid. I hope I'm near a phone.'

He laughed. It wasn't meant as a joke, actually.

The last thing I did before leaving my apartment was arm myself. Normally, though I'm licensed to do so, I don't like to carry a gun. Lots of times they can get you *into* trouble faster than they can get you out. But I didn't feel normal, especially in the neck area.

I gave the matter some thought. I own two handguns, a .38 Colt Police Positive revolver, and a 7.62 mm Walther PPK automatic. The Colt has more stopping power and is highly jam-resistant. But the Walther is lighter, more comfortable to tote, and has less recoil, which might be important given the state of my right wrist. To tell the truth, neither of them looked like much compared to what was in Commander Zero's war chest. I opted for the PPK, holstered it, and clipped it to my belt at the small of my back. I dropped a couple of extra ammunition clips into my jacket pocket. Hopefully, Zero was just some loony who lived out in the deep woods and didn't know anything about anything except how to survive a nuclear war.

As best as could be, I was now prepared to hear whatever message the voice of Babel might have for me.

95

13

I parked my VW next to a Volvo again. Chaudri was out on the front stoop, presumably taking a break from the CRT.

'Mr Swift,' he said. 'And how are you finding Babel?'

'It's a strange place.'

'I am sure that it would appear so to you. You are discovering perhaps that things are not always as they seem?'

His expression was neutral, as usual. Since it varied so little, I was less inclined to think that he was mocking me than I'd once been. Still, I never felt really sure.

'I hope there aren't too many more surprises,' I said.

'Each moment of our existence is a wonderful surprise, is it not?'

'Rags, you know, I really don't want to get in a philosophical discussion with you. Your ancestors were pondering the nature of the universe for five thousand years before mine knew there was anything more to life than sex and olive oil. That's an unfair advantage.'

He smiled. 'Perhaps. But then, you were not raised amid conflicting systems.'

I got the distinct impression that there was a double or even triple meaning to that one.

'Your parents were Hindu?'

'One Hindu,' he said, 'one Buddhist.'

'Ah. Put 'em together and you get a computer jock.'

'Science does have its attraction, yes.'

'What kind of a scientist was Temple Ballard?' I asked quickly.

'As a scientist, he was a . . . poet.' He looked wistful.

'I didn't know he wrote.'

'We all leave our poetry in one another's hearts, do we not?'

'Yeah, I guess we do at that. Best you can do is hope to write the good stuff. Tell me, Rags, what do you think of Commander Zero?'

'The Commander prepares for war. He does not realize that he is already *at* war.'

'I thought he was pretty paranoid,' I said.

'It would not be so if he recognized the enemy within.'

'I heard that he hated Temple Ballard.'

Okay, I might have overstated the case a little. But it was like I'd suddenly shaken him from the inside out. A series of divergent emotions fought it out behind his face. I was fascinated. Though I didn't have the first idea what those emotions might be, I felt certain that if I could find out, it would be to my benefit. I watched as his demeanour settled slowly back on to neutral ground. What was the key to this man?

'Temple believed that we had obligations to the world,' he said finally. 'Commander Zero does not believe this. Their viewpoints were inevitably at odds.'

'Do you think that Zero is capable of killing if he feels sufficiently threatened?'

Again he lost his composure, this time only briefly.

'I do not know what you are suggesting,' he said. 'Do you believe that Temple Ballard was murdered?'

'I don't believe in anything except possibility at this point.'

'If you find that Temple Ballard was murdered, you will . . . undermine the principles on which Babel was founded. You realize that, of course.'

'I'm not interested in principles,' I said. His manner was beginning to grate on me. 'I'm interested in what happened.'

'Spoken like one whose mind works in but a single direction.'

'C'mon, Chaudri, we're talking about taking an innocent human being's life here. Don't you *care*?'

That hurt him. 'Yes,' he said softly, 'I care. I care for the man, not the circumstances.'

'It wouldn't matter to you if he was murdered and his killer just walks around scot-free for the rest of his life?'

'It would not matter. A murderer will ultimately be punished beyond what we can devise.'

'You know what *I* don't care about?' I said harshly. '*I* don't care about a lot of mumbo jumbo that God is continually judging us or that we'll get what we deserve in the afterlife. What I *do* care about is whatever imperfect justice we can come up with here and now.'

'That is your prerogative.'

'You're damn right it is. So what's the answer in plain English, Mr Raghu Chaudri?' I leaned closer to him, using the leverage of the standee over someone sitting down. 'Tell me. Do you think we might have a killer living out in the woods? Huh?'

He was rattled, I was sure of it. But say this for the man, he

97

wasn't about to let it control him.

'Excuse me,' he said. 'I have much work to do.'

And he got up and went into the core house. I kicked the cement step. That didn't help, so I followed him inside. When I passed the office, I could see the back of his head and the glow of the screen. He didn't turn around. I continued on into the living area. There was no one in sight.

'Hello!' I yelled. 'Anybody here?' I wanted to see Sally.

No answer.

I went to my room and dug out my map of Babel. Ike Bender lived in a cluster that I hadn't yet visited. You followed the road below the Ark and then turned up the ridge at the farther end of the cornfields. There was a cul-de-sac back in there, with several houses. I called Bender, and he told me to come up anytime.

I made myself a sandwich. No one arrived while I was eating. So I headed for Ike's place.

Out on the gravel drive, I ran into Spock Jackman. He seemed to spend his time wandering up and down roads. I'd seen several kids since I'd been at Babel, but no others his age. I imagined that it would be pretty boring for him without someone to relate to.

'Spock,' I said.

'Yeah.'

'Well, how are you doing?'

He folded his arms across his chest and stared at me like I was barely there. His hair was day-glo in the sun. I found myself seeing it as colourful rather than weird. Maybe there was magic in Babel.

'You like the Clash?' I asked, pointing to one of the stencils on his jacket.

'Uh-huh.'

'I saw the Clash two years ago, when they played the university.'

'You did not.'

'Sure I did. "London calling, a nuclear error",' I mimicked.

'What were *you* doing there?'

'Ah. Funny you should ask. I had a, um, girlfriend who went to the U.'

'*You* were going out with a *student*?'

'Come on, Spock, I may be twice your age, but that's not *that* old. I mean, well, maybe I was a tad old for this particular lady. She left me for someone in grad business. But, anyway, she was queer for the Clash.'

He didn't say anything.

'It's hard living in a university town,' I said. 'The girls all stay the same age while you get older and older.'

I saw something like a smile. Just a trace.

'How'd you like the concert?' he said.

'Musically or politically?' Another polite smile.

'I liked the band,' I said. 'But the acoustics . . . ' University Hall had been very well designed. For basketball. 'It was kind of hard to hear the words.'

'I know. I'm not going there again.'

'Look, what are you doing now? Anything special?'

He looked at me suspiciously.

'It's just that I'm walking to Ike Bender's house, and I wouldn't mind some company. I'm not a bad guy, really. As a matter of fact, I like X too.'

'They used to be a good band, but they sold out.'

'Oh.'

'It always happens.'

'Too bad,' I said. 'They had a hell of a guitar player. Old Billy Zoom. Really fine. And the greatest ear wiggler I ever saw.'

He laughed and we started walking.

'Yeah,' he said.

'You must be pretty bored around the farm,' I said.

'You wouldn't believe it. There's *nothin'* to do here.'

'Why don't you leave? Go away to college.'

'Maybe. If we get some . . . money.'

That was a subject best quickly changed.

'Where'd you get the jacket?' I asked.

'This guy at school. His big brother was in the war.'

'Me too.'

'Oh, yeah? What was it like?'

'It was like a war, except that the people we were fighting against wanted to win a whole lot more than the people we were fighting for. That was discouraging. Also, it was hot and it rained a lot. Everyone got these little boils all over their bodies.'

'Gross.'

'It was,' I said. 'You couldn't imagine how happy I was to get home.'

'You kill anyone?'

'Not up close. Maybe in the distance. It was kind of hard to tell.'

'You see a lot of dead bodies?'

'Yeah. After a while it gets so it doesn't mean that much

99

anymore. Unless it's one of your buddies.'

'I wouldn't mind being in a war,' he said.

'Spock,' I said, 'it's horrible. That's all I can tell you. Do anything else. Don't fight until they're attacking Nelson County.'

'What does it matter? The world's just gonna get blown up, anyway. None of it matters.'

'You sound like you've been talking to Commander Zero.'

'Oh, did you meet him?'

'I not only met him,' I said, 'I went to his hidey-hole. It's quite a place.'

'I know. He's got some neat guns there. I wanted him to be my friend, but he told me there wasn't any reason to have friends. I think it was that he saw me as Temple Ballard's kid more than anything. Him and my father didn't get along.'

'How'd *you* get along with Ballard?' I asked casually.

His expression got stony. This was getting monotonous. They might have loved him collectively, but whenever I talked to anyone individually about Temple Ballard, they got all bent out of shape.

'He was an asshole,' Spock said bitterly.

'How so?'

'Faggot. He treated my mother like shit. I lived with him for five years and he never told me — Ah, forget it. I don't want to talk about him.'

He'd been about to tell me something. I cursed silently. They were always *about* to tell me something and they never did. I decided not to press him. He'd opened up to me remarkably well, and I didn't want to jeopardize that. There'd be time.

'What do you think of Fred and Nancy Evans?' I asked.

'They're okay. I don't have much to do with them.'

'How about Chaudri?'

'Faggot,' he said disgustedly.

Oh, ho. Now that was an interesting piece of information. If it was true.

'Jeff's a strange bird,' I said, 'isn't he?'

Spock smiled. 'Yeah. Him and Freddie got into it once. You shoulda seen. That Freddie's a little guy, but I don't think he's afraid of nobody. I think he woulda killed him if Ike hadn't of pulled him off. I just *laughed*.'

'Jeff pretty much have trouble with everyone?'

'Yeah, sure. Nobody likes him. Except maybe Lisa.' The way he said Lisa, I felt that he knew of her relationship with his mother.

'How can you like somebody who's trying to save your soul all day long?'

'Spock,' I said, 'I solemnly swear never to try to save your immortal soul.'

'Thanks. What a buddy.'

We'd come to the end of the far field. We stopped. The river ran past, low because of the dry spell. There was a small cleared area nearby, with a path leading down to a natural swimming hole. It made me nostalgic for the kind of past that never existed.

'Spock,' I said, 'it's been a pleasure.'

I held out my hand for a low five. Surprisingly, he gave it to me. I returned it.

'Really,' I said, 'I've enjoyed it. But I truly think you should get away from this place.'

'You do?'

'Yeah. It's nice, but there's nothing for you here. Get away. Go to college. See the world. Chase women. Whatever you want to do. People here are doing what *they* want to do. You should too.'

'Nobody tells me that. All they talk about is how great Babel is.'

I laughed. 'Well, maybe someday you'll want to come back to this great place. But in the meantime there's a lot to do. Believe me.'

'Uh, okay.'

'It's not half as scary as you think. Catch you later.'

14

I followed the road into the woods. The cul-de-sac was in a clearing, short of the ridge top. It was a nice, protected spot. The houses had a lot of south-facing glass and were earth-bermed to boot. They'd be cosy.

Ike Bender's house was very small. Just one room over one. Good-sized rooms, but still, not a lot of square feet. Adequate as long as he stayed single.

Ike was sitting out on his miniature front deck. He got up and greeted me with a big smile and a hearty handshake.

'Swift,' he said, 'it's good to finally be able to get to talk to you.'

He gestured me to sit in one of the webbed-plastic lawn chairs. I sat.

'And can I get you anything?' he asked.

'Coffee?'

'Fine. And anything in it?'

'You have Irish whiskey?'

'No, I'm afraid not. How about American?'

'Just a taste.'

He scurried off and returned in a moment with the coffee. It must have been waiting in the pot. He seated himself next to me. I tasted the coffee. It was very good.

'Ah,' he said. 'It's beautiful, isn't it?'

'Yes,' I said, and it was. His location featured a view across the fields and the river, clear to the western edge of the Rockfish Valley and the Blue Ridge. The leaves had already turned at the higher elevations. Lower down, they were beginning to. In Virginia, only the flowers of spring are more colourful.

'And so,' he said, 'what do you think of our little experiment here?'

'I think it sounds like a good idea,' I said.

'An insurance investigator who quotes Gandhi. I'm impressed.'

'I read a lot. A few of us remember how.'

Ike laughed. 'Well said. We try to encourage the habit among the children. There is only one TV set on the land. It's less enticing if you have to go out of your way to see it. And no video games!'

'Thank God for that.'

'Yes. But your answer to my question suggests that you don't think we've been entirely . . . successful.'

'No one's *entirely* . . . successful.'

'What is the trouble? Have you not been made welcome?'

'No,' I said, 'I feel welcome.'

'From what I hear,' he said with a grin, 'we might even say more than.'

'News travels fast.'

'Of course.'

'No,' I said, 'I'm fine. It's just that this job has turned out to be a lot more complicated than I thought it was going to be.'

'That must often be the case in your business,' he said.

'Ike, I understand that you and Temple Ballard were friends for a long time.'

'Temple and I knew each other from college. But there was a rather lengthy stretch where we didn't keep in touch at all. Our

102

lives went in very different directions after graduation. No one was more surprised than I when he wrote me here.'

'You were happy that he and Mary Beth came?'

'Good heavens, yes. Spock, too, of course. It's good to have young people around. Mary Beth was the real shocker, though. I never could have imagined that they'd be back together.'

'What do you mean by that?'

'By what?' he asked.

'By "back together". How'd you know they had split up?'

He looked puzzled. 'Well, I was there. MIT. You said you knew that.'

'Are you saying that Temple and Mary Beth knew each other in *college*?'

'Why, yes. She was at Radcliffe. He was . . . They met at a mixer. Didn't she tell you?'

Just what I needed. Yet another complication.

'No,' I said wearily. 'She told me they met in San Francisco about five years ago.'

'Met again. Oh, dear. Perhaps I shouldn't have . . . She must have her reasons.'

'It's done now. Did you know her then too?'

'No, it was a very casual relationship. Temple was getting ready to graduate, and then it was on to Houston and NASA. She was only first-year. There was no future in it.'

'Hence your surprise,' I said.

'Yes. There they were, reunited. Quite by chance, as I understand it.'

'And how did they seem to be getting along?'

'Pretty well. Every marriage has its ups and downs, of course. Especially when you've got someone like Temple.'

'Meaning?'

'Well, you've heard how good-looking he was. He wasn't entirely . . . faithful to her.'

'Who with?' I asked.

'I don't think it's my place . . . '

'I heard he was bisexual.'

'That would be correct, yes.'

We paused. I asked for another coffee, this time with a little more whiskey in it. He got it for me.

'Swift, you think that Temple was murdered, don't you?' he said.

'I think it's possible.'

'So do I.'

'Huh?'

'So do I,' he repeated. 'And so does everyone else here. Haven't you felt that there was something you weren't being told?'

'I sure have.'

'That's what it is. Since Temple's death, we've all been walking on eggshells. You can imagine what it's been like, wondering if there's a murderer here, eating with us, tilling the garden, and chopping firewood with us. And also wondering: Why Temple? Wondering if someone else is next.'

'Why don't you go to the police?'

'With what? The sheriff investigated. There's nothing to find unless someone confesses.'

'Can't you talk about it?'

'To who?'

I got the point. You couldn't talk when you couldn't be sure who was listening.

'Swift,' he said, 'do you know what Babel stands for?'

'Sort of.'

'Let me tell you. Babel stands for light. It opposes the forces gathered on the dark side.' He gazed into the distance. 'We had a dream for this place. You have to understand, we were the Kennedy kids. We believed that the world could be made right. Through service to your fellows, yes. But also through technology. In the mid-sixties we were on the threshold of the greatest technological explosion in the history of the world, and we knew it. To place that at the disposal of all humankind, that's what we wanted.' He smiled. 'Sounds naïve, doesn't it?'

'Uh-huh. I remember Kennedy as the guy who dragged us into Nam.'

'You're a vet?'

'Yes.'

'I'm sorry,' Bender said. 'To those of my era, though, Kennedy was still a positive figure. He embodied our vision. At that time we probably didn't even know the dark side existed. But we found out in a hurry. Kennedy was killed, Johnson committed us to war, eventually we got Nixon. It's a story too often told, but it's true. The dark side got the upper hand. We watched our dreams turn to rubbish.

'And technology, the saviour, we learned that it has its dark side, too, mirroring that of its creators. We watched the missiles and the bombs piling up. We watched the environment being slowly

104

ravaged. In the end, we questioned that we should ever have believed in the first place. It looked like technology and destruction were only two sides of the same coin. A lot of us went mad.'

'Is that what happened to Ballard?' I asked.

'No, Temple never really believed in anything but himself.' There was condemnation in his voice. 'He played the game for what *he* could get out of it, and damn the consequences. When he fell to the bottom, it was due to his *personal* failures.

'But there were half a dozen of us who refused to give up. We founded Babel. It was our goal to make technology the servant of light once again. We set out to create something that would meet the needs of the people here while having minimum negative impact on the environment. The Ark achieved just that. It was my . . . It was a tremendous accomplishment.

'Then . . . Temple died. We could feel the dark side closing in on us again. It was the technology that killed him, whether helped along by human hands or not. Time alone will tell if the community can recover.'

'I'm sorry,' I said. 'It must have been terrible.'

'It was.' He slapped his knees, and his far-off gaze returned to the present. 'But you want to know if someone killed him, and if so, who, don't you?'

'That's more or less it. Do you suspect someone in particular?'

'No. I don't suspect anyone. Don't get me wrong, Swift. I've told you all this only to show you our worst fears and how they play upon us.'

'Didn't you say . . . ?'

'I merely said it was possible. And it is. If it wasn't, we wouldn't be so afraid. But when we told you we all loved Temple Ballard, that was the truth. We just neglected to add that it was a love/hate relationship. On the one hand, he did a great deal for us. On the other, he was an arrogant, selfish, ill-tempered son of a bitch who couldn't work cooperatively with anyone. He was brilliant, but he was no communitarian. He used Babel like he'd once used NASA, to show the world what he personally could do. And, of course, there were his sexual involvements.'

'Great,' I said. 'I've got a dead man, and everyone's suspected.'

'You need to look at it that way, I agree. I have. We all have. But do you want my candid opinion?'

'Sure.'

'I think Temple Ballard's death was an accident. I really do.'

'Thanks a lot, Ike. You're a big help, you are.'

105

'Don't mention it, my good man!' He laughed. The hearty, genial fellow had returned. 'Consider me at your disposal. Who knows, perhaps you'll be the one who brings the light back to Babel. Perhaps you are the very Keeper of the Flame!'

I trudged back along the road bordering the hayfield. There was a small herd of cows grazing. One of them interrupted her meal to mount one of her neighbours. It was a common sight, and I'd often wondered about it. Why *did* cows attempt to impersonate bulls? Were they envious? Were the dynamics of some bovine pecking order being worked out? Or were they just having a good time, was it all a big joke that we couldn't fathom because we didn't know the sound of their laughter?

I didn't know much about cow behaviour, but I thought I'd known something about human behaviour. I'd learned a couple of tricks in my years as a detective. One of them was that if you assume the simplest explanation for a puzzling series of events, you nearly arrive at the truth. As Deep Throat had put it: Follow the money. That's another way of asking the cop's foremost question, the first one I'd asked Sally Friday afternoon: Who profits?

Nine times out of ten, you can reduce everything to greed. Usually greed for money, as Deep Throat recognized. But it could be greed for something else on occasion. Sex or social status or political power.

So what do you do when you've got a little bit of all of the above? Because that was certainly what I had. There was money: Mary Beth. Sex: Mary Beth again, Lisa, probably Chaudri, and undoubtedly several others. Power and status, possibly: the three remaining founders. As if all that wasn't enough, I had to throw in religious mania: Jeff. Paranoia: Commander Zero. And intra-familial hatred: Spock. And that was only what I'd uncovered over the first two days!

It was an incredible witches' brew that might never come clear. I had to admit it. All I could possibly do was continue to peel away the layers and hope that somewhere I'd stumble across a critical fact, something that would point me in one direction only.

Toss a coin to determine the person I next needed to talk to. I flipped it and it came up Mary Beth Jackman. Only because her house was on the way. I went down the fork in the road that led to her cluster. Her house was empty. I left a note on her door asking her to call me when she got in. I walked back to the core house.

Chaudri was in the office, working at the computer. I came up behind him.

'Rags,' I said, 'I want to talk to you.'

'I'm quite busy just now,' he said without turning around.

'It's important. I think you knew Temple Ballard a lot better than you've told me.'

'It is possible.'

'I think that the two of you were lovers.'

That got his attention. He stopped typing and slowly swiveled in his chair until he was facing me. His face was composed, as usual, and then abruptly it shattered. The placidity was replaced by horror. I was stunned. I couldn't imagine that . . . And then I realized that it wasn't me he was looking at. I spun around. Jeff was standing in the doorway. His expression was icy.

'Do you mind?' I said to him.

He gave us a nasty last look and walked away.

'I'm sorry,' I said to Chaudri.

'The damage would appear to be done,' he said. He was composed again, but not entirely so. 'It is of no value to speculate on what might have been, is it?'

'No, but I still want to talk to you. Not here. Let's go somewhere.'

We walked up to the barn and rested ourselves against a board fence. There was no one around but us and the pigs.

'Is it true?' I asked him.

'Yes.'

I didn't really know what else I wanted to ask him. I watched the pigs groveling about in the dirt. They lived in a pretty restricted universe, but it was probably not an unpleasant one. When I looked at Chaudri again, he was crying. It wasn't a sobbing kind of cry. The tears were just trickling down the impassive brown face as if they'd made the whole trip on their own.

I suddenly realized how my own biases had coloured the way in which I saw Chaudri. He'd seemed to me to be almost asexual. Yet he wasn't that at all. His style had merely resisted my attempts at classification. I tend to stereotype other people, just like everyone does. Heterosexuals go in one slot, homosexuals in another, bisexuals someplace else. Rags hadn't fit anywhere. I'd then made the mistake of assuming that that was because he didn't *belong* anywhere, rather than that I was misperceiving him. I felt guilty. At the same time I wondered how many other people at Babel I was seeing incorrectly, and in what ways.

'I'm sorry,' I said. 'Everything I do around here I seem to cut loose someone's feelings.'

The tears ebbed. He wiped them away with his sleeve. I wondered if he ever totally let go. I doubted it.

'It is why I have never returned to India,' he said. 'There I would be merely a disgrace to my family, unless I chose a celibate religious order. Here at least there is the chance of acceptance.' He paused. 'Temple Ballard was a wonderful man. He had an ugly side, it is true, and there were those who could not see beyond it. But he was kind and thoughtful and a good friend. I was in love with him from the first moment I saw him.

'I could not *have* him, of course. To possess is to destroy. And Temple could not be satisfied by one lover, or even two. He gave himself freely, to whoever needed.

'Do you suspect that I killed him?'

I looked at the round gingerbread face. It was impossible to imagine Rags killing anyone.

'I don't know what I suspect any more,' I said.

'In the end,' he said, 'it was Mary Beth. Perhaps it was always Mary Beth, that he didn't know it until he had lost her. He had loved others, I don't think realizing how it had hurt her, and eventually she had scorned him. Then, of course, he had to have her back, no matter the price. She had once given him back his pride, but then she had taken it away. This he could not bear.

'It cost me his love, Mr Swift, but I did not kill him. I could not have.'

'Who did?'

'I believe that his pride did. He was intent on fixing the water supply, and he ignored the signs of carbon monoxide poisoning. He was like that; he had a disregard for personal discomfort that you or I would find astonishing. He didn't trouble with what was happening to him, and he died. I do not think it is more complex than that. It was an accident.'

I put my hand on his shoulder and started him back toward the core house.

'I hope you're right,' I said. 'I hope to *hell* you are right.'

15

I finally got to see Sally late in the afternoon. We greeted each other warmly, walked down to the river, and sat on its bank in the waning sunlight. Willows overhung the water. Near the bridge was a level area that had been used for some time as a refuse dump.

'I'm beginning not to like this, Swifty,' Sally said.

'Not like what?'

'All of it. This prying into people's lives and trying to get them to confide in you. Is this what you usually do?'

'Sometimes,' I said. 'Sometimes you end up hurting people, and sometimes you're able to help them. You can be a nice guy or a complete heel. I do my best to maximise the good things, but it's kind of hard to predict ahead of time what's going to happen.'

She hugged her knees and rested her chin on them.

'It seems so bogus,' she said. 'You get someone to trust you, and then maybe you wind up using what they tell you against them.'

'I know how you feel. When you've done it for as long as I have, you develop a certain detachment. It's probably not healthy in any larger sense, but it's the only way to survive.'

'We could quit. Just go home. Tell Devin that we couldn't find anything.'

I watched the river flow. It mindlessly carried its collection of autumn flotsam from one place to another. She was right. We could walk away. Turn our backs on Babel and all of its resident crazies. It would be easy.

'You can if you want, Sally,' I said. 'But I can't. I've explained about Patricia.' She nodded. 'There's more too. The thing has gotten under my skin. Temple Ballard may not have been one of the world's swell fellows. I probably wouldn't have liked him. But he didn't deserve to die like that. If someone killed him, I want to know *who*. And *why*. When I get caught up in a real puzzle like this one, resolving it becomes much more important than the money. It's the real reason I do what I do. Can you understand that?'

'Uh-huh. It's just never been so . . . personal for me before.'

I reached over and idly began to massage the back of her neck.

'You have talent, Sally Hatch,' I said, 'but you may be too good a person for this kind of work.'

She smiled. 'Maybe not,' she said. 'I really want to know what happened too.'

'You're not quitting?'

'Nah.'

'Excellent.' I smiled. 'How'd you do today?'

'I found out that Nancy was sleeping with Ballard.'

'I guess I shouldn't be surprised.'

'No. It was a very emotional thing for her to talk about. She got very weepy.'

'Sounds like my day,' I said, and I told her about the scene with Chaudri.

When I'd finished, she said, 'Looks like we've got us a lengthy list of suspects.'

'That it do. And there's more to come. Ike told me that Ballard was in the process of trying to woo back his wife when he died. That could have made for a touchy situation with his two lovers. Put that on top of the jealousy that Freddie and Lisa may have been into, and we've got ourselves a real mess.'

'What was your take on Bender?' she asked.

'It's hard to say. He seems the least uptight about the subject of anyone I've met so far, and I haven't heard any rumours indicating that his sex life was relevant. On the other hand, he'd known Ballard from college. Something could have happened between them in the past. Plus I think we have to consider what all of the founders were facing. They'd put years of sweat and money into this place, then along came Ballard and turned everything around. They've been a little too quick to say how much they approved of what he was doing, in my opinion. There were bound to have been ego conflicts. Ike strikes me as someone who might have been particularly susceptible to that.'

'But, of course, if what he told you is true, then you have to take a closer look at Ms Jackman too.'

'You still think I'm apt to go a little light on her?'

She held her thumb and forefinger about an inch apart.

'Okay.' I laughed. 'How do you mean?'

'If he was trying to start up with her again, that might have really made her angry. It wouldn't surprise me at all.'

'You're right,' I said. 'I'm going to try to talk to her tonight. I'll bring it up. I also want to know exactly what happened between her and Ballard back in college. I've got some suspicions. Unfortunately, if I'm right, things are going to get more complicated, not less.'

She shrugged. 'Well, what the hell . . . '

'Yeah.'

We let a few silent moments pass, then she said, 'I picked up something else today too.'

'Uh-oh. What?'

'I think you're right that Freddie's holding back.'

'You talked to him?'

'No,' she said. 'I got it from Nancy. There were times I felt like she wanted to tell me more, but then she'd clam up, so I didn't pry. It all centres around what happened that night, I think. And since Freddie discovered the body, it's logical to assume that she's keeping a secret on his behalf. It wouldn't likely be her secret because by the time she got to the Ark, there was a crowd of people there.'

'Better not assume,' I said.

'I know. But I still have an intuition that that's what it is. Anyway, as I was leaving, Nancy said to me, 'I really feel comfortable talking to you. I wish I could tell you everything sometime.' It was a real tough moment for me. I like her very much, and I was flattered that she considers me a confidante, and I didn't want to hurt her. At the same time I was dying to know what she had to tell. I guess that makes me at least part detective.'

'Yup. Did you ask her what "everything" was?'

'Yeah. She just dismissed it with some generalization about her life. It didn't make me believe she hadn't been referring to something specific.'

'I guess it's time for me to see them.'

'You think?'

'Yes. I haven't spoken to Nancy since the dinner party. I don't want her getting suspicious. And I can be as abrasive as I want to. It might trigger something. If it doesn't, it might get her to open up even more to you later.'

'That's an ugly way of looking at it.'

'Look, Sally,' I said, 'you don't think Nancy was involved in Ballard's death, do you?'

'Not directly, no.'

'And you think she'd feel better if she got whatever's on her chest off of it, don't you?'

'Uh-huh.'

'Then we're going to be doing her a favour by bringing it all out

111

into the open. *That's* the way I see it.'

'You're probably right,' she said wearily.

'You can see her again tomorrow if you want. I won't be able to get the two of them together until evening.'

'Okay. I guess I should be working on other people too.'

'You might try Lisa,' I said. 'You seem to have some rapport with her.' She looked at me and we both laughed. 'I didn't mean to imply anything by that.'

'No problem,' she said. 'I think we've learned that at Babel every word carries a double meaning. Or more.'

'Thanks. There's Jeff, as well. I think you're a whole lot more likely to get something out of him than I am.'

'You're a pal, old man. Save me all the choicest assignments. What else you got, little latrine detail?'

'I knew you'd be pleased.'

'Well, I'll see what I can do,' she said. 'But don't expect much. That kid'll probably crack his own coconut before we do it for him.'

Mary Beth called just before dinner. I asked to meet her later in the evening. She was civil but not overly enthusiastic about my coming over. I made as if I only had a couple of very simple questions, and she agreed to see me.

Then we sat down to eat, Sally and Lisa and I. I didn't know where the other two were, and I didn't much care. I waited until we were nearly finished before I asked Lisa what she had thought of Temple Ballard.

'Well, I didn't know him as long as some of the others,' she said. 'He was a brilliant man.'

'No,' I said, 'what did you *really* think of him?'

She gave me that look she had, then shrugged. 'I didn't have much use for him.'

'Didn't have much use for, or didn't like?'

'All right.' She sighed. 'He was an arrogant prick. Is that what you want to hear?'

'I don't *want* to hear anything. I'm neutral.'

'You're not acting like it,' Sally said.

Lisa flashed her a thank-you smile.

'I am,' I said. 'I'm just trying to get a feel for some guy I never met.'

'Okay,' Lisa said, 'he was arrogant and he was manipulative. He felt like he had to control — I don't know, everyone.'

'Including your lover?'

112

'Meaning who?' Her tone was a little unfriendly.

'Meaning Mary Beth Jackman.'

'Swift,' Sally said, 'don't you think that's *her* business?' Her manner and her timing were perfect.

'Sure it's her business. But I was under the impression that everyone around here thought it was very liberating to discuss each other's sex lives.'

'I have nothing to hide,' Lisa said firmly.

'Good. Then how did you feel about his attempts to manipulate his wife?'

'He wished. He could never control Mary Beth.'

'Who could? You?'

'Mary Beth is a very strong-willed woman. No one can force her into anything she doesn't want.'

'But Temple Ballard tried, didn't he?'

'I suppose.'

'How'd you feel about that? I understand his feelings for her ran very deep. And hers for him.'

'What is this?' Lisa said. 'What are you suggesting?'

'I'm not suggesting anything. I'm simply asking you how you felt.'

'I think you should tone it down a little, Swift,' Sally said. 'She hasn't done anything to you.'

'Thanks, Sally,' Lisa said. Then to me, 'You think I cared if Ballard went slobbering around her door? He was pathetic, like some kid whose favourite toy has been taken away. Mary Beth wouldn't have fallen for that crap. She's much too perceptive.'

'How about you?' I asked. 'Are you that perceptive too?'

'Oh, I get it,' she said. 'You think I got frightened of his attempts to get her back and bumped him off.' She rolled her eyes. 'God, are you ever out to lunch.'

She never even missed a beat. If she wasn't blameless, she was way too quick to be caught in a trap as crude as the one we were setting.

'How did Mary Beth feel about his efforts?' I asked.

'Right. Now you want me to implicate her. Go fish somewhere else, will you?'

'Nicely put,' Sally said.

'Thanks. I hope he's better in bed than this would lead us to believe.'

Lisa and Sally both laughed. It didn't matter that the remark was off-target. I still turned red.

'No complaints,' Sally said.

I probably turned red all over again, because they had another good laugh.

'Lisa,' I said, fishing around, 'I understand that Mary Beth's other lover might not have your confidence.'

'Oh, come off it. There isn't anyone else and you know it. We don't need anyone else. Look, what do you want me to say, that I'm glad the creep's dead? Okay, I'm glad the creep's dead. So I'm a monster for being happy that he's finally off Mary Beth's back. You satisfied now?'

I shook my head. 'Did you kill him?'

'Nope. Didn't have to.'

'Because someone else saved you the trouble?'

'You want my candid opinion?'

'Yes, I do.'

'Okay,' she said. 'Yeah, I think somebody killed him. And so does everyone else in this godforsaken place. This is a lunatic asylum, Swift. You got some people here who've been afraid to turn their backs on certain other people for six months now. It ain't no way to live.'

'Why do they stay around?'

'You oughtta be able to figure that out. People have a lot of their lives invested in Babel. A lot of their money, too, some of them. And we *all* still believe in the principles. We actually do. There's a kind of a general hope that there is justice in the universe and things will work out in the end. Babel's a very hard place to leave.'

'You don't seem like you'd have that much trouble,' I said.

'I don't, do I? That's because I won't. Just as soon as the money comes through, Mary Beth and I are splitting for the Coast. I can't wait. We tried here, but it's all over now.'

'You realize that I'm convinced Mary Beth shouldn't get the money?'

'Yeah, but she will. You should just forget it, Swift. You'll never be able to prove somebody did Ballard in. What're you gonna do, tell them the whole *community* done it?'

It was a point well made. I couldn't help but smile.

'All right,' I said. 'In that case, who do *you* like for the killer?'

'I wish I knew, brother,' she said. 'But I'd be flipping coins, just like you.'

16

By the time I left Babel, I figured, I'd at least be an expert on their road system. I was going up and down it every day, on foot. I knew where all the potholes were.

It was a moonless night, but once my eyes adjusted, I could easily follow the ghostly path of the gravel drive. I walked down the left fork, toward Mary Beth's.

After dinner Sally and I had had the opportunity to spend a few minutes alone together. We agreed that she'd probably made a good start toward winning Lisa over and that if Lisa hung around, Sally might profitably put some effort into that relationship.

Now, out on the road, I thought back to Lisa's remark about reporting to my employers that the whole community had 'done it'. Well, maybe it had, like the passengers on Agatha Christie's Orient Express. Or in some even more mysterious fashion. The dark side, Ike had called it. It was certainly running wild at Babel. The problem was that the dividing line between light and dark could be very fuzzy, similar to the line that divided your experiences from your imaginings. A lot of the time it wasn't easy to tell the difference. And the two would be constantly interacting. Suppose that the ill feeling toward Temple Ballard had reached such a level that his desired demise became an actual one? Was it so farfetched? After all, voodoo really killed. Why couldn't the community's collective dark side disable an alarm system?

I stopped myself. The place must be getting to me. I'd begun to postulate death by ESP. I didn't need that; I had a whole bagful of perfectly good human suspects to consider. Besides, that had been no phantom at my bedroom window. A physical blow had knocked me out. The message stuffed into my pocket had been written by a mortal hand.

Every day this case starts over at some new point, I thought as I settled myself into Mary Beth's bentwood rocker. Tonight that point is right here.

'I didn't think I'd see you again so soon,' Mary Beth said.

'Do you mean you hoped you wouldn't?' I asked.

She was dressed in jeans and a sweater again. I rated a little more colour this time, yellow on blue. The room wasn't warm, but it was comfortable. Spock wasn't there.

Mary Beth tucked one leg up under her as she sat on the couch. It was a position that served to emphasize her small stature in a very appealing way. I could believe that her obvious toughness was not incompatible with a need to be held through the night. The contrast stirred something in me. I clamped a lid on it.

'That too,' she said. 'It means that you've been uncovering things. I wasn't fooled by your few-simple-questions routine.'

Once again I got the impression that we could transcend our adversarial roles if only I said the right thing. Setting the tone of our conversations seemed to be critically important. I decided to take a small chance.

'Yes,' I said, 'I've picked up a couple of things I didn't know. But before we talk about them, I'd like to ask you one question, Mary Beth. Do you want the money so much that you're just not interested in what happened to your husband?'

She studied me across the empty space between us. I felt that I could see the cluster of warring emotions behind her face. Trouble was, I hadn't a clue what those emotions were. The conflict could be between wanting to know the details of Ballard's death and not wanting to know. Or, if she already knew those details, it could be between what to tell me and what to continue to hide. In the best of all possible worlds, she was deciding whether or not to trust me. I pretended for the time being that I lived in the best of all possible worlds.

'Loren,' she said, 'what do *you* think happened to Temple?'

'I think someone knew about the carbon monoxide leak and deliberately disconnected the alarm. I'm sorry.'

She was silent for a long moment, then she sighed. 'I haven't allowed myself to think that,' she said. 'It's been so much easier to believe that it was a horrible accident. I guess you've found out that Temple and I weren't getting along.'

'Yes.'

'It was the worst stretch we'd ever been through. I was very angry with him. There were plenty of times when I wished him dead. But I never . . . I can't bear the thought of someone, some-one I know, maybe someone I'm close to, having . . . murdered him.'

Her eyes were no longer deep and mysterious, nor did they

116

smoulder with her inner fire. They merely pleaded with me to say it wasn't so.

'That is what I think happened,' I said softly.

'God,' she said. She put a hand to her head and squeezed her temples. Then she looked hard at me. 'It's ironic, you know, Loren? Even dead, the son of a bitch is still trying to control my life. Don't look shocked. I'm not coldhearted. Sometimes I wish I were, but I'm not. You're right. I could ignore it as long as I kept my head in the sand, which you are not going to allow me to do. So here I am. Yes, if someone killed him, then I want to know who it was. I owe him at least that much for the good times. What the hell, it's only ten million.'

I was convinced. All except in that one corner of my mind where a tiny voice was saying: *Go with it, only remember, if she wanted to mislead you this is how she'd do it.*

'What do you want to know about?' she asked.

I cleared my throat. 'I understand that you knew Ballard in college,' I said.

'Who told you *that*?' she snapped.

'I'd rather not — '

'Don't bother. It had to be Ike. I'd talk to him a couple more times if I were you.'

'Why do you say that?'

'I don't trust him,' she said. 'Neither should you.'

'Did he and Ballard get along?'

'Superficially. But they were both brilliant engineering students. They competed. I think Temple had the edge. I think that Bender always felt overshadowed by him.'

'But you're prejudiced.'

'Maybe so.'

'Did you know the both of them back then?' I asked.

She shook her head. 'Only Temple. There wasn't all that much mixing between the two schools in those days. Occasional socials and the like. No common classes or anything.'

'Ballard never talked about him?'

'No. We were pretty heavily into . . . each other.'

'Once you got here, there was an obvious rivalry?'

'In my opinion.'

'Ike didn't go along with the changes in Babel?'

'Oh, he went along,' she said. 'But I always felt it was more because everyone else was excited by them. He gave the impression of a man who had been top dog and was just biding his time until

117

the scales tipped his way again. In the meantime, he'd go with whatever the crowd wanted.'

It was confirmation of a possibility that I'd considered myself. Or perhaps it was just a neat bit of misdirection.

'Interesting,' I said. 'Why'd you lie to me about when you met Temple Ballard?'

'I — I don't know,' she said. 'I've told the story that way for so long now, it's a habit, I guess. I suppose I thought that it wouldn't come up. It doesn't make any difference.'

She'd been caught off-guard by the question. There wasn't any sincerity in her reply.

'I think it does,' I said.

'What are you getting at?'

'The obvious. I had a talk with your son earlier today. We got on the subject of Commander Zero. Spock said, 'Him and my father didn't get along.' I realize that it's not uncommon for kids to refer to their stepfather as 'father', but in light of what I know now, I don't think that's what he meant. He's Ballard's natural son, isn't he?'

There was a long pause before she nodded.

'Do you want to tell me about it? You don't have to if you don't want to.'

'What does it matter? You already know.'

She closed her eyes, looked into the past. Then she began.

'I was a freshman, a teenager,' she said. 'What did I know except here was this big, gorgeous, brainy senior and he was hot for me. I didn't even know that birth control had been invented. He told me he loved me. I suppose he did, too, even then, at least the way that he understood it. The difference between us was that for me love was the world and everything in it, for him it was something that couldn't be allowed to get in the way of his career. When I got pregnant, he wanted me to have an abortion. I was appalled. If ever there had been a love child, this was it. How could he even suggest that? I should have realized that the simple fact that he wanted to get rid of it meant that it wasn't as much of a love child as I thought it was. But I didn't. I stuck to my guns. Come hell or high water, I was going to have that baby.

'As time passed, Temple seemed to get more comfortable with the idea. We made plans to be together. I was willing to drop out of school for a while, to take care of the baby. I could go back later. After graduation Temple took off for Houston. I went to California. The plan was for me to work over the summer, save a little money. Then in the fall I'd join him in Texas. You can probably guess the rest. I waited to hear from him, and I waited some more. I don't think I really accepted that he'd left me until the moment Spock was born. But I accepted it then, all right. I also determined that no matter what, I was going to get on with my life. And I did.'

She paused. 'It was twelve years before I laid eyes on Temple Ballard again.'

'In San Francisco?'

'It was like I told you. An accident. I walked into a party, and there he was.'

'You punch him out?' I asked.

'If he'd been like I'd known him,' she said, 'I probably would have. But he wasn't. He'd never used to drink, and he was drunk. He'd lost a lot of weight. He was gaunt. His face was yellow-looking, he had about five days' growth of beard, and his eyes were red and watery. He was pathetic. There was no way I could hate him. In fact, I just took him in my arms and held him.'

'And then helped him back.'

'Yes. I still loved him, after all those years. It seemed like there wasn't anything to do but do it. He came around. We made up for a lot of lost time.'

'Did you tell Spock?' I asked.

'How could I? Tell the poor kid that this derelict was his father, and even though he'd abandoned me for twelve years rather than start a family, I was just gonna move right back in with him?'

'How long did you keep it from him?'

'I told him in January.'

'You didn't tell him until he was seventeen?' It was a little hard to believe.

'Don't look at me like that. You can't understand. I was always about to, but it never seemed like quite the right time, or I lost my nerve at the last minute. I'm not proud of it.'

'Didn't Ballard want him to know?'

'No. Temple was more ashamed of what he'd done than I was. He'd been given a second chance, and he didn't want to blow it this time. As far as he was concerned, we shouldn't ever have told him.'

'Mary Beth,' I said, 'that's a very strange story.'

'I suppose it looks that way. But it worked. Temple and Spock really took to each other, I'm sure more so than if Spock had known. In spite of everything, those were good years.'

'But you finally decided he ought to know?'

'Yes. Temple was away for a couple of weeks. I worked up the courage . . . No, that's not the way it happened. Spock and I had a fight. I told him in the middle of it.'

'Spock didn't seem too pleased with the way Ballard was behaving,' I said. 'Is that what you were fighting about?'

'In part. They had stopped getting along when Temple began playing around. After we moved to Babel. The atmosphere here encourages you to explore sexual . . . possibilities. Temple was ready for that, especially where other men were concerned. He'd never let those feelings out before. Our relationship kind of deteriorated.'

'And Spock was . . . confused?'

'Confused and hurt. He finds male homosexuality very threatening. We had some blowups about it. The wrong time to tell him about Temple, but it just popped out.'

'How'd he react?'

'He was horrified. At first he didn't believe me, but then he realized that I'd never have lied about something like that. I couldn't approach him for weeks. He was still working through his feelings when Temple died.'

'How did Spock take his father's death?'

'He didn't grieve,' she said. 'I suppose it seemed like a vindication of his values. That'll change as he gets older.'

It was time to redirect the conversation. She'd gotten into talking, and I didn't think she realized how bad her son was beginning to look. She'd told him about Ballard in January, and he'd been very angry. A month later the man was dead. I didn't want to destroy any rapport we might have by pursuing things.

'It will,' I said. 'So is it safe to say that after you moved to Babel you and Ballard drifted apart?'

'Sure. He took his lovers. In retaliation, I took mine. You know how it works.'

'I've heard that just before he died he was trying to win you back.'

'You have been busy,' she said tersely.

'You don't sound like his attention pleased you.'

'How would *you* feel? I never wanted to screw around. He encouraged me. "Time to liberate our relationship," he said. He jumped in with both feet. Then when I began to develop relationships of my own, he tried to put the leash back on, the only way he knew how. He came on with all this undying love crap, we really needed each other, and so on. I was damn mad!'

'What about the other people he had relationships with? How did they feel?'

'I'd say they were damn mad too. That was Temple's ugly side. He always wanted to have everything under his thumb. When it came to people, that got him in real trouble.'

'Maybe it got him killed,' I said.

She stared at me as if she'd never thought of it that way. How could she not have?

'You mean . . . ? Oh, no. Not Nancy. She couldn't have.'

'Rags?'

'I — I don't know. I don't think so. He's always so . . . under control.'

'Mary Beth, whoever disabled that alarm went back in there, reconnected it, and walked away. He or she was very much under control. Temple Ballard did not die during an argument.'

'I see what you mean.'

I let a few moments pass before I said, 'Lisa told me that you're going to move to San Francisco if the money comes through.'

'We might. Lisa's really anxious to get away from here, but of course she won't leave without me. What of it?'

'It gives her motivation.'

'*Lisa*? No, no way. She's an artist.'

'Artists sometimes do extreme things to get what they want.'

'Loren,' she said, 'now you're talking about somebody that I know really well. It's ridiculous.'

'She gives the impression of being very confident of her relationship with you.'

'I'm sure she is. You need a lot of self-confidence to succeed as a dancer. It carries over.'

'How did Ballard take that?'

'You mean, did he try to scare her away from me? He may have. It wouldn't have been beyond him.'

'And how would she have responded?'

'Look,' she said, 'let's drop it, okay? She's incapable, take my word for it.'

'For what it's worth,' I said, 'I believe you.'

She relaxed a little. 'Do you have a theory?' she asked.

'As a matter of fact, I do. Are you sure you want to hear it?'

'I'm not sure. But go ahead.'

'Okay. My number-one suspect is Commander Zero. What do you think of that?'

'I think it's nonsense.'

'Why?'

'Zero didn't care a thing about Temple,' she said.

'I disagree,' I said. 'I think that he felt Ballard was a bad influence on the community, that if he got free rein, Babel would eventually be in the national spotlight. I think Zero's paranoid about things like that.'

'Enough to — '

'Yeah, enough to. I've seen his type before. The urge toward violence is so close to the surface in them that you never know when it's going to break the skin.'

She thought about it for a while, then shook her head. 'I still don't see him.'

'Do you see Jeff?'

'That's closer to the mark. But wouldn't he be likely to strike out in a more physical way?'

I thought about my attacker in the night. She had a point. On the other hand, he might well be capable of both.

'The main problem I have right now,' I said, 'is with Freddie Evans. He knows more than he's telling, I'm sure of it. Since he discovered Ballard, that makes it look real bad for him. And Nancy's covering up for him too.'

She looked at me for a long time, as if trying to see inside my head. Finally she said, 'Well, Freddie is the only one who knows exactly what that room looked like before any of the rest of us saw it. Yes, you should talk to them.'

It was a little oblique, but her meaning was clear. I'd been right all along. Freddie *knew* what had happened that night. Or worse. Now that I knew that he knew, I was positive I could get it out of him.

But why had she said that to me? Was it another attempt at misdirection? It didn't figure that way. If he really didn't know anything, then it was wasted. And if she pointed me toward the person who had the key, it would surely come back to haunt her, if she, too, was hiding something. Unless she was the most devious person I had ever met, the alternative must be true. She had decided to help me get to the bottom of Ballard's death.

'Thank you,' I said. 'I will.'

There was another lengthy pause, then she said, 'This is strange for me, for all of us. We are used to sharing. But you, you want to know everything about us, yet don't want to share anything of yourself.'

'I know,' I said. 'There's just so much to do. Underneath all this there is not a bad fellow.'

'I'd like to meet him someday.'

'All right. When I'm finished, assuming we're still on speaking terms, maybe we can get together and talk like normal human beings.'

'Maybe. Is that it for tonight?'

'That's it.'

17

I stepped out into the cool night air. The countryside was still. That must take the most getting used to, living out here. The silence. And it was a deceptive silence. All around me the life of the forest went on. Creatures were eating and getting eaten.

The trouble with new information was that it was like a drug that suppressed pain. It worked only on symptoms and left the root cause of the problem untouched. In the case of Babel, who was doing what to whom, who knew what about what, all of these were merely symptoms. The root was Ballard's death. I was actually no closer to an understanding of how that had come about than I had ever been.

There was, however, someone who might be able to cast some light in that direction. Freddie Evans. There were things that only he knew. I debated dropping in on him unannounced. On the one hand, he might get angry, he might not let me in, he might close himself off from me for good. On the other hand, the element of surprise might work in my favour. He wouldn't have time to prepare for my visit. He'd be off-guard from the gitgo. If I could get my foot in the door, I might be able to control the situation to my advantage.

It was a calculated risk. I decided to take it. The conversation with Mary Beth had whetted my appetite for more. I just wasn't in the mood to go back to the core house and fritter away the rest of the evening.

I headed down the road. About twenty-five yards from the cluster, someone came out of the dark and lightly took hold of my arm. I must have jumped a foot in the air. Thoughts of my unknown stalker flashed through my head. I was spinning and in the process of drawing my gun when I recognized the kid.

'Spock,' I said.

'I'm sorry, Swift,' he said. 'Did I startle you?'

'Jesus, kid, don't do that. I almost . . . Never mind.' No point in advertising the fact that I was carrying.

'I only wanted to talk to you.'

'Okay. Let's walk,' I said, brushing some nonexistent dust from my sleeves.

We started walking.

'Mr Spock, you now have my undivided attention. What's on your mind?'

'Well, I was thinking about what you said the other day.'

'What specifically?'

'Oh, I don't know. Nothing. Just the way you talk. You don't talk down to me.'

'Why should I?' I said. 'It's not a crime to be a teenager. You're still a real person.'

'That's what I mean. Everyone else treats me like a little kid, which they probably don't know any better. If I wasn't the only one my age here, it might be different.'

'I don't know. People get older and they develop blind spots. It seems impossible that they can forget what it was like to be seventeen. I know I never have. But they do.'

'Would you help me out if I was in trouble?'

I stopped and looked at his shadowed face. The tough-guy punk façade was gone. I'd suspected that it was just surface, anyway. Spock hadn't had the kind of inner-city upbringing that breeds the serious hard cases. Now, in the dark, you'd never know he had pink-and-yellow hair. He had become just a likable kid with normal adolescent problems, wanting adult acceptance but afraid to seek it among the adults around him. And who could blame him? As I'd said, he needed to get away from Babel.

'Of course I would,' I said. 'Why, are you?'

124

'Would you protect me?'

'Spock, what are you trying to say? Why do you think you need protection?'

'Commander Zero's the only other one,' he said. 'But he'd never help me. He doesn't even like me.'

'Are you afraid of Commander Zero?'

He jumped a little. 'No,' he said quickly. 'He's the only other one who knows what he's doing. Besides you.'

I put my hand on his shoulder. Whatever the subject was, it was extremely difficult for him to get down to it. And I'd been considering him as a suspect. Right now, nothing seemed more implausible.

'Spock,' I said, 'does this have anything to do with your father's death?'

'How'd you know he was my father?'

'You told me. You called him "my father". I put two and two together.'

'Oh.' Some air seemed to go out of him. 'I'm not sad he's dead.'

'Why not?' I said. 'Whatever else he may have been, Temple Ballard is still the man who loved your mother enough to want to merge his spirit with hers. And that's you. He'll always be your father.'

He was staring at the ground. I didn't have to see his face to know what he was going through. The amazing thing was that he wasn't an emotional basket case. He had every right to be, I thought. There must be a real resiliency to him.

'Maybe I miss him a little,' he said. 'I know Mom does.'

'Yes, I know she does too. Tell me what's bothering you, will you?'

He looked up at me.

'It does have to do with your father's death, doesn't it?'

He nodded. 'He'll kill me if I ever tell anyone.'

'Who will?'

'Rags.'

'*Rags*?!'

He nodded again. 'He was out there that night,' he said.

'I know that. He went to the shed after the alarm went off. He was the next one to get there after Freddie.'

'No, I mean before. Before the alarm went off.'

'Where did you see him?' I asked.

'Out here. I was walking. He was coming across the field, from the direction of the Ark, instead of using the road. It's the shortest way to his house.'

'He lives in the same cluster as you and your mother, right?'

'Yes. He came over to me. He was acting weird. Usually he's so . . . cool, y'know?'

'I know.'

'But not that night. He was nervous, and something else too. I don't know, like his balance was off or something. Like he wasn't exactly sure where he was. He wanted to know what I was doing there. I told him I was out walking, obviously. I've never liked him much. Even before. . . . Anyway, he didn't say anything else. He just walked away, toward his house. I made like I was going down the road, but once he was out of sight, I stopped in the shadows. About five minutes later he came back out and went back across the field and into the woods toward the Ark. I started walking again. A little while after that the alarm went off. I didn't think anything about it at the time. I don't even know why I spied on Rags. They didn't have a thing to do with my life.'

'What time was this?' I asked.

'I don't really remember. I'm sorry. I don't pay much attention to time. It was dark.'

'Okay. When did Rags threaten you?'

'The next day. He said never to tell anyone I'd seen him that night.'

'He told you he'd kill you if you did?' I said.

'Yeah. I mean, I — I think so. I could see it in his eyes, though. They scared me. I'd never seen him looking like that. He's a foreigner. I don't really know what they're really like.'

'They're mostly like us. Greedy and afraid. Don't worry about him. He's as frightened of you as you are of him.' But still, I gave him a lot of credit for having borne up under the threat for so long. In a real crunch situation, I'd be willing to bet he'd come through.

'You think so?'

'I know so,' I said. 'Besides, I'll make sure he doesn't bother you.'

'You won't tell him . . . ?'

'No, I won't have to. Unless he's gonna be leaving us permanently.'

'You think he . . . ?'

'I don't know. Do *you* think so?'

126

'Maybe. I've thought about it. It means that someday he'll want to kill me, doesn't it?'

'Stop it, Spock,' I said firmly. 'It's not going to happen, I guarantee it. Now, did you tell the cops about this?'

'No.'

'Why not?'

'I didn't know what Rags would do.' Then the punk put in a brief appearance. 'Besides, I don't talk to *cops*.'

'I don't think it would've made any difference if you did. Have you told anyone else?'

'No,' he said softly.

'Good. Don't,' I paused. 'Spock, you do want to know what happened to your father, don't you?'

'Yes, I want to know.'

'It may cause you a lot of pain, and it may cost you a lot of money too.'

'I still want to know.'

'That makes me happy,' I said. 'Because I'm going to find out. It's important to me that you not be holding it against me.' And I meant it.

'Okay,' he said. 'See ya.'

He went off in the direction of the core house. I stood in the middle of the road. It was one of those moments when you look at the sky and wonder what in hell you are doing in this particular universe.

I didn't know what I wanted to do next, either. I started down the road, toward the connecting road to the Evanses' cluster. Then I stopped, turned around, and headed back the other way, toward Rags's. I'll never know what my ultimate choice would have been. . . .

This time it wasn't Sally's pretty face, it was the sound of shouting. Why were they doing that? There was no need to raise one's voice, it was too cold for . . . Cold. There was pressure in the small of my back. My gun. I was on the ground, on my back. It was cold.

My first emotion was anger. My first thought was: Ah, for Christ's sake, not again. I raised myself on to my elbows. My anger churned me up inside. Where *was* the bastard? Why wouldn't he *show* himself to me? I wanted to strike out, at anything. But there was only the night and . . .

The shouting.

It was as if I'd just heard it for the first time. From up in the cluster. Two people arguing, impossible to tell what they were saying. I lurched to my feet, stumbled, fell, found my balance point, and began to run toward the noise. The voices were people I knew, that was certain, but I was too fuzzy to put the right names to them. I didn't like the tone, I knew that.

There was a crash as I reached the edge of the cluster. Only two of the houses were lit. One was the Jackmans'. It wasn't from there; it had to be the farther one. I ran toward it. The door to the Jackmans' came open, and Mary Beth rushed out.

I wasn't sure she'd recognize me in the dark, so I yelled out, 'It's Swift!'

She caught up to me, pointed. 'Rags,' she said.

We raced toward the house. There was another crash. It was followed by a high-pitched shrieking, the words unintelligible. Some banging. My leg was aching. I ignored it. I went through the door fast, in a semi-crouch.

It was a small living space, very spartan. Without thinking, I mentally photographed it. One table, one chair. Shelves with books, a couple of pictures, some kind of dried flower arrangement. A small kitchen area.

That's where the action was.

I skidded to a stop. 'Hold it!' I yelled. No response. I rushed over, grabbed one of his arms. Mary Beth grabbed the other. He sloughed us off as if we weighed nothing, and returned to his work. I jumped back up and pulled my gun. Mary Beth shrank away. I went over to him and jammed the gun in his ear, hard, so he could feel what it was.

'*Jeff*!' I screamed. 'I'll blow your fucking head apart, I *swear it*! Let him *go*!' I shoved again with the gun.

And he stopped. He let go. Chaudri's head lolled in the same spot where Jeff had been beating it methodically against the floor. There was a lot of blood. Scalp wounds bleed a lot, I told myself. Rags's eyes were glazed, but he was conscious. I lifted under Jeff's arm, leaving the gun where it was. He was like a rag doll. Mary Beth looked on in horror.

'Up,' I said. 'Slow.'

We both got to our feet. When we were upright, I detached myself from him. I moved away, keeping the gun pointed. I motioned him to the chair at the other end of the room. I tracked him at a safe distance.

'Sit,' I said. He did it without a word. I never took my eyes off him. 'Dial 911,' I said to Mary Beth. 'I want the sheriff and the rescue squad here right away.'

She went to the phone. I leaned my back against the wall, across from Jeff. My leg hurt, but I continued to stare tough. If he ever decided that I wouldn't be able to shoot very well with a cast on my arm, anything could happen.

'They're on their way,' Mary Beth said.

'Good,' I said. 'See about Rags.'

She went over and began to talk to him in a low voice. I tuned them out. I still wasn't feeling all that clearheaded myself. I had one thing to concentrate on, and I did it.

'I think he's okay,' Mary Beth said to me. 'I don't want to move him until they get here, though.'

'They won't be long.'

They weren't, if you don't think twenty minutes is a long time. The rescue squad arrived first, by about a minute. I explained what had happened, and they gave Rags a quick check.

'I'm certain he'll be all right,' the EMT told me. 'But he should go to the hospital.'

A deputy walked in. I ran back through the story. The rescue squad bundled Rags up and got him on to a stretcher.

'Can he hear me?' the deputy asked them.

'As far as I know,' the EMT said.

The deputy bent over him. 'I'm a sheriff's deputy,' he said. 'Do you understand me?'

A cracked yes came from the form on the stretcher. At least that's what it sounded like.

'You have to answer one question,' the deputy said. 'The man who was beating you, do you want to press charges against him?'

Come on, Rags, I thought. Come on. I felt that at least a part of it was my fault.

'Yes,' came the croaked reply. I relaxed.

'All right,' the deputy said to the men in white. 'You can take him.'

Very efficiently, they hustled Chaudri out the door. The deputy went to the phone and called the sheriff. The deputy had to explain that he thought the incident was serious before Jakes agreed to come.

It was a half hour until the sheriff appeared, a quiet half hour for a while. I felt all right about closing my eyes and resting. The details of the night bounced around in my head in the random movement of molecules. Then other members of the community

129

began to show up. Word was spreading. Someone had seen the emergency lights and had called someone. . . . Mary Beth directed them to her house, should they want to wait for the sheriff to be done with us.

At one point I realized that there was something in my pocket. I should have thought to look, of course, but I didn't really blame myself. I pulled out the piece of paper and unfolded it. Two words again, same block printing: FINAL WARNING. I looked up. Jeff was staring at me. Was it his? I looked down at the note, then back at him, trying to penetrate his mask. Nothing. He gave me no clue. I might as well have been trying to get the dried flowers to tell me what it was like being alive.

'What is it?' Mary Beth asked.

She was still looking at me somewhat like I was from another planet.

'Nothing,' I said. 'A note reminding me of something I was supposed to do. I'll get it later.' I returned the paper to my pocket.

Another deputy preceded Faber Jakes through the door. He held it for the boss. Seeing him out with the foot soldiers, I couldn't avoid the comparison to a German SS officer. It was in the wire-rimmed glasses, in his bearing, in the little ways the deputies deferred to him. I was being unfair, but I didn't care.

'This the kid?' he asked, pointing to Jeff.

The first deputy nodded. When Jakes looked away, the deputy gave me a glance that said, 'Who in the hell did he think it was?' The sheriff turned to the second deputy, the one he'd come with.

'Take him to Lovingston,' Jakes said.

The second deputy dutifully read Jeff his rights, with Jakes seemingly scornful of the procedure. Then the two deputies took him out to the car. Jeff didn't resist. I wasn't sure he'd understood any of what had happened, except for the gun in his ear. He'd known what that was. Outside, a car started and pulled away. The first deputy returned.

'You lock him in the back?' Jakes asked. What a question.

'Of course, Sheriff,' the deputy said with no irony that I could hear.

Jakes took the chair that Jeff had been using. He turned it around and straddled it, resting his forearms on the back. The deputy squatted on the floor. It was the only other place. Mary Beth and I were already there.

'So,' Jakes said, 'what's going on here?'

'I let Mary Beth tell it. It didn't take long. She confined herself to what she'd actually seen and heard. She'd recovered her composure, and her description of the events was straightforward and clear. Even Faber Jakes couldn't think of much to ask her when she was finished. Among her accomplishments, she made an ideal witness.

I was grateful. I had the sneaking suspicion that I was the one who was going to get grilled. The extra preparation time was good for me.

As it turned out, I was right. Jakes asked me to corroborate her story and I did. Then he told her she could go, but that he'd want her to come to Lovingston and sign a statement as soon as they could get a stenographer. She told him fine. I started to rise, too, but he held out the palm of his hand. I sighed and sank back to the floor. No harm in trying.

'Loren,' Mary Beth said from the door, 'I'll wait for you. I'll have to explain things to the others, anyway.'

'Okay,' I said, and she left.

Jakes settled himself in. He took a tin of smokeless tobacco from his shirt pocket and stuck a pinch between his lip and gum. The way he did it, it was almost obscene to watch, as if he were fondling himself in front of me. I had to keep myself from laughing at the image.

'What's the story?' he asked me finally.

'Mrs Jackman told you,' I said. 'I don't know any more than she does. I'd been visiting her. I was out on the road, returning to my room, when I heard the fight break out. I ran back here. What we found was what she said.'

'You don't have no idea what they was fighting about?'

'Sure, I've got an idea.'

'Swift, I hope I don't have to keep asking you to get on with it. Tell me what you know,' he said sternly.

'I don't mind,' I said.

I told him that Chaudri was homosexual. It was going to come out. When I said it, the deputy sneered, but Jakes kept his SS poker face. I told him that Jeff was a good Christian and homophobe who believed it was his duty to show them the light. I offered the opinion that Jeff may have felt obliged to beat Chaudri's sin out of him, though I stressed that I hadn't heard any of the specific words that Jeff had been yelling.

'That ain't no Christian,' Jakes said.

131

'I quite agree, Sheriff. I think the kid is more than a little nuts.'

'We'll let a doctor decide that.'

'Of course.'

He looked at me for a long moment, letting me wonder what he was thinking. I got the distinct impression that in a real interrogation he would be merciless. That frightened me a little.

'This business you're here on,' he said, 'the Ballard death. That tie in any way with these two?'

'I don't know,' I said, and that was the truth.

'Funny thing,' he said. 'You show up here, and a couple days later there's violence. Funny thing, wouldn't you say?'

'Sheriff Jakes, I don't think it's humorous, believe me. You're making me feel like *I'm* suspected of something.'

'Nope. But you come all the way to Lovingston to tell me you thought Ballard's death wasn't an accident. Plus you told me somebody wanted you gone enough to hit you over the head about it. Now this Hindoo fella's had *his* head broke up about something, maybe his sex life, maybe not. What do you think, I might like to know what's going on?'

I didn't know what I wanted to do. Earlier I'd been after the sheriff's help, it was true. But now? I was making a lot of progress on my own, or at least I thought I was. If I told him any more of what I'd learned, not to mention that I'd been knocked out yet again, he'd certainly have sufficient cause to jump into the case. He and his men would be back asking people a lot of questions. Did I want that? No, I didn't. It would make it awfully difficult to proceed. I might never work up my momentum again. If I didn't say any more, he'd likely confine his attention to Jeff and Rags, both of whom were currently off the land. That would allow me to move around unhindered, for the time being. Maybe for long enough.

I was right on the edge of the crevass, though. Not revealing what Spock had told me about Rags, not recounting the second attack on me, these omissions could later be construed as obstruction of justice. I might not be formally charged, but this man could go a long way toward getting my licence pulled if he wanted to.

For an instant I hung there. Then I decided to chance it.

'I'm sure you'd like to know what's going on,' I said. 'So would I. It's what I was hired to find out. I'm telling you, I haven't yet. I believe that Ballard's death was not an accident, but I don't have any evidence to support that belief. I'd suggest that you talk to these two about the fight.' It was a decent compromise. 'Maybe

132

they'll tell you something they haven't told me. I'll be the first to thank you if they do.'

While I was talking, he peeled off the wire-rimmed spectacles. He breathed on each lens and polished them with his shirt. He put the glasses back on. I continued to revise my opinion of his cop talents. The action was just enough to disconcert you if you were nervous. At the same time it would give the unwary the erroneous impression that he was not paying full attention. Then, if he was going to, he'd jump on you. That apparently wasn't his plan for me.

'Swift,' he said casually, 'you're telling me everything, ain't you?' It was more effective than any threat. I was as evasive as I dared to be.

'I've told you what I know,' I said. 'I've also told you what I'm guessing. I think that's everything.'

'Good. We're working together on this thing now.'

'Fine with me. I appreciate your attitude.'

'And here's what I think you oughtta do next. I think you oughtta continue with your investigation, like you been doing. And I think you oughtta check in with me, what you're finding and all. How's once a day sound?'

'It sounds okay to me,' I said.

'We cooperate, I believe we can get to the bottom of all this.'

'I do too.'

He went through his snuff routine again. More distraction. Patience is a habit in the business. You cultivate it. I'd done that, and so had he. He was making sure that mine was equal to his. It was. I blanked my mind for the duration. It would be grateful for the inactivity.

'I guess that's about all we got to talk about,' he said finally. ''Less you got something else.'

'No, nothing else.'

'That gun you had to show the kid, you carrying it?'

I dug it out for him and handed it over. He examined it cursorily.

'Nice,' he said. 'For a automatic. Prefer a revolver myself.'

'Me too. But this one's a lot easier to pack.'

'There's that. You got a permit?' He accented the second syllable.

I rummaged in my wallet and produced it. He gave it a more perfunctory look than he'd given the gun. He knew I wouldn't try a phony permit on him.

'Okay,' he said, passing them back with just the trace of a smile. 'Gotta be sure we don't have people running around with guns, they don't know how to use them.'

'I know how to use it,' I said. 'If I have to, which I hope I never do.'

'Right.' He got up. 'Well, that's it, then.'

I got to my feet. My legs had cramped up. I rubbed them, one at a time, using my good hand. Jakes watched me with some amusement.

'The man don't believe in furniture, do he?' he said.

'Maybe it's against his religion,' the deputy said.

'Perhaps. Let's go, Martin. And you take care of yourself, Swift.'

'I'll try,' I said.

They went out. I heard the cruiser leave. The circulation was coming back into my legs. They were still weary from the running. Other parts of me began clamouring for attention too. I suddenly thought of an old Jimmy Buffett tune, and I smiled to myself. The song was called 'My Head Hurts, My Feet Stink and I Don't Love Jesus'. Well, *my* head hurt, too, and my feet probably stank. As for Jesus, personally I didn't have a thing against him. Unless someone like Jeff was a faithful representative of his ethics. Then I didn't love him, not at all.

18

So Lisa had been wrong, after all. Jeff was very capable of violence. Unfortunately, the man he'd been committing violence against had also been vaulted to near the top of my suspect list.

And the same incident, I had to admit, was going to force me to drop Jeff down a few notches. He *could* have bopped me on the head and then gone on to try to kill Chaudri, but I didn't think he had. The first was a carefully premeditated attack, the second an explosion of uncontrollable rage. In my mind the two didn't go together, maybe not at all, but certainly not within a few minutes of each other. Then, too, there was this question: Why stun me so close to the cluster, where I'd be likely to hear the ensuing fight and might be counted on to intervene? The logical conclusion was that

134

he hadn't been the one who'd sapped me. And if he hadn't done that, then he probably wasn't Temple Ballard's killer, either.

I also felt that it was time to start trusting the old occasionally reliable sixth sense. It was telling me that Mary Beth had not murdered her husband and that Spock had not slain his father. I'd warmed up to both of them, to the point where I could no longer believe in their involvement. I was ready to strike them from the list entirely.

Lisa I was less sure of, but again, my gut feeling was that it hadn't been her. She just didn't fit the role. I couldn't, however, forget that she was a dancer, a performing artist. All artists are to some extent masters of make-believe. Her innocence could always be another act. I placed her in the highly improbable pile.

All of this still left me with an unwieldy collection of likelies. My favourite continued to be Commander Zero. The second attack on me had been a carbon copy of the first. It was cool and professional and had once again completely surprised me. That was remark- able. I hadn't evidence that any of the other Babelonians possessed that kind of expertise.

Rags, of course, had to figure as a near co-favourite after what Spock had told me. The Indian had obviously been involved in *something* on the night of Ballard's death. That didn't mean he'd been involved in the death itself, but I had to assume the possi- bility.

Ike Bender remained somewhere in the middle of the list. At this point I didn't have compelling reasons to suspect him, but I didn't have any not to. He would bear another conversation or two.

Finally, there were the Evanses. They were hiding something — both Sally and I were sure of it. I wanted to know what it was. Long as the night had already been, I knew that I wouldn't sleep until I tried to find out.

I plodded the short distance to the Jackmans' house. As I did, the thought came to me that there might be more things stuck to the underside of Babel than just the murder of Temple Ballard. If so, there'd be more long nights like this one.

Only Mary Beth and Spock were left in the house. I slumped into the rocker while Mary Beth set some tea brewing.

'You look like you're the one got beat up,' Spock said.

'I am,' I said. 'One of them, anyway.'

'Huh?'

I held up my right arm. 'See this? It used to be my wrist before some lunatic decided to play Beat the Snake with it. And this leg worked better before the bullet went through it. They hurt me right now. You'd think people would give me a break. But *nooooo*. Since I've come to Babel, someone has been testing his rabbit punches on my neck.'

Mary Beth was staring at me. 'What on earth are you talking about?'

'I'm talking about having my lights extinguished. Twice. Once on this side. Then, for variety, once on this side.'

'When?' she asked.

'Tonight, for one example. Last night, for another.'

Spock whistled softly.

'You never told me,' she said.

'Mary Beth, in the investigation business there is what is politely called the Need to Know. If you don't have it, then you don't get the information. Prevents the accumulation of clutter. Last time I talked to you, you didn't have the Need to Know. Now you do. You, too, Spock.'

'How come?' he said.

Mary Beth served the tea. I asked her if she had any whiskey to put in it. She said no, they'd gotten out of the habit of keeping it around, because of Temple Ballard's problem. I thanked her, anyway. The tea was strong and hot, at least. I added some sugar to the caffeine. My energy reserves needed a booster shot.

'The reason how come,' I said to Spock, 'is that you were almost a witness.'

'Me?'

'You. Whoever it was clipped me right after that talk we had out on the road.'

'What talk?' Mary Beth asked.

It was a delicate moment. The two of them were looking not at each other but at me.

'Spock and I have been discussing his future,' I said to her, 'what options might be open to him. Whenever we meet, we talk.'

I was prepared to let it go at that. But there were forces in the night that were pushing us together, compelling us to be more honest. The subject wasn't going to drop.

'Thanks, Swift,' Spock said. 'He's just covering for me, Mom. He's a good guy that way.' And he told her about Chaudri. The whole thing. You could almost see him lightening up. When he'd finished, Mary Beth hugged him. I had the feeling their communication had been permanently improved.

136

'You should have come to me,' she said without it being a reproach.

'I know.'

'But I understand why you didn't. You've been brave.'

Spock looked embarrassed, so I said, 'If y'all don't mind, I still have a few questions.'

They turned to me.

'You see why I have some suspicions about your husband's death,' I said.

She nodded. 'And you got knocked out,' she said. 'Does that have something to do with it too?'

'I believe so. My attacker left me a note in each instance, warning me off the case.'

'I see,' she said. 'That's why you're carrying that . . . pistol.'

'Right. Tonight's note said it was the final warning. I have no idea what's next on the agenda.'

'I— I guess I'm convinced,' Mary Beth said.

'About what?'

'About Temple. I'll help you if I can.' Spock nodded his support as well.

'Thanks,' I said. 'What you might be able to help me with tonight is timing. Now, Spock, did you hear the fight between Jeff and Rags?'

'No,' he said. 'I was down at the core house. I didn't come up until the ambulance got here.'

'And how long was it between the time I left and the fight starting?' I asked Mary Beth.

'I'd say about twenty minutes,' she said.

I did some hasty figuring. 'That doesn't leave much,' I said. 'I had to have time to talk to Spock, and he had to have time to get out of earshot. The yelling was pretty loud. I'd say I was only out a minute or two and that I woke up right when the fight began. You didn't see or hear anything in those twenty minutes?' I asked Mary Beth.

'No, nothing unusual.'

'And you didn't see anyone on the road?' I said to Spock.

He shook his head. 'No one.'

'I see what you're getting at,' Mary Beth said. 'The timing is too tight for Jeff to have been the one to knock you out.'

'Exactly. But I didn't figure him for it, anyway. He's not subtle enough. The more important thing may be that it couldn't have been Chaudri, either.'

I let the implications of that sink in.

'But,' Spock said, 'what about . . . ? You mean, he didn't . . . ? Then why . . . ?'

Mary Beth said, 'He might have been doing something else that night, Spock. Something that he didn't want anyone else to know about. And that's why he wanted you to keep quiet.'

'Right,' I said. 'Another possibility is that Chaudri's a killer and the person who keeps bopping me isn't.'

'How can that be?' Spock asked.

'I don't know,' I admitted. 'Maybe there are more dimensions to the crime than we yet realize. And for God's sake, don't ask me to explain *that* one.'

'Or your assailant could be involved in something unrelated that will nevertheless come out if the truth about Temple is discovered,' Mary Beth said.

'Yes.'

She chuckled to herself. I asked her what was funny, although there was no mirth in her laugh.

'It's ironic,' she said. 'You know one of the big reasons why we came here? Because we wanted to simplify our lives. Looks like it was all just an illusion, doesn't it?'

'There's nothing wrong with wanting something better,' I said. 'Even if it never works out.' There was a pause while we examined whatever dreams we still had. Mine was easy: for Patricia Ryan to wake up and be the person she'd been before.

'So, what do you think about tonight?' I asked.

'God,' Mary Beth said, 'we haven't even talked about that yet. What did the sheriff want with you?'

I gave her a brief summary of my meeting with Faber Jakes and asked if she knew him well enough to offer an opinion about him.

'I don't know him personally,' she said. 'The word in the county is that he's not a man to make an enemy of. Otherwise, he minds his own business, doesn't bother the boys making 'shine or running cockfights. He lives alone, doesn't have any friends, doesn't drink or party. Rumour says he might have had a wife who died young, but no one seems sure. If you want my advice, I'd say play it straight with him. But then, you're already playing it not quite straight, aren't you?'

'Yeah, I already am.'

'Well, if you dig up something important, you better go to him with it first thing. There are a few stories floating around about

138

folks who got injured in the county lockup. It's always because they try to escape, you know. Keep him more or less on your side and I imagine he could be a help to you. He knows the county.'

'How about the scene at Rags's?' I asked. 'Any ideas about that?'

She shrugged. 'What's to say? It looks like Jeff finally went off the deep end. I feel sorry for him; he must have had something really awful happen to him in his life. But I can't say that I'm surprised.'

'Jeff goes berserk, attacks the nearest homosexual. You think that's all there is to it?'

'Sure. What else would there be?'

'Damned if I know, Mary Beth, but I've got to ask. Every time I think I understand things here, somebody pops the cork on a new bottle and it's here we go again, Jack.'

'I'm sorry,' she said.

'It's not your fault.'

'No, I know that. I'm sorry that it's so difficult for you. You might consider what it is that you're trying to do. You're trying in three days to understand patterns of personal interaction that have been developing for *years*. That's not going to come easy. Some of these people have been bouncing around inside a fairly closed society for a long, long time. Hell, I've been here two years, and the early history of Babel is still a mystery to me, a lot of it. Don't expect miracles.'

'It's frustrating,' I grumbled.

'C'mon, Swift,' Spock said, 'lighten up.'

'It hasn't exactly been an evening of light entertainment.'

'No,' Mary Beth said. 'I don't think I've ever . . . I was terrified that you were actually going to shoot Jeff. I haven't stopped shaking yet.'

'I don't know if I would have,' I said. 'And I'm glad I didn't have to find out.'

'I wish I would've been there,' Spock said.

'Spock!' his mother said. He looked sheepish, but I understood. Real violence has precisely the same appeal as what we've seen on the big and little screens. There is no longer any way to tell them apart.

'You would have been disappointed,' I said to him. 'There's nothing fun about watching a man's head, wondering whether it's gonna turn into watermelon in the next second. It's not even fun to see someone you hate being beaten to death.'

'I— I don't hate him anymore,' Spock said. But I felt it was only

139

a concession to me.

'Good. So, there's nothing else I need to know about Jeff and Rags.' They looked at each other, shook their heads. 'Then I guess I'd better get moving. Were Nancy and Freddie over here tonight?'

'Yes, earlier,' Mary Beth said.

'When did they leave?'

'Not long ago.'

'Okay, I think I'll go see them.'

'I'll go with you,' she said.

'You don't have to do that.' Now what was she up to?

'I know. But I'm still keyed-up from tonight. I don't feel like sitting around here. You don't mind, do you?'

She might be telling the truth. Or it might be a subtle offer of her help in prying out whatever secrets there were to be pried from the Evanses. Or she might for reasons of her own want to be present when I went to work on them. Or anything. The question was, did I mind her tagging along? Nope.

'It's fine,' I said. 'Why don't you call them and not mention me?'

She smiled like someone who was pleased to have been assigned a part in the deception. I couldn't imagine why she should be. She went to the phone.

'Do you like your job?' Spock asked me.

'Sometimes.'

'How do you get a job like that?'

'There's a lot of ways,' I said. 'You can apply at an insurance company. They'll probably start you out driving around, writing estimates on car wrecks. And you might be asked to wear a suit.' He grimaced at that. 'You can join the cops. That's where a lot of investigators start.' He grimaced again, and I grinned. 'Different kind of suit. The army'll train you, too, if you're willing to commit the years. Or you can just take a course, get your licence, and see if anyone wants to employ you.'

'I don't know,' he said.

'It's not for everyone. Most of the time it's incredibly boring. You get to be your own boss, though.'

'I think I'd like that.'

'It's nice. But you've got to be able to blend in. Usually, the last thing an investigator wants is for people to remember what he looks like.'

Spock looked self-conscious. Mary Beth returned from her call.

'It's on,' she said. 'They're kind of like us, sitting around wondering what to do next. There're going to be a lot of people

140

asking serious questions about our admission policies after this.'

'Okay,' I said. 'Let's go, then.'

Mary Beth took me the short way, across the field and back over the ridge. The same path Chaudri had followed the night of Temple Ballard's death. Twice. Coming and going.

I wasn't quite ready to lay a murder charge at the Indian's feet, however. It wasn't that I disbelieved Spock. I didn't. And it wasn't that I thought Chaudri incapable: a jilted lover is an unpredictable beast. Rags had method: he knew the setup at the Ark as well as anyone. He had motive, obviously. And he had opportunity: my witness could place him in the vicinity of the 'accident' at just the right time.

It was a hell of a lot of circumstantial evidence. It might even be enough for Fail-Safe Detection Systems, Inc. to be able to pressure Mary Beth Jackman into a very modest settlement. But in the end it was still only circumstantial evidence, not proof. It wouldn't convince even the most easily persuaded juror, especially not with so many other highly motivated people swimming in the same tank.

Rags might well have done it. Or he might have seen what had happened and was now covering up for someone else. Or he might have done it in *conjunction* with someone else. And so on. The possibilities were limited only by my imagination.

As if reading my mind, 'Mary Beth asked, 'Do you think Rags was involved?'

'In your husband's death? Yeah, probably. Do you?'

'Maybe. I'd like not to think so. I've always been fond of him. Somehow, there was never any petty jealousy there. He loved Temple. I could see that and I accepted that.'

'Love's a powerful motivator.'

'True. But killing the one you love. I have a hard time picturing that.'

'It happens all the time. You have a murder, the first person the cops want to talk to is the husband, wife, lover or whatever.'

'The police are cynical,' she said.

'Cynical and realistic, both.'

'And you? Do you think that way too?'

'To some extent. When I first came here, I figured you'd probably killed your husband.'

'I knew there was a reason I disliked you. And am I still a suspect?'

'Nah. Do you still dislike me?'

She laughed. 'I guess not. But I wouldn't want to have to live like you do, being suspicious of everyone.'

I admitted that there were times when I felt the same way. 'Right around three o'clock every morning,' I said.

'But you keep on doing it.'

'Yeah, I seem to be unfit for any other kind of work. And speaking of work, tell me something. Did Ballard cut off the relationships with his other lovers when he decided he wanted you back?'

She chuckled. 'I can see you still don't know Temple,' she said. 'He never allowed that anything was final. Depending on your point of view, you could say that he was an enlightened man who'd learned how to live completely in the present, or that he was a selfish son of a bitch who always kept his options open. The specific answer to your question is that he put his other relationships on indefinite hold. The way he did things, it wouldn't have been difficult for someone to take that as a polite form of permanent rejection.'

'How about Nancy? Did she love him too?'

'Yes.'

'As much as Rags did?'

'Surely you don't expect me to be able to make that kind of judgment?'

'Give me ball park,' I said.

'It's impossible,' she said. 'The two are so different. Rags is a single man. Nancy has been with Freddie for fifteen years. That complicates things. She might have loved Temple madly, but she never wanted to leave Freddie. Her feelings would always have to be somewhat ambivalent. On top of which, Freddie was insanely jealous — ' She stopped as though she'd only just realized what that might mean.

'A jealous man with a quick temper. Did he and Ballard ever fight?'

'Not physically, no. We don't settle our disagreements that way . . . usually. They had some screaming arguments, though. After a while, they stopped trying to communicate. They didn't talk at all.'

'How long had Ballard been seeing Nancy before he died?' I asked.

'Oh, maybe three months.'

'And Rags?'

'About six.'

'Was Rags jealous when he took up with Nancy?'

'I wouldn't know,' she said. 'Look, I didn't talk to Temple much about how things were going with his other lovers. I had plenty to take care of in my own life.'

'Your own relationships?'

'Relation*ship*. I told you Temple was the one who wanted multiple S.O.'s.'

'I meant friends as well as lovers.'

'Sure, those. And my son, and my job.'

'What kind of job did you have?'

'I was doing counselling for the community action agency in Charlottesville.'

'But you're not now?' I said.

'No.'

'Why? If you don't mind my asking.'

'I don't mind. Temple's death was a major event in my life, even though we weren't getting along at the time. It made me evaluate everything about myself. I decided that I didn't want to be doing what I was doing.' She hesitated, then continued. 'I'd been wanting to . . . write a book for some time. So I quit my job and started.'

'A book?' I said. 'What's it about?'

'It's an overview of intentional communities in this country. I still believe that in the long run, community is the way to go. If I move back to California, I'll look for one to join there. Plus I'll eventually have to get out and do some field research. It's not going to be just about Babel.'

'Ambitious.'

'I like to keep busy. If you believe the insurance charts, my life's about half over.'

'Don't remind me. My charts aren't as good as yours.'

'How about you?' she asked. 'Isn't there something you've always wanted to do?'

'I don't know,' I said, thinking aloud. 'I used to want to travel, until Uncle sent me sight-seeing in Southeast Asia. That made me realize that I like it here just fine. For a while there I thought I might make a good politician. Then I realized I had some pretty clear convictions, and that's the last thing people want in their elected officials. Actually, I *have* always wanted to try hang gliding.'

'Why don't you?'

'I'm chicken.'

She laughed. 'Well,' she said, 'I should have guessed. A man chooses a profession where he has to carry a gun, he's bound to be afraid of *some*thing.'

That may have been uncomfortably close to the truth, so I let it ride. We walked with our thoughts for a few minutes.

Then I said, 'Mary Beth, I'd like to ask you a question. Why did you file the suit against Fail-Safe?'

'Is that personal or are you working?'

'Both. But mostly personal. I'm curious.'

'It's simple either way. I need the money.'

'You need ten million dollars?'

'No,' she said, 'I don't really need ten million dollars. I'd like to be free to be able to work on my book and not have to worry about money. I could do it on less. But what if it happened to someone *you* cared about? How much would that person's life be worth?'

'At least ten million,' I said. I was prepared to fork it all over if Patricia would only wake up.

'There you have it. I consulted with a lawyer, and that's the figure we arrived at. If the detector truly cost Temple his life, the company should pay gladly.'

'I doubt they do anything that costs them money gladly. But why'd you wait so long before you filed the suit?'

'Oh, you know. I was confused about a lot of things. I had to do some healing, emotionally. I wanted to believe it had been an accident, yet I had my doubts. It was a while before I could deal with something like a lawsuit.' She paused, then went on. 'Ah, why am I going through all this? It's crap, I know that now.' She stopped walking and looked at me. Though her face was shadowed, I could feel her intensity. 'I think I only finally put it together tonight. When I saw Jeff hunched over Rags like that, and you with your gun stuck in the kid's ear, well . . . '

She shook her head sharply, as if ridding it of some long-stagnant water. 'You know,' she went on, 'I *hated* you when you first came. That was part of it, part of what I wouldn't let myself face. I'm glad you turned out to be who you are. If you'd pushed back, we'd still be fighting. As it is, you've helped me to see. I didn't sue for ten million bucks because some greedy lawyer talked me into it. And I didn't wait for so long because I had to feel sure it was an accident. I sued for that much money because I *knew* that they'd be forced to send someone like you to investigate. And I

144

waited because I wanted to believe it was an accident, and I couldn't.'

'Uh, I'm not sure I understand,' I said.

'Neither did I at the time. I thought my motivations were straightforward. But my subconscious was apparently working overtime, setting it up so I'd get what I *really* wanted: someone down here to do a full investigation. The police weren't going to do it. I knew that. The only way to ensure it was to give someone with the resources a very compelling reason.'

'Fail-Safe.'

'Right,' she said. 'I'm sorry if it seems calculated now, but like I said, I didn't know myself what I was doing. It must have been that in my heart I'd always felt Temple had been murdered.'

'You don't have to apologize to me, Mary Beth. Fail-Safe can afford me out of their walking-around money. And none of this changes what I'm trying to do.'

We started walking again. We were entering the housing cluster where Nancy and Freddie Evans lived.

'Except for one thing,' she said.

'What's that?'

'I imagine that your primary interest is in getting me to drop the suit entirely.'

'That's what Fail-Safe wants. Of course.'

'*Or* get me to settle out of court, for some piddling amount.'

'Mmmm,' I said. 'Yeah, that too. They'd be happy with that.'

'If it was the money, you see,' she said, 'you might be able to do that. Raise my doubts enough that I wasn't willing to let it drag through the courts. But now I want to *know* what happened to Temple. Reasonable doubt won't do it, I'm afraid. I'll never drop the suit until I'm sure.'

'I see,' I said. 'Well, for what it's worth, I believe we want exactly the same thing. That happens, you know. You can start out on a job for one reason, and halfway through your reasons get bent every whichaway. I've come to want to know the truth about your husband.'

'Thank you. I know it's going to be difficult for you.'

'Already has been. But maybe it's about to get easier. Let's start here, shall we?' We were at the Evanses'.

'Let's.'

145

Mary Beth knocked on the door and Nancy let us in.

The door opened into what is sometimes called a 'mud room', an entryway for hanging coats, storing snow shovels, scraping the dirt from your boots. I hung my jacket on one of the wooden pegs. Nancy led us into the house proper.

The kitchen area came first. It was small and tidy, with a bathroom off it. The stove was gas, and so was the refrigerator. The Evanses also used kerosene lamps. They wouldn't be paying much to the electric company.

Beyond the kitchen was the living/dining room. It was about fifteen by fifteen, large by Babel standards. It was also cluttered. There was a round oak table with the memories of dinner still on it. There was a couch and a couple of overstuffed chairs, all nonmatching. Clothes were strewn here and there, over the backs of chairs, in corners. One end of the couch held a stack of newspapers and magazines. And there were pillows everywhere, from small throw pillows with patchwork covers to large fluffy ones meant for sitting on. Against the far wall was an open toolbox with various hand tools next to it on the floor, as if someone had just been rummaging around in there and hadn't found what they were looking for.

A lot of people would have said, 'Excuse the mess.' Nancy didn't. I liked that. This was the way they lived, and what concern was it of mine?

Freddie was sitting on one of the straight-backed chairs around the table. He didn't apologize, either. Instead he said, 'What's he doing here?'

'We've been talking,' Mary Beth said, 'trying to make some sense out of all this. It's been a difficult night for both of us.'

'I don't want him here.'

'C'mon, Fred,' Nancy said, 'don't — '

'I don't have anything to *say* to him!'

He turned and stared out of one of the south-facing windows. There wasn't anything to see but the unilluminated night. Nancy looked at me as if to say that Freddie would calm down, I should only be a little patient.

In truth, I didn't really want him to calm down that much. This was a good time to dredge up old memories, and it would be better to have him a little agitated. What I had to be careful of was not to let control of the situation get away from me.

'Would you like some coffee?' Nancy asked.

'No, thanks,' I said. 'Look, why don't we all sit down for a minute?'

Nancy and Mary Beth nodded, and the three of us moved into the living room. They sat. I remained on my feet. It's the oldest trick in the book, and still one of the best.

'Now,' I said, 'what happened tonight, grotesque as it was, should serve to remind us that back in February a man died here. He died by violence. Not the kind of violence Mary Beth and I recently witnessed, but violence just the same. He died at the hands of someone else.'

'Mr Swift,' Nancy said, 'Temple Ballard's death was an accident. Can't you accept that?' She was pleading and seemed on the verge of tears. Unconsciously, she glanced at her husband. She wasn't good at this. I didn't know what her silent question was, but it was obvious she was asking one. His reply was a strong stare. She looked back at me and then down at her feet.

'I wish I could, Nancy,' I said, 'but I can't. I've learned too much. I've seen the current of violence that runs beneath the surface here. Jeff's outburst is not an isolated incident. Ballard was murdered. I know it, and so do you.'

I gazed at her sympathetically, encouraging her to open up to me. She moved her lips silently, then said, 'You think Jeff . . . ?'

'I don't know. I think everybody. Who do you think, Nancy? Tell me who *you* think.'

I leaned toward her. There were tiny beads of sweat forming at her hairline.

'Leave her alone, Swift,' Freddie said.

I turned quickly to face him. 'Why, Freddie?' I said. 'Why don't you want her to talk to me? Because she was Temple Ballard's lover and she knows how he died?'

Mary Beth gasped. It was dirty. I felt like God's ugliest child saying it. But I'd said it.

'You bastard,' he growled at me. 'How *dare* you? Nancy didn't have anything to do with his death.'

147

'How do you know *that*? How do you *know*, Freddie?' I took a step toward him.

His face was turning the colour of his hair. 'Get out of my house,' he said through clenched teeth.

'Sure,' I said. I took another step. 'Just give me a couple of answers. What happened that night, Freddie?'

'I've told you—'

'I'm not convinced. I want to hear it again, Freddie. What *really* happened?'

'Mr Swift—' Nancy said.

'Loren, stop it!' Mary Beth said at the same time. I ignored them both.

'What is it, Freddie?' I said. 'What are you *afraid* of?'

He came up out of his chair, his fists knotted at his sides.

'Please, Fred,' Nancy said, 'just—'

'Get *out!*' he snarled.

I raised my voice, as if I might be just as angry as he was.

'I want some *answers*, Freddie! Someone's been hitting me over the head and I'm just pissed enough to think it's *you*. Tell me the *truth*, goddamn you!'

His mouth twitched. Something unintelligible escaped from it, and then he took the swing at me. He telegraphed the punch. I was leaning away, and I caught a lot of it on my good left arm. The remainder landed on my jaw. It wasn't really enough to put me down, but I went down, anyway.

Freddie stood over me, seething. The two women had gotten to their feet and their eyes were darting wildly from me to Freddie to each other. Oddly, my thought was: There are no killers in this room. But my mind was still clicking along down its single track. I looked Freddie in the eye.

'Why'd you do it, Freddie?' I said calmly.

He howled his rage and pain and jumped on top of me. He grabbed for my throat. Mary Beth had seen enough of that for one night. She latched on to one of his arms. Nancy quickly took hold of the other. They pulled at him.

'Fred,' Nancy said, 'for God's sake, let's just tell him!'

Freddie's voice came out as a high-pitched shriek. It was aimed at me. 'I killed him! That's what you want me to *say*, isn't it? I killed him, I killed him, I killed him! It was an *accident*, god-damnit! I'm sorry! Why can't you leave me the hell alone? I'm *sorry!*'

Mary Beth was gaping at him, her mouth hanging open like a

148

cartoon character's. Freddie stood up, shedding the women from his arms, and bolted from the house. The kitchen door crashed shut behind him, then the outer door. The silence that followed made the house feel like a burial vault. I wasn't at all sure I'd done the right thing.

Mary Beth reacted first. She stood up, sighed, and ran her hand slowly back through her hair. The movement had a ritualistic air to it, as if she were re-enacting a scene that had been played out countless times before, in all ages and all places. It stirred something in me at a level that I didn't even know existed. I could not have spoken to save my own life.

Nancy sat back on her heels and was very still. Her baby face, which I had once thought unremarkable, now captivated me. In repose it was like one you might see in an old, richly toned oil painting.

Mary Beth started to speak, but the words caught. She cleared her throat and began again. 'I'll go after him,' she said, and she followed Freddie out the door. Considering what he had just said, it was an extraordinary response. There wasn't a trace of anger in it. She wanted to know what had happened, and she wanted him to tell her. Somehow she knew, even then, that whatever he had to say would not cause her to turn on him. It was a gamble I'm not sure I would have had the strength to take.

I didn't follow her. There was no reason to. Nancy would be able to tell me what I wanted to know. Freddie and Mary Beth could use the time alone. I sat up and absently massaged my jaw. Nancy turned her attention to me. She began to resemble a painting less, and a routinely troubled person more.

'I'm sorry,' I said. I felt as lame as I ever had offering an apology.

'No,' she said, 'it's all right. I'm glad. It goes against our grain — and I mean everyone here — to lie and hide things. We've had to live with it for too long now. It's time that the truth came out.'

I got up and went over to her. I offered my hand, and she pulled herself up. We went and sat at the table. It seemed like the most appropriate spot for the kind of discussion I was expecting to have.

'Are we going to talk?' I asked.

'Yes,' she said.

'All right. I guess I should say one thing at the beginning, Nancy. I don't believe that your husband killed Temple Ballard.'

'Yes, he did. But it was an accident.' She looked like she was talking about some uninvolved third party.

149

'Do you want to tell me about it now?'

She nodded. 'The day Temple died,' she said, 'was Freddie's turn to maintain the gasifier. You know that. Did someone show you what that entails?'

'Yes. Rags did.'

'Good. Well, that was kind of a bad day for Freddie. The previous night we'd had a fight about my relationship with Temple. Even though he and I were barely seeing each other any more. But Freddie can keep an issue alive for years if he wants to. So we fought. It wasn't a horrible fight, it wasn't a particularly meaningless one. In the morning Freddie was in a foul mood. When he's irritated like that, he doesn't do his best work. Normally, he's very conscientious, but . . .

'He went through all the things he was supposed to do at the Ark. I don't doubt that he did. But I also know that his mind wouldn't have been focused on what he was doing. He was in the state where you make mistakes. And he made one.'

She sighed, then went on. She was looking me in the face now. She wanted very much for me to understand what she was saying. 'It's the kind of thing,' she said, 'where you ask yourself forever after: "Was it truly an accidental mistake or was the subconscious carrying out its real wishes?" You can't help asking that. Yet it's a question that can never be answered, no matter what. The only thing I'm sure of is that he didn't do it deliberately. I'm sure of that.

'Anyway, you know what it looks like in the shed. There's the filter unit that removes particles from the gas just before it's burned.' She looked at me questioningly, and I nodded that I knew what she was talking about. 'Inside are several kinds of filters. Freddie was supposed to clean them and he did. Before he fired the gasifier for the day. To get at the filters all you do is remove the top and pull them out. When you're done, you slide them back in place. The only thing you have to be careful of is fastening the top back on properly. It has to be fitted so that it seals the filter housing. If you don't get it right, gas − carbon monoxide and the rest of them − can . . . . leak out.'

She paused, so I said, 'And that's what happened?'

'Yes, that's what happened.'

'But the police were told that the leak occurred at the exit gasket in the filter box, not in the top. Isn't that right?'

'That's what they were told. It wasn't true.'

'Why did you lie to the cops?'

150

'You have to understand,' she said, 'what it's like to try to run a small business these days. That's what the Ark is, a small business. More important, it's a business where we use dangerous equipment. That makes a lot of people interested in us, federal and state safety offices and what have you. They give us as much attention as they give the big factories. If they decide that our working conditions are unsafe, they can close us down. We depend on the Ark in many ways, Mr Swift. Can you imagine what a disaster it would be if we didn't have it?'

'I think so,' I said.

'I'm not sure you do. Babel could be destroyed. No matter who dies, we can't let that happen. Babel would still represent life for the ones who remained.'

'I can understand that. So you reported a death due to negligence as one due instead to a mechanical failure beyond your control.'

'Yes, that's what we did. The filter top was replaced correctly and the gasket seal was deliberately broken. It didn't matter; Temple was dead already. Now the agencies couldn't claim negligence on our parts, which is the one thing that they come down the hardest on. I don't think it was the wrong thing to do.'

'Yeah,' I said, 'I don't know what I would have done in your place.'

'But naturally, it's made us crazy, especially Freddie. For different reasons, of course. There's the cover-up that we did. But Freddie has to live with suspicion of himself. That's a lot harder. It's been tearing him up.'

'Who exactly decided on changing the shed around, Nancy?'

'The three of them, Freddie and Ike and Rags. They were the first ones on the scene. Though once they discovered what had really happened, Freddie wasn't in much shape to decide anything.'

'You weren't there?' I asked.

'Not until later.'

'Did they tell you right away?'

'Yes.'

'Who else knows?'

'No one.'

'*No* one?'

'No.'

'You haven't told Mary Beth?'

'No.'

'Jesus.'

151

'We were afraid to. I'm sure you understand.'

I understood. But Mary Beth was going to find out now. I wasn't at all sure that that was the best way for it to have happened.

'It's done,' I said.

At that point Mary Beth returned with Freddie. I could tell by looking at them that he had told her. He must not have gone far. He hadn't been running from her, I thought, not so much as he had been running from what he might conceivably have done to me.

The two of them sat down at the table with us. Everyone waited for someone else to start the conversation. Nancy finally did it.

'What happens now?' she asked no one in particular.

There was no immediate response, so I said, 'I think that's up to Mary Beth.'

'Me?' Mary Beth said somewhat dazedly.

'Yes,' I said to her. 'I'm not a cop. I don't have to report anything unless I see evidence of a crime having been committed. That's not exactly what happened here. Now that *you* know, I doubt there's anyone else the Evanses want to tell. But if you want the investigation officially reopened, you could probably attract the cops' attention with this.'

'I . . . I don't know,' Mary Beth said.

'It's all right. Don't hurry it, Freddie,' I said, turning to him. 'Nancy has told me what happened, as much as she knows. But I need to ask you some questions. Will you talk to me?'

He nodded dumbly after a moment. The fight was out of him now. What I'd done hadn't been pretty, but it had succeeded in lifting a weight from him. He had no reason to hate me any more.

'I need to know the sequence of events that night,' I said. 'Beginning with why you were down at the core house.'

'I was using the computer,' he said. There was no inflection to his voice at all. 'To do our taxes.'

'Was anyone else around?'

'No.'

'Where were Jeff and Lisa?'

'I don't know where Jeff was. Lisa was there when I arrived, but she went out early and I didn't see her again all night. After a while, it started to get cold in the core house, so I went outside to split some wood for the stove. That's when the alarm went off.'

'And as soon as it went off, you ran up to the Ark,' I said.

'Yes.'

'Did you see anyone on the way?'

'Spock. I saw Spock. He was on the road. It didn't look like he

152

cared that the alarm was going off.'

'So it took you what, a couple of minutes to get to the Ark?' I asked.

'Uh-huh.'

'And what did you do when you got there?'

'I shut down the gasifier and vented the lines. Then I found Temple. And Rags arrived.'

Yeah, I thought, he was on his way.

'We didn't know what to do,' he went on, 'so we tried to call Ike. He didn't answer, but he got there a few minutes later. He'd started down when he heard the alarm, but he lives farther away, so it took him longer. The three of us found where the leak had been. It was my fault.' He stopped. I waited until he was ready to resume. I noted that he said Ike had arrived on his own, where he'd originally told me that they'd called him. That was confirmation of the fact that he'd previously been telling a well-rehearsed story. It made me feel that I was getting the truth.

'Temple wasn't my friend,' he said. He looked from one to the other of us. 'But I didn't want him dead. You've got to believe me.' No one spoke, so he continued. 'I never wanted him dead, but he was. There wasn't anything we could do about it. We realized that what I'd done could really hurt Babel. So we . . . changed things a little. We didn't think it would hurt anyone, and it was for the good of the community. I never wanted to, to lie, but we . . . had to.'

'When did you call Nancy?' I asked.

'Right after that. I couldn't have kept it from her. She was the only other person who knew.'

'Okay. Now, Freddie,' I said, 'there's just one more thing I need to know. Who originally suggested changing the scene around? Was it you?'

He thought about it. 'No, not me. I wasn't thinking very . . . clearly.'

'Who was it, then?'

'It was . . . it was Rags.'

'Are you sure?'

He nodded. 'It was. Ike didn't think we should touch anything at first. But Rags saw the danger. He's more . . . logical than we are.'

'Thank you,' I said. 'I understand how difficult all this is for you.'

He had his hands folded in front of him on the table. His chin dropped to his chest. His eyes were closed.

153

'Come on,' I said to Mary Beth, 'let's walk back to your house. I don't think there's anything more to talk about tonight.'

She nodded. We got up and left. The Evanses sat mutely at the table as if the stage lights were going to go down and in the next scene it would be tomorrow. I was momentarily overcome with the feeling of how little we ever really know about what's going on. I'd live through whatever happened to me the rest of the night, but I'd never know what happened to these others.

Outside, Mary Beth took my arm and we walked. I decided to talk only if she wanted to. We were halfway back before she did.

'You know what I keep thinking?' she said. 'It doesn't have anything to do with anything, but this is it. That I missed a lot that other people take for granted, and I'm different from them. I didn't have the chance to be in love when I was a teenager. Temple and I didn't have that chance. We just passed through each other's lives at that point, and the consequences have been in charge of my life ever since. But we never went to the beach to watch the sun come up, even though it was only an hour away. It's corny, but I think that's what you're supposed to do when you're a kid. Even if it's not important in the long run. I didn't have it, *we* didn't have it, and it makes me sad to realize that we never did.'

'And never will?' I said.

'No. That's not so bad. It's a lot worse that we never *could* have.'

That was it. When we got to her house, she left me with a simple good night. Appropriate. She certainly wasn't going to thank me for what I'd done.

I walked slowly back to the core house, trying to put the night into its proper niche with regard to the overall story. And it didn't quite fit. I bent and twisted everything I'd seen and heard since I'd first telephoned Devin Pethco. The pattern had to be there, didn't it? I didn't know. All of my questions should have been answered, shouldn't they? I didn't know. I only knew that the many voices of Babel were still babble to me.

When I got to the core house, I went directly to Sally's room. I let myself in as quietly as I could. To my relief, she was sleeping alone. I went over to her bed and shook her gently.

'Sally,' I said in a whisper, 'I've got to talk to you.'

The tangled blond curls came up toward me. She didn't screw around about waking up, she just did it. There was no sign that I'd startled her at all.

154

'What is it?' she said.

I let myself down to the floor, until I was comfortably seated, leaning against the bed. My head dropped back. Sally reached over and ran her fingers lightly through my hair. It felt great. I let myself drift for a couple of minutes.

Then I said, 'It's a long story,' and I told it to her, hoping that my whisper didn't carry beyond the walls of the room. I told her everything. As I did, I realized that it was quite a list for one night: the first chat with Mary Beth; Spock on the road; getting knocked out; Jeff and Rags; the sheriff; Mary Beth again; and the scene at the Evanses'. When I finished, I think she was in shock. Like me.

'God,' she said finally.

'Yeah, I think we need His intervention.'

'What does it all mean?'

'I wish I knew. No matter how I try to piece it together, there are still holes. I'm about ready to give Mary Beth Jackman her money. I'm not sure any of this is worth it.'

'You ain't a quitter, Swifty.' She ruffled my hair.

I sighed. 'Nah, I suppose not. We keep turning up new stuff, we're bound to come to the end of the line eventually.'

'The problem is,' she said, 'even with Freddie's story, we still don't know why the alarm failed. We're not much better off than we were.'

'Yeah. I think Freddie's been torturing himself for nothing. Somebody loosened the filter top *after* he'd replaced it, I'm sure of it. It's diabolical. They'd know that Freddie would take the fall.'

'Uh-huh. It'd be the same person who disabled the alarm. Do you think it was Chaudri?'

'Well,' I said, 'it sure as hell looks like it. We can put him in the vicinity at the right time. Spock said he was acting strangely. And then, he *was* the one to suggest the changes at the scene. That's suspicious. But it's all still circumstantial. You can't hang him on it. And the thing that really bothers me is, it couldn't have been Rags who hit me over the head.'

'Right. I almost forgot about that.'

'I haven't.'

'Sorry. Why don't you get into bed?'

'I don't think I'd be worth much tonight.'

'That's not what I meant,' she said.

I turned and smiled at her. 'I know. Thanks.' I got some clothes off and slipped in beside her. When my head fell on to the pillow, I

155

realized that I was more tired than I could have imagined. Sally held me. She was soft and warm and the sort of friend we should all wish to have a dozen of.

I was drifting a little when she said, 'I spent some time with Lisa tonight.'

'Oh, yeah?' I mumbled. 'No major revelations, I hope.'

'Only that she's sleeping with Ike Bender.'

'Izzat all? I wouldna thought he was her type,' I said, and then I passed out.

20

In the morning I felt better, and I was a bit more interested in Lisa Berlinger. Before getting up, Sally and I had another of our whispered conversations.

'How do you know about Lisa and Ike?' I asked.

'Well, I can't be positive,' she said. 'We stayed around here last night, chatting. She was in a strange mood. Distracted. Like something was about to happen to her, you know? Maybe not something good. That was my feeling. After a while I was certain that she had something she wanted to do and was trying to figure out how to get rid of me. So I made it easy on her. I told her I was going to my room to read.

'I thought her behaviour was on the odd side, so I watched out my window. Sure enough, about fifteen minutes later she slipped out the back. She didn't head down the road, she lit off directly across the hayfield. I followed her.'

'And how, pray tell, did you do that in an open field?'

She grinned. 'Simple. From the direction she was headed, I figured she must be going to the far cluster. So I borrowed one of the bikes out back and took the road. I'm very fast on a bike. I got there way ahead of her. Then I just hid in the trees and waited.'

'Ms Hatch, I'm impressed,' I said. 'Once again. And Lisa went to Bender's house?'

'Right. I stayed outside, of course. In a few minutes the lights went out. I'd say that was pretty good evidence there's something on between them.'

'Sounds like.'

'After that I returned to the core house. A while later the ambulance arrived. I went to the cluster to see what was up. Other people were on their way there too. The cops kept us away from Rags's, but when they'd finished with Mary Beth, she came out and told us the story. I was going to wait for you, but then I figured I might get in your way, so I split.'

'Did Lisa show up there?' I asked.

'Yeah, she and Ike both. She really wanted to stay with Mary Beth. She wasn't there when you got through with the sheriff?'

'No, everyone was gone.'

'I'm not surprised. Mary Beth was not in the mood for company. She was moving the crowd out right after she filled us in. She said there wasn't anything we could accomplish by hanging around.'

I gave some thought to what I'd just heard, then I said, 'Sally, I thought you were sure Lisa was gay.'

'She is. You know that.'

'But she must be bisexual, mustn't she? Otherwise, what's she doing sleeping with Ike Bender?'

She shrugged. 'It's very peculiar. I would never have pegged her as bisexual. Especially considering how strong her relationship with Mary Beth is. And Ike Bender? His name came up last night, and she didn't seem hugely fond of him. Frankly, I'm puzzled. Maybe I'm misreading what I saw. Or maybe there's more to this than meets the eye.'

'*That* wouldn't surprise me at all. Let me think about it. In the meantime, keep digging. Let's start by getting up, shall we? There's things to do this day.'

We looked at each other, suddenly acutely aware of where we were. I smiled and gave her a little kiss.

'Thanks,' I said.

I decided to drive back down to Lovingston. Before I left, Sally and I arranged a message-drop system. It was long overdue. We simply agreed that if anything came up and the other person wasn't around, we'd leave a note detailing what was happening. Under the carpet in the appropriate bedroom. It wasn't elaborate; we weren't going up against the KGB, after all. The important thing was that we know what the other was doing.

The road south was not as cheerful as it had been. The sky had clouded over and the air was cool. Indian summer was gone, like a misplaced childhood toy. It might be found again, briefly, but it would eventually be lost for good.

157

The mountains ringing the road were no more solid than the barriers inside my head, the ones that prevented me from an understanding of Babel. I'd hoped that getting away would liberate my thoughts a little. It didn't. They continued to bounce around at ground level, never able to enjoy the view from the top.

I found myself remembering a long-ago September, back in Boston, with my ex-wife, Marilyn. The Red Sox were in the process of blowing yet another August lead, and I was living and dying with the team every day.

Marilyn failed to comprehend this. 'I don't see how you can get so wrapped up in a bunch of grown men playing a kids' game,' she said. 'It's not important.'

'It is to me,' I said.

'And why is that?'

'I spend a lot of my time trying to decipher people's motivations. It's never easy and sometimes it's impossible. Baseball is simple. The pitcher tries to throw the ball past the batter, and the batter tries to hit it. Simple. You don't need a Back Bay psychiatrist to explain why the opponents are doing what they're doing. I need to know there is someplace in the world I can go and predict exactly how people are going to behave. The ballpark is one of the few places I know of.'

'What a waste,' she said. 'You could be putting your energy into so many more worthwhile things about which you could be equally certain.'

'I doubt it.'

'You doubt that there are more worthwhile things?'

'No. I'm sure there are. But I doubt that I'd be equally certain.'

'It's still true,' she said wearily. 'You've only got tunnel vision because you have a job in which you always come into contact with the ignoble side of people.'

'So does everyone. That's why there's baseball.'

'Great. What an unselfish, enlightened philosophy of life.'

'You don't understand, Marilyn,' I said. 'I simply don't believe that you can *choose* one philosophy or another. There is only what you can see for yourself. That's it.'

'You're impossible,' she muttered. 'No wonder you like children's games. You refuse to grow up yourself.'

It would go on like this, sometimes for days. I thought it was the way all married couples acted. Maybe it is. If Patricia didn't wake up soon, I'd never get the chance to find out. I'd probably end up a crusty old bachelor like Faber Jakes, the gentleman seated across

158

the now familiar desk from me.

'You didn't need to check in quite this soon, Swift,' the sheriff said.

'I know,' I said. 'I don't really have anything to tell you, either. I was hoping to have a few words with your guest.'

'What about?' He didn't switch completely over to suspicion; he stopped at something more than mild interest. 'You suspect him of something?'

I shrugged. 'Not directly. But he might be able to shed some light on things. Never know.'

Jakes gave me one of his patented stares. It didn't bother me. For once I wasn't hiding anything. Well, hardly anything. I looked back neutrally.

'Sure,' he said finally. 'You can talk to him. Maybe you'll have more luck than we've had.'

'He playing it quiet?'

'Ain't spoke a word since we've had him. I'm gonna have to get the judge to tell me what to do next.' He picked up his phone and punched a button. 'Bring the Ringwold boy to the talkin' room, would you?'

I never knew his last name, I thought.

The sheriff hung up. 'You know anyone over at Babel who'd take responsibility for this kid?' he asked.

'No,' I said. 'As far as I know, he's not close to anyone. Most of them can't wait till he leaves.'

'Why don't they just kick him out, then?'

I laughed. 'Good question,' I said, and I proceeded to explain, as best I could, about Babel's admission procedure. Jakes grunted a couple of times.

'Sounds like a nest of damn copperheads to me,' he said when I'd finished.

'It sort of is,' I said. 'That's the main reason I want to try to talk to Jeff. I figure that the more I understand what goes on there, the more likely I'll be to discover what happened to Temple Ballard.'

'If there's anything to be discovered.'

'Of course.'

'You know, Swift,' he said after a pause, 'I'm beginning to hope I was wrong about you.'

I asked him what that was supposed to mean, but he refused to elaborate. He led me instead to the talking room. It was in the basement, just like his office. It was small, about eight by eight. The walls were concrete, painted institutional green. There was

159

one window, high up, and it was barred. The furniture, at least for this particular talk, consisted of a table with a lot of doodles scratched into it and two hard wooden chairs. I took one of them.

Jakes left me alone there. He gave me the following advice: 'Do it legal.'

A few minutes later they brought Jeff in. The deputy dropped him off and let us be. I reminded myself that this looked like a private conversation but that that didn't mean it *was* one. Even in rural little Nelson County they might wire their interrogation room. I'd have to be a little careful of what I said.

Jeff was wearing the same clothes he'd had on the previous night. He looked bad. Not the kind of bad that's signalled by bloodshot eyes and sunken cheeks. No, it was the kind that comes from staring too long into the empty night. I'd seen the look before, in Southeast Asia, on the streets of Dorchester and Southie, once or twice in the genteel Commonwealth of Virginia, even. It was the look a man had just before he stepped off the kerb against the light, oblivious of whatever might be coming his way.

'Sit down, Jeff,' I said, and he sat. I asked him how it was going, and he stared at me blankly.

'Look,' I said, 'I feel sort of responsible for what happened. It'd make me feel a lot better if you'd talk to me.'

There was no response.

'Why'd you attack Chaudri?'

No response.

'Was it because of what you overheard us talking about?'

Nothing.

'Your left trouser leg is on fire.'

He didn't even glance at it.

I sighed. 'Okay,' I said. 'You don't want to talk to me. I think it'd be easier for you if you did. You're eventually going to have to talk to *someone*. Me, the cops, a doctor somewhere. People will want to know why you beat up Chaudri. People want to know about Temple Ballard too. Somebody killed him, Jeff. There are those who think it was you.'

And he smiled. He smiled broadly, as if he'd just learned the most pleasant news in all the world.

'Yes,' he said. 'Yes, I did.' His voice was dreamlike. 'It was just. It was neither more, nor less, than what was deserved.'

'What are you saying?' I said. 'Are you telling me that you killed Temple Ballard?'

He smiled and said, 'The Lord is just.'

160

'C'mon, Jeff,' I said. 'I don't believe this. You're gonna have to do better than that.'

He kept on smiling, but that was all he said. I cajoled him as best I could. Nothing. Eventually, the smile faded as well. He looked again like the ill-fated fellow facing the oncoming traffic. There was nothing more to do. I fetched the deputy and he took Jeff back to the lockup. I made my way to Jakes's office.

'Sheriff,' I told him, 'you're not going to believe this, but Jeff just confessed to the murder of Temple Ballard.'

Jakes gave me the piercing stare, then he went to his snuff tin and loaded up.

'Now, that's very interesting, Swift,' he said when he'd had time to consider my openers. 'Why would he want to say a thing like that, do you think?'

'Search me.'

'All right, let me put it like this: How'd you happen to get on the subject?'

'He wouldn't talk to me. So I kept asking him questions. Finally, I told him that there were people who thought he'd killed Ballard. He smiled and said yeah, he'd done it. Then he shut up again, and I didn't get another word out of him.'

'Why'd you say that to him?'

'I don't know,' I said. 'I was hoping he'd open up. Maybe I thought it might jar him. But it made him happy.'

'You got any reason to believe he *did* do it?'

'No. In fact, I doubt it. He's a loony. I don't think a loony murdered Temple Ballard. A loony would've killed Ballard the way Jeff tried to kill Chaudri.'

He nodded. 'Might could be,' he said. 'You think this "confession" is more loony tunes?'

'Yeah.'

'He repeats it to me, I'm gonna have to take it serious.'

'I know that.'

'I think it's best the boy sees a doctor.'

'I agree.'

'And what do you reckon we oughtta do next?'

'Hell, I don't know, Sheriff,' I said. 'I wish I had something concrete to give you, but I don't. All I have is my suspicions, and they aren't worth squat. What I'd like is some more time to poke around. If I can find out who bopped me on the head, I just might find you a murderer at the same time. It's worth a shot.'

'You poke around all you want,' Jakes said. 'I ain't gonna bother

161

you. There ain't much I could do, anyway. If we got a killer out there, I don't suppose he's gonna run off someplace, or it woulda happened already. Tell me, who might you be suspicious of?'

I laughed.

'Like to share the joke?' he asked.

'Sure,' I said. 'I suspect the lot of them. You wouldn't believe the ins and outs of the way these folks behave with each other. Who loves or hates which one, and why. It's a mess that I'm only beginning to sort out. Only thing I'm sure of is that there's a whole slew of people with sufficient reason to want to see Ballard dead. There is one guy who stands out, though.' I told him about Commander Zero and the survival hole back up in the hills. 'He seems the logical candidate,' I added, 'and he's the only one I think would've been able to sneak up on me in the night.'

'You think right much of yourself, do you?'

'It's all relative. I'm a professional and they aren't. Except maybe him.'

'Well, it's possible,' he said. 'We had us a little trouble with some of these survivalists a couple of years back. Thought they could just take stuff that didn't belong to them. Account of their guns. We cleaned them out.'

'I'm glad you've got the experience,' I said. 'If Commander Zero is into what I think he is, I'm sure as hell not going after him alone.'

'See you don't.'

'You need anything else from me right now?'

'I don't suppose so,' he said. 'Looks like I got a fella in my lockup who wants to confess to a crime I don't even know has been committed. Oughtta keep me busy sorting that out.'

'I'll be taking off, then. If I dig up anything, you'll be the first to know.'

'Good. You can get me at 911. I'll be sure all the dispatchers know to put you through to me if you call.'

'Thanks, Sheriff.'

He nodded and I left. I still wasn't able to read Faber Jakes. Maybe he wasn't a neo-Nazi, after all. He didn't seem to have much use for survivalists. I was glad of that. But then again, he probably didn't have much use for private cops, either. Maybe behind the emotionless exterior he was planning how to bust *me* for something.

21

I parked Clementine in Babel's used Volvo lot. The core house was the sort of place that seemed to take on the coloration of the atmosphere. On the warm, sunny days it was bright and friendly. Now, under cloudy skies, it felt sullen and full of ill tidings.

The only person around was Lisa. She was in the kitchen working on something. I decided that it might as well be now as later. I'd been thinking a lot about Lisa.

'Hi,' I said. 'What's up?'

'Nothing much,' she said. 'Just putting together some garbanzo salad for a potluck tonight. What's with you?'

'I saw Jeff.'

'Oh.' She looked at me as if acknowledging my presence for the first time. 'Well, how is he?'

'I think he's insane.'

'That's a pretty heavy judgment.'

'He's a pretty heavy dude. Last night he tried to kill a man.'

'I don't know that you could say that for sure.'

'I was there,' I said. 'Believe it. That's what he was trying to do.'

'What are they going to do to him?'

'That all depends. Right now he's only charged with assault. But that could change.'

'What's that supposed to mean?' she said.

'It means that he told me he murdered Temple Ballard.'

'Oh, come off it. That's absurd.'

'Why?'

'Jeff wouldn't kill —'

'Yes, he would, Lisa. And you know it. He almost did, right in front of me. What makes you so sure he didn't do Ballard as well?'

She looked at me. I felt that she was working a major effort to hold on to that strength of character, that unflappability she'd projected since I first met her. But somewhere in there I could see the tiny traces of doubt, and perhaps the first faint rustle of fear. I thought I detected the sudden scent of musk, though it may have been just the shampoo she'd used on her freshly washed hair.

If she tried to dance away, I wasn't going to let her. Not this time. I wanted to ask her a couple of questions, and I wanted her to answer them. I kept the conversation on track.

'He hated homosexuals, didn't he?' I said.

'Yes, of course,' she said. 'Everyone knows that.'

'Then here's what I think happened. I think Jeff tried to get Temple Ballard to see the evil of his ways. And I think Ballard laughed at him. I think Jeff killed him for it and walked around for eight months stewing in guilt over what he'd done. Then I showed and opened the whole thing up again. I think that drove him so crazy that he went after Ballard's old lover. How's that sound to you?'

Actually, it even sounded pretty good to me. In fact, I believed the second half of it. But the first half, where I had him killing Ballard, I believed that about as much as I believe that the friendly folks at General Dynamics seriously want peaceful coexistence with the Russians.

'It sounds farfetched,' she said.

'Why, Lisa?'

She turned back to her garbanzo beans. 'I don't know,' she said. 'Forget it, maybe you're right. How the hell should I know?'

'Yes, how *should* you know? What were *you* doing that night?'

The question startled her, as I'd intended it to. She stammered a little.

'N-nothing,' she said. 'I— '

'Where were you? I know you weren't here. Freddie was down here, and he said you left early and he never saw you again. Where were you? Were you with Ike Bender?'

She whirled and glared at me. Bingo. It had been a calculated shot, and it had been on the mark.

'What are you talking about?' she said. Her tone was menacing.

'It's a simple question,' I said. 'I asked you if you were with— '

She slapped me. Hard. Her slender body packed a surprising amount of power. Enough to rabbit-punch me unconscious? I couldn't be sure. But I rocked back on my heels.

'Son of a bitch,' she growled. She took a step forward and tried to slap me again. This time I caught her wrist. Once should have given her sufficient satisfaction, as far as I was concerned.

'Lisa,' I said. 'I don't give a good goddamn about your personal life, but I want to know what happened to Temple Ballard. Tell me what you were doing that night.'

She tore loose of my grip.

164

'Go to hell,' she said.

She stalked out of the kitchen, leaving the salad unfinished. She walked across the living area, headed for the front door. I went after her.

'Hold it,' I said, grabbing her arm.

'Take your hands *off* me!'

'Look,' I said as hard as I could, 'I might not care what you do, but that doesn't mean nobody does.'

At that moment she hated me, I have no doubt. I thought she might even go for my throat.

'You rotten bastard,' she said.

Yeah, I was that. If this little interchange didn't produce something of value, I was going to feel very ugly about myself. I watched her eyes as the options ran past them.

'You would, wouldn't you?' she said. 'You'd tell her.'

I shrugged. But actually, I wouldn't. There are things I draw the line at. Like intentional cruelty. Not to mention that I liked Mary Beth and didn't want to hurt her. Unfortunately for Lisa, she was never going to know just what my limits were. She deflated audibly and I let go of her arm.

'What do you want?' she asked listlessly.

'Tell me everything you know about that night,' I said. 'And my mouth stays shut. You can trust me.'

She grimaced. 'Yeah, sure.'

'You can.'

'Well,' she said, 'what choice do I have?' She looked around her. 'But not here. Let's walk.'

'All right.'

We went down to the river. When she was sure we were alone, she said, 'How did you know? Nobody knew.'

'You weren't careful enough.'

'Last night?'

I nodded. 'Just before the fight. I was out on the road. . . . ' I let it go at that. Maybe the sequence wouldn't hold if I got too specific. It was enough that I knew and that she knew I knew. She wouldn't look too closely if I didn't point out where to look.

She accepted it. 'I tried to tell him it was a lousy time,' she said, 'but he wouldn't listen. What does he care? The harder it is on me, the more he enjoys it.'

'This is not a love relationship, I take it.'

She snorted derisively. 'Hardly.'

165

'Well,' I said, 'I don't really care what it is. You don't have to tell me anything about it if you don't want to. All I'm interested in is what happened the night Ballard died. What were you doing? Did you see anything?'

'Right. Simple questions, huh? But it's all connected. All connected. . . . '

I'd suspected as much, but I didn't say so. It was her show from here on. I stared at the river for a while. I waited. Then I looked over at her. She had been watching me. Her eyes were large and glistening. She won't cry, I thought. She's not the sort of person who will cry. I looked down.

A quick breeze sprang up, out of the west. It carried some dead leaves on its leading edge. They defined the flow of the air, following the course of the river, spinning and tumbling, dancing just out of reach of the water. Abruptly, the breeze died. The leaves dropped into the river and were swept away. Like people from your past you once cared about.

'What do you do, Swift?' she said finally.

'I'm not sure what you mean.'

'I'm a dancer. What do *you* do?'

'I don't know,' I said. 'I guess I don't have any real talents. Not like that.'

'It's all I've wanted to do, since I was a little girl. It's the reason I'm in Virginia. Because my teacher is here. I've worked hard. I doubt that you have any idea how hard. Hours and hours a day, every day, until my body screamed at me to stop it. And do you know what? I'm good, but I'm not quite good enough. Do you know what that's like, to not quite have it?'

I thought of a beautiful teenage girl who'd died once upon a time because I hadn't been quite good enough.

'Yeah,' I said. 'I know.'

She looked at me closely. 'I believe you do,' she said. 'Well, it nearly killed me. I even took pills once, but I screwed that up too. Then I came to Babel and I met Mary Beth. She put me back together again. I would . . . I would do anything for her.'

Would you kill for her? I framed the question in my mind. I didn't ask it, but she must have seen it lurking in there.

'No,' she said, 'I didn't kill Temple Ballard. I would have, willingly, but I didn't.'

She picked up a handful of pebbles and began flicking them into

166

the water. The sound they made seemed to be muffled by the cool, heavy air.

'I love Mary Beth,' she said. 'When I met her, her life was in almost as bad a shape as mine. But she was strong enough for both of us. She's remarkable. Unfortunately, her husband realized that too. After he'd been running around screwing anything that would bend over far enough.'

'He had lovers besides Rags and Nancy?'

'Sure he did. They were just the ones that lasted longer than a night or a weekend. He didn't care; age, sex, nothing mattered except himself and his own satisfaction. If he hadn't been so good at other things, he would have alienated everyone here.'

Randy Temple, I thought. The first thing I'd learned when I arrived at Babel.

'He wanted her back,' she went on. 'All of the misery he'd caused her and then he has the gall to try to get her back. Just when we'd found each other and had begun healing some of our wounds. Just when I'd finally realized that it wasn't the end of the world if I couldn't dance as well as I wanted to. Mary Beth made me see that. She showed me that the talent I do have is wonderful in itself, that I'm still capable of giving pleasure to other people and to myself, even if I'm never going to be one of the best.'

She paused, then continued. 'I don't know if I could have done it without her. You never really know, do you? At the time I didn't think I could have. Temple threatened all of that. I hated him. God, I hated him. I sat around and dreamed up ways I could kill him and get away with it. I would have done it too. No point in kidding ourselves. I'm capable and I was very motivated.'

'But you didn't,' I said.

'No, I didn't. Someone saved me the trouble. Or maybe God did. It might well have been an accident, you know. People still get what they deserve by chance. Every now and then.'

'What do you think of Jeff's confession?'

'Sure, he could have done it.'

'Where was he that night?'

'No one knows. Somewhere on the land. He never told anybody, and there wasn't a great deal of interest in pressing him on it.'

'Okay. Back to you,' I said.

'Back to me. The night before Temple died, he and I had a fight. A real screamer. I hadn't planned it. It just happened. Down at the core house. He told me in no uncertain terms to stay away from Mary Beth. I told him the same. We probably would have gone for each other right then, only we weren't alone. Jeff was there. And Ike Bender. They saw the whole thing. That was the beginning of it. If they hadn't . . . Ah, no point in playing "what if", is there?'

I shrugged. 'Not unless you want to get trapped inside your own head,' I said.

'Right. The next day I was still steaming. After dinner I went out and drove around for a long time. Maybe an hour, or longer. When I got back, I parked the car and sat there, trying to figure things out. That didn't work. My only recourse, it seemed, was to confront Temple Ballard again. I knew he was going to be at the Ark, working on the water supply. We all did. So I went up there. I didn't take the road. As I got close to the Ark, I saw someone cross the road above it and duck into the woods. He was headed toward the cluster at the far end of that big field, though I didn't wait to see what he did when he came out of the woods.'

'Did you recognize him?' I asked.

'Well, it was dark. But I'm pretty sure it was Rags. He was the right size and shape. The only thing was that he didn't move like Rags. Rags is a graceful person; he's almost like a dancer himself. This guy was kind of . . . lurching.'

'Did he see you?'

'No, I don't think so.'

'All right, Lisa,' I said, 'what did you do then? Did you go into the shed?'

'Yes. I mean, no. I didn't actually go in there. I opened the door, and . . . there was Temple. He wasn't far from the door. I'd never seen a dead person before, but there was no doubt in my mind that he was. He was just lying there, on his side. One arm was stretched out, like he was reaching for something. His eyes were open and the eyeballs were bulging out. His mouth was open too. His tongue hung out the side of it. He was a funny colour in the face. It was horrible.'

She closed her eyes against the sight. I let her catch her breath.

'I let go of the door,' she said, 'and it slammed shut. I just stood there and stared at it. I'd never felt more unsure of what to do, not in my entire life. That's when Ike arrived.'

'Bender? What in hell was *he* doing there?'

'I don't know. He'd come down to talk to Temple too. I'm not sure what about. He took charge right away, as soon as he realized

Temple was dead. My friend,' she said ironically. 'At least, that's what I thought at the time. He persuaded me that I should get out of there. It seemed right. Temple was gone, and we didn't know how at that point. Enough people hated him that it could have been . . . murder. It would have been bad for me to have been there with the body, considering the fight we'd had the previous night.'

'I can understand that,' I said. 'So you ran away?'

'Walked away. Ike went with me. Reassured me that he believed I didn't have anything to do with Temple's death, and so on. Mr Sympathy. We went to my friend Mary's, who lives out beyond the Evanses. I decided I should make like I'd dropped in on the spur of the moment, to talk about my personal problems, and that I should stay put no matter what happened. It was the longest night of my life.'

'But you stayed put?'

'Yes.'

'Ike stayed with you?'

'No, he didn't go inside. He turned around and went back toward the Ark. No one had seen us, so I thought it better if no one knew we had been together. I figured he was going to go back and "discover" the body. But it didn't work out that way.'

'Did you tell him about having seen Chaudri?' I asked.

'No.'

'Did you hear the alarm go off?'

'No. I was on the back side of the ridge, and besides, Mary likes to play the stereo all the time. I wouldn't have.'

'All right. So you pretended to learn about Ballard in the morning?'

'Uh-huh. I hadn't been seen. I was safe.' She said the last word as if it were a snake that had struck at her unexpectedly.

'Meaning that we now get to the reason you became Bender's lover,' I said.

'I suppose you've guessed,' she said grimly.

'Yeah, I've guessed. You don't have to talk about it if you don't want to, Lisa.'

'I *hate* him!'

As she said it I realized something. There was a different level of emotion behind her words than there had been when she talked about her hatred of Temple Ballard. In the latter case it had been intense and immediate, heartfelt, like he was still alive and screwing up her life. I'd never questioned whether she was being honest or not. But the denunciation of Bender was stronger still, almost exaggerated in its severity. Somehow, it didn't ring true. I was instantly reminded that I might not be getting the whole truth and nothing but. Ike Bender *was* alive and presumably screwing up her life. Then again, her relationship with him might be considerably more complex than I could yet imagine. Don't draw premature conclusions, I warned myself.

'Blackmail?' I asked.

She nodded. 'He came to me a couple of weeks later, after all the furore had died down. He'd always wanted to sleep with me. Occasionally, he said, that was all he was asking. In return, Mary Beth would never find out about my fight with Temple, or that I'd been at the Ark that night.'

'Lisa, did you kill Ballard?'

'No,' she said softly. She didn't look at me.

'Then why go along with him?'

She sighed. 'You haven't been listening, have you?'

'I've been trying,' I said, and I thought I had.

'No, you haven't. If you had, you'd realize that Mary Beth means more to me than I do to myself. Have you ever felt that way about anyone?'

I didn't say anything. I wasn't sure, and I envied people who were.

'Probably not,' she said. 'Well, it's true. If she thought for a minute that I had anything to do with Temple's death, it'd be all over between us. And that would be the end of me. Yeah, I know, if the idea were put in her head by someone else, she'd reject it. Sure. But I wouldn't be able to deny the facts. We *did* have a bad fight. I *was* at the Ark that night. I couldn't lie about that; she'd see through me in an instant. I'd have to admit it. And then the seed of doubt would be there forever. Eventually, it'd grow, until it was out of control and we just blew apart. No. No way. It's not worth it. Bender is a bastard, and I loathe him, but what does he get? Occasional use of my body; not an ounce of *me*. It's a meaningless act. There can't be much pleasure in that for him. Which is what he deserves.'

Again I wondered whether her vehemence didn't sound a little hollow to me. I couldn't be certain.

'Are you sure he won't betray you when you and Mary Beth

finally leave Babel?' I asked.

'I don't think he will. What would he gain? That's the bottom line for Ike Bender. Besides, I'd ki — I'd make him very sorry.'

'Do you think *he* murdered Ballard?'

'Sure, maybe. He was there. I hope he did and they put him away forever.'

'Rags was also there. Might he have done it?'

'He might have. He was torn up over Temple.'

'And Jeff we don't know about,' I said.

'Hey, he was there, too, for all I know. Grand be damned Central Station.'

'How about Commander Zero?'

She looked at me with what seemed to be genuine surprise. 'Zero?' she said. 'Nah, I don't think so. He plays at being bad ass, but I've never seen him . . . *do* anything.'

'Well, Lisa . . . ' I said. 'Christ, I don't know what to make of all this. What do *you* think happened?'

'To Temple?'

'Yeah.'

'I think it was an accident. I think you should leave us.'

22

I didn't know what I had.

The pattern continued: the more I learned, the less I knew. I could now place no less than three people in and around the Ark on the night Temple Ballard died. Any one of them might have offed him. They were all sufficiently motivated. On the other hand, it could have been an accident, as some believed. And on yet a third hand, if I had one, someone else entirely still might have been involved. Because all of the people I could so far put in the vicinity of the Ark had been there, as far as I could determine, *after* Ballard went to work on the water pipe. Whoever set up the carbon monoxide leak and disabled the detector would obviously have to have been there *before*.

The man to see was Ike Bender. It appeared that he had some

171

knowledge of that night which he'd kept from me. Of course, I hadn't been looking for anything specific the first time I talked to him. And, in addition, Lisa's story cast him as a rather unsavoury character. He might be. Then again, her story might be only half true, or it might be a complete fabrication. He deserved a hearing before I began to form opinions.

I found him in the Ark, tending to the maintenance of the fish ponds. Since I hadn't seen him in a while, the resemblance to Eisenhower struck me anew. With his infectious Midwestern prairie smile, he seemed like the sort of fellow you'd trust to invest your life savings. I had a hard time picturing him as a sexual blackmailer. But if I based my investigative work on appearance, I'd have been out of a job long ago.

'Swift,' he said genially, 'nice to see you again.' Then he became serious. 'But it must have been a dreadful night for you.'

'It wasn't great.'

'I'm sorry.'

'Y'all do seem to have your problems here.'

He chuckled. 'Yes, there are problems everywhere, I'm afraid. Do you know why the Blue Ridge is blue?'

'I didn't know it was,' I said.

'It's not, really. But it *looks* blue. The reason is terpenes.'

'What's that, the stuff that takes paint off?'

'Related. They're natural resins produced by trees. When humidity's high, the two factors combine to produce a blue haze. Hence the name. At least, that's the way it used to work. Look at the Blue Ridge in the summer nowadays and what do you see? A dull white haze, if you're lucky. If you're not, it'll be yellow or brown. Pollution. We think of ourselves as living in a clean rural environment, but the mountains are telling us otherwise.'

'Yeah,' I said, 'it's the same with the night sky, isn't it? Some people I know still go out on a clear, moonless night and ooh and aah over how many stars there are. Me, all I can see is how many fewer there are than when I was a kid. Even twenty years ago there was a noticeable difference.'

'You're right. Astronomers are among the most depressed people in the world.'

'What was it like the night Temple Ballard died?'

'Just a moment.' He inspected a set of dials on one of the tanks and jotted some notes in a small spiral notebook. 'It was clear, I believe.' He smiled. 'Though perhaps not by your standards.'

'What were *you* doing that night?'

He looked at me carefully. 'I understand that you've spoken with Freddie Evans,' he said.

'Yes.'

'So you know of our . . . deception.'

'Uh-huh.'

'Does it bother you?'

I shrugged. 'I can't see anything to be gained by publicizing it at this point,' I said.

'Thank you.'

'But I continue to be bothered by the way Temple Ballard died.'

'You still don't think it was an accident?'

'I'm sure it wasn't.'

'I see,' he said. 'And you want me to account for my time that night?'

'Yeah, I'd like that.'

He took a deep breath, let it out again. It wasn't exactly a sigh of resignation. In fact, it appeared to energize him.

'I was at my house in the early evening,' he said. 'It was a bad time for us all. Half the people at Babel resented Temple for one reason or another. I'm sure you've heard a lot of them. Something had to be done. I was Temple's oldest friend, as well as one of the founders, so it was pretty much up to me to do that something. I would have liked to have had Freddie's and Nancy's help, but I couldn't go to them, for obvious reasons.

'So I went to see him alone. I knew he'd be at the Ark, working on that leaky pipe. I thought he'd be alone too. I walked down there. When I came around the far corner of the Ark, I saw someone standing outside, staring at the door to the shed where the generator is. It was Lisa. I wasn't surprised to see her there; she and Temple had been having a particularly bad time of it. But I couldn't imagine what she was doing just standing there. It was chilly out.'

'Did you see anyone else on your way to the Ark?' I asked.

'No, no one.'

'Okay. Please continue.'

'I went up to her, of course,' he said. 'She really jumped out of her boots. She was a little spooky. She'd just seen Temple lying dead on the other side of the door. I looked in, and there he was. I checked his pulse, even though I didn't really need to. Some things you just do automatically, you know? As if they might somehow have brought him back to life.

'But he was gone. I went back outside to Lisa. At that point we had no idea what had happened to him. He could have had a heart attack, or he could have been poisoned, anything. Lisa was frightened. She wanted to get out of there. I told her I didn't think that was a good idea, that we ought to notify somebody first. She said she was afraid to be the one to find his body, because of all of the fighting they'd been doing lately. Especially not knowing how he'd died. She didn't want to take the chance that it'd been by violence. She begged me to let her leave.

'I allowed her to talk me into it. Maybe I was wrong. I don't know. I just didn't believe that she'd done that to Temple. And he was dead. I didn't feel that it made a lot of difference. So I walked her up to her friend Mary's house. I told her I'd go back and find the body, and I promised not to tell anyone that I'd seen her down there. If it turned out that Temple had been poisoned, I didn't have to keep that promise.'

So their stories jibed. Either it was the truth, or else Ike and Lisa were into something together.

'But Freddie actually "discovered" the body,' I said.

'Yes,' he said. 'I'd fully intended to do it. I was halfway up the far side of the ridge when I heard the alarm go off. I hurried to the top and looked down.'

'Did you see anyone?'

'Only someone running up the drive. It turned out to be Freddie.'

'It sounds like you still could have gotten there before him,' I said.

'Yes, I could have. Why didn't I? I'm not sure, exactly. But it was like I was transfixed by the scene. I felt as if I were meant to be a spectator, to see from afar how it played itself out. I knelt down and watched.

'Freddie got to the Ark and did all the right things. Shut off the gasifier, vented the gas that was still being produced, opened the door to the shed. That's when he would have seen Temple. He didn't go inside immediately; I think he was afraid the fan might not have cleared the place yet. But eventually he went in and shut the alarm off. About that time Rags came out of the woods to the west of the Ark.' He pointed the direction. 'He met Freddie.

That's when I decided I'd better get down there, so we could figure out together how to handle the situation. We were probably the best three people to do that.'

'And the decision was to rearrange the scene?' I said.

'Yes. I believe it was the right thing to do under the circumstances. Are you going to tell anyone?'

'Not unless it has something to do with Ballard's death.'

'Well,' he said, 'he was already dead, of course.'

'Of course. It probably won't need to come up. But tell me, whose idea was it to go ahead and alter things?'

'We all agreed on it. It was unanimous.'

'No, I mean, who first suggested it?'

'Let me see. It was Rags, of course. Freddie was in shock. I didn't think it was a good idea initially, but I changed my mind.'

'He persuaded the two of you?' I said.

'He didn't have to. We came to realize the problem soon enough. Are you trying to insinuate something?'

'What's your relationship with Lisa Berlinger?'

'I beg your pardon?'

'C'mon, you heard me.'

'I don't get the point,' he said.

'The point is that I want to know how you feel about her. What's so difficult about that?'

He crossed his arms. 'I don't think this is relevant,' he said.

'I think it *is*,' I said. 'Are you sleeping with her?'

'That's not your—'

'Ah, for Christ's sake, Bender, people here *love* talking about their sex lives. It's part of what Babel's about, isn't it? Open? Free?'

'Your attitude is hardly conducive to openness.'

'Look,' I said, 'I got a woman here who's in love with somebody else, who's openly gay on top of it, and I hear she's sleeping with you. That strikes me as rather odd. I want to know if it's true.'

He stared at me. Then he turned his back and walked over to one of the fish tanks. He rested his hands on its rim and looked down into it. I let him be. He'd been backed into a corner, and it wouldn't work just to shut up. He'd come out of the corner. I didn't know how, but I knew he would.

After a few minutes he faced me again, leaning back against the tank.

'How did you know?' he asked.

175

'Rumour. I wasn't sure. But I am now.'

'We have no future, of course. But I do care for her. It's an . . . unusual relationship.'

'How long has it been going on?'

'That's a difficult question to answer. Physically, since just after Temple died. But in actuality, since the moment we first saw one another.'

'I guess you'd better explain,' I said.

He was looking past me as he searched out the words.

'Have you ever had a real love/hate relationship with someone?' he asked me.

'I don't know,' I said. 'I don't think so.'

'For most people those are just words in a textbook. They don't mean anything real. For Lisa and me they describe us very well. The people we basically are, we just don't like each other a whole lot. We're completely incompatible. On the other hand, from the moment we met there's been an overwhelming physical attraction.'

'She *is* gay, isn't she?'

'That's a convenient category, Swift. It simplifies life, like all categories. Also like all categories, it distorts reality. No one is *completely* one way or the other, are they? We make choices depending on our feelings of the moment. Some people never have a heterosexual relationship, some never have a homosexual one. Some bounce happily from one to the other, and some switch back and forth frequently, but it's agony for them.' He shrugged and gave me a rueful smile. 'Real life is a complicated thing. Lisa is committed to being gay in general, and to Mary Beth Jackman in particular. Yet the electricity between us was undeniable. We ignored it for a long time, but eventually it demanded to be experienced. And so we do. Does that make any sense to you?'

'Well,' I said, 'it makes about as much sense as anything else around here.'

'An unsurprising reply.'

'And an honest one. You can't truly understand what you haven't experienced. You say the physical relationship with Lisa began shortly after Ballard died. Is there some connection?'

'I suppose so,' he said. 'She was already in a highly emotional state, from the conflicts with Temple. When we found his body together, it really set things in motion. We looked into each other's eyes and we knew implicitly what was going to happen.'

'Do you think she feels guilty about what you're doing?'

'Quite possibly.'

'Has she tried to end it?'

'Several times. It will burn itself out eventually. Or she will leave Babel.'

'Ike,' I said, 'do you think Lisa could have killed Temple Ballard?'

'Do you mean, is she capable? Yes, she's capable. And motivated. But she didn't do it.'

'How can you be sure?'

'Come on, Swift. Your theory depends on someone disabling the detector and then reconnecting it. She couldn't have done that. I was with her. She couldn't have sneaked back to the Ark and set off the alarm before I got there. There wasn't time.'

'You could have done it, if the two of you were working together.'

He laughed. Really laughed. That one had struck home.

'If you only knew how comical it is to imagine Lisa and I cooperating on anything,' he said. 'But sure. We could have. Almost anyone at Babel could have. Only not Lisa alone.'

'You truly believe it was an accident?'

'Yes, I do.'

I looked around the Ark. It enclosed the life unfolding within, protected it, nurtured it, created an environment not subject to the whims of the world outside. In a way Babel did the same for its people. If the generator broke down, the Ark could be breached. Where was the functional equivalent of the generator in Babel as a whole, I wondered? If I couldn't find it and somehow shut it down, I'd probably never get far enough inside to discover the truth.

'Why is it,' I said, 'that I never seem to get a straight answer around here?'

'I've just given you a lot of straight answers.'

'The second time around.'

'We're normal people,' he said. 'We're afraid to reveal things about ourselves to someone who could bring the law down in here. How can you blame us? We're already suspected by our neighbours of God knows what. We don't want trouble. But I'll tell you something: I think that ultimately we'll be glad that you came here. Too many people have residual doubts about Temple's death. I'll be happy when those doubts are finally put to rest. And I think that you can do that. People are watching you. I think they're prepared to believe that if you can't find any evidence of a crime, then there wasn't one.'

'You have any suggestions of what I should do next?'

'Talk about that night with everyone who was there. Have you

177

spoken to Lisa?'

'Yes.'

'And the Evanses, of course. What about Rags?'

'Not directly yet.'

'Talk to him,' he said. 'Once you've heard the story from everyone who was involved, perhaps a conclusion will naturally come to you.'

'Yeah. And maybe the Rockefellers will start paying taxes too.'

I went back to the core house. Fortunately, Sally was there, having lunch, and we were able to get off by ourselves. I'd certainly done a lot of walking since I came to Babel. If it was as good for you as they said it was, I was going to come out of this case in excellent physical shape.

Sally had had an uneventful morning. I filled her in on Jeff's confession and the talks I'd had with Lisa and Ike.

'Good work,' she said when I'd finished, 'but where the hell are we now?'

'Well, we've got someone who'll admit to murder,' I said. 'That ought to be enough for Fail-Safe if you want to go home.'

'But you don't think he did it, do you?'

'I'm not sure. He might have. I'd much rather have something more substantial than the word of a loony, though. He could change his tune any old time.'

'Yeah, we're a little short on supporting evidence.'

'And I don't know what to make of this business between Ike and Lisa. We've got two versions of the thing, either of which sounds to me like it could be true. What's your reaction?'

'I agree with you,' she said. 'It could go either way. Being gay is a constant struggle for some people. She might feel she had to test her commitment. On the other hand, nothing suggests to me that Ike Bender would be above what she accuses him of.'

'I know. Mary Beth told me not to trust him too.'

'I think the most important thing may have been Lisa seeing Rags. That makes two witnesses. Plus we now know he was actually at the Ark.'

'*If* everyone is telling the truth.'

'Right,' she said. 'We can't even be sure of that, can we? For all we know, Rags never went near the Ark, Lisa killed Ballard, and Ike found out, but because he loves her, he covered up for her. How's that for an alternate scenario?'

'Well, I must admit I hadn't considered that one. But it's pos-

178

sible, all right. Along with about fifty-seven other kettles of soup.'

'I guess that means we keep digging.'

'Yeah. I just hope we don't fall into our own hole.'

'What next?' she asked.

'Well, you seem to be doing just fine on your own. I think what I'll do is go to town and talk to Chaudri. He's still in the hospital, isn't he?'

'As far as I know.'

'It'll give me a chance to see Patricia too. In fact, I think I'll spend the night at home. Maybe tomorrow too. Why don't we do this? I'll stay out of sight for the next day and a half. I'll leave a note on the bulletin board saying that my investigation is complete and I've left the community. You can spread the word that I got discouraged and decided to file a report saying Jeff did it. People will believe that. Say that I've moved on to a new case. Be a little sad because it means that our relationship is over too. After I'm gone, things should loosen up. You might hear something important. Whoever's been beating up on me may even accidentally reveal him- or herself. And I might get something out of Rags. Then, day after tomorrow, slip off to the store in the morning and give me a call if you've got a line on anything that looks hot. Otherwise, I'll come back that afternoon. Leave me a note under the carpet in your room if you're not going to be here. What do you think?'

'I like it,' she said. 'If I can't turn up anything in the next two days, I shouldn't be doing this sort of work.'

'Don't get ahead of yourself. And be careful, please. If there is a killer, and if he or she suspects what's really going on, it could get dangerous.'

She saluted me. 'Yes, *mein generale.*'

'And try not to be such a wiseass. I know damn well I don't have to play the protective male with you.'

She laughed as she took my arm and started me back toward the core house.

'Lucky thing you've got *me* to protect *you*,' she said. 'The way I see it.'

I'd just finished posting my message to the Babelonians on the bulletin board. Lisa came scurrying by me. She paused with the door half open.

'Oh, yeah,' she said. 'Some guy called for you a few minutes ago. A Dr Pastreich. Wants you to call him back.'

My heart sank. Lisa slid out the door.

'Wait!' I yelled after her. 'What'd he *say*?'

'That's it!' she called over her shoulder. 'Just call him back. I gotta run.'

I made the long walk to the living room, my feet like blocks of stone. From somewhere deep within me came the message: *It's over. It's all over now.* I went to the phone.

Sally was nearby. 'What is it?' she asked.

'Patricia's doctor,' I said. 'He wants me to call.'

'Oh. It could be good news.' She smiled hopefully.

'Yeah, sure.'

I waited, not patiently, while somebody at the hospital put me through to somebody else, who put me through to somebody else, who finally put me through to the man.

'Dr Pastreich,' I said, 'Loren Swift.'

'Thanks for calling, Mr Swift. I have some news for you. Patricia Ryan woke up this morning.'

'Huh?'

'She came out of the coma. She's awake now.'

'Oh, Jesus Christ. I— Uh— Hold on, I'll be right there!'

'That will be fine,' he said. 'Please come to my office first, if you will.'

'Sure. Half an hour. Thanks.'

I cradled the phone and turned to Sally.

'She woke up,' I said, still not quite believing it myself.

Sally ran over and threw her arms around me. I hugged her and spun her in crazy circles to the music inside my head. I leaned back and screamed at the top of my lungs.

'Okay,' she said after I put her down, 'now get the hell out of here, will you?'

'You know it. Look, it might be an extra day or so before I get back to you, all right? I don't have any idea what I'm going to have to do.'

'Don't worry.'

I headed for the front door.

'Hey, Swifty,' Sally said. I stopped and looked back. 'I'm real happy for ya.' She was showing all of her teeth, and one small tear was slipping down her cheek.

I blew her a kiss and took off for town.

23

Pastreich sat behind his somewhat forbidding doctor's desk and looked at me over the bristly dark moustache. The thing made him appear to be glowering all the time. A false impression – I knew him to be a helpful, considerate fellow – but perhaps one that he deliberately cultivated in order to preserve that distance doctors need to maintain between themselves and their work. They're a lot like cops, and P.I.'s, in that way. Lose the distancing and you'll be sucked under faster than you can imagine.

I'd been apprehensive heading into Pastreich's office. I'm one of those people who generally expects that the worst will happen if it possibly can. When good fortune strikes, I'm immediately wary, wondering what the catch is.

In addition, I was nervous about my relationship with Patricia. She'd been out for a long time. What would she remember? Would she blame me? Was the way in which we saw each other going to be forever changed? I wanted the answers, and yet, now that they were available, I didn't want them, either.

It is at times like this that the little details run through your head: the way she groans and rolls her eyes at one of my rotten jokes; the glow of her auburn hair when the afternoon sun catches it at just the right angle; the hoarse, strangled cry she sometimes gives out while making love. The images grab at you and your chest tightens, and you wonder if it can really be true that they'll soon be yours again.

'You must be a happy man,' Dr Pastreich said.

'Actually, I'm scared shitless,' I said.

He laughed. 'Well, if you're worried about Patricia,' he said, 'you can relax. She's fine.'

'When did it happen?'

'Early this morning. Fortunately, there was a nurse with her at the time. Patricia was a little disoriented, as you might expect.'

'And she's okay?' I said.

'As far as we can tell. We checked her out very thoroughly this morning. All of her functions are normal. We'll need to monitor her closely for a few days, of course. Get her started eating again. But in general, I'd say the prognosis is excellent.'

'Has she . . . asked for me?'

'Yes, she seems quite anxious to see you.'

It was the question I had most dreaded asking, but it was the answer I wanted to hear. I loosened up a little.

'What should I expect?'

'You mean, for now? Or for the future?'

'Both,' I said.

'All right. For now, she's going to be physically weak. It'll take time for the muscles to regain their tone. Psychologically, expect her to continue to be disoriented. She doesn't remember what happened to her, but she's been told, as much as we know. Seeing you may bring more of it back, or it may not. There's no way to tell. I don't know the complexities of your relationship with her, of course, but I would think that it'll be much the same. Just don't push her to recall anything that she has trouble with.'

'Don't worry about that. I'd just as soon she never did.'

'Good. As to the future, that's really up to the two of you. We'll make certain she's ready before we let her go. But even after we release her, she'll need to come back every day for a while, to work with the physical therapist. In addition, we'll give her a home exercise routine to follow. See that she sticks to it, but otherwise pamper her. Give her a chance to readjust to the world slowly. There's no reason why things shouldn't be close to normal in a few weeks.' He grinned. 'And whatever you do, just make sure she doesn't bang her head on anything for a while.'

'You mean she could relapse,' I said.

'Highly unlikely. But we like to play it safe. Oh, yeah, also, if she starts having headaches, dizziness, blurred vision, anything like that, see that she gets herself over here right away.'

'I will.'

'Excellent. Well, I don't suppose there's a reason to wait any longer, is there?'

'Just one thing,' I said. 'Could I ask you a favour?'

'Sure. What is it?'

'There was a fellow brought here last night for observation, by the name of Raghu Chaudri. He'd been in a fight. I wonder if you could find out for me where he is. I'd like to talk to him before I leave here.'

'Sure,' he said, making a note. 'No problem. Friend of yours?'

'Sort of. I'm the one who broke up the fight.'

'I'll arrange it. As long as it's okay to visit him.'

'It should be. The EMT from the rescue squad didn't think he was hurt that bad.'

'Okay,' he said. 'Ready to see Patricia?'

'I guess.'

'We've moved her to a different room. I'll take you there.'

He led me down some corridors, up an elevator, down another corridor, to a room like any other hospital room. Except that Patricia was in it.

'Patrick's in there too,' Pastreich said, referring to Patricia's kid brother. 'I've got a couple of things to take care of. I'll check back with you in a while.'

He left. He had a long, gangly stride. I don't know why I was noticing things like that.

I went through the door and almost yelped in fright. The woman in the bed had white hair. Her skin was wrinkled and sallow. Her breath ratcheted. It didn't look like she was going to last out the day. Then I realized that I must have the wrong room. I turned to go. Then I realized that, of course, there were two beds in the room. A white-fabric folding screen separated them. I walked over and peered around it.

It was the bed by the window. There was a nice view out over the campus of the University of Virginia. Students were walking from place to place, doing student things. From here the world seemed an orderly place.

Patrick was near the bed, sitting in his wheelchair. He'd needed the thing since a late-night encounter with a drunk driver, from which the drunk had walked. For many people, such an accident would have been devastating. Not Patrick. He was an energetic, physically active young man who ran his own business and would break your arm if he caught you using words like 'handicapped' or 'confined'. Not to mention that once upon a time he'd saved my life.

'Swift,' he said.

Patricia lay with her eyes closed. For one terrifying instant I thought that she'd relapsed. Then she opened her eyes, the green eyes I hadn't seen in so long.

'Loren?' she said.

I went over to the bed. She reached out, and we clung to each other for the longest time that there is, the time that celebrates a moment that might never have been.

'I see you two have already met,' Patrick said. 'Well, get

acquainted, anyway, why don't you? I'll be back. And, uh, keep it clean, y'hear?'

I listened to him wheel out the door. We were alone except for the woman dying on the other side of the screen.

'You don't know how good it is to see you,' she said.

'Me too.'

'I feel like I've been reborn. Does that sound corny? Everything looks like something I've never seen before.'

'You make it sound like fun.' She smiled. 'How do you feel?'

'I don't know,' she said. 'I feel fine. Like I went to bed last night and had the most refreshing sleep of my life and now I can't wait to get out and do things.'

'You're supposed to take it a little easy for a couple of days.'

'Oh, I know.' She paused. 'Loren, what happened to me?' She looked at the cast on my arm. 'And what happened to you too?'

I pulled over one of those hard steel hospital chairs and sat next to her. We held hands. It was as if, now that we'd made contact, we didn't want to risk losing it.

I explained to her what had happened, in general terms. She remembered a lot of it. The part she'd lost was where the maniac had come to my apartment to kill me and had ended up nearly killing both of us. As I told the story it seemed as if I were talking of some remote period in my life, rather than the recent past. When I got to where I had to shoot the guy, I found that I still had difficulty with it. I could still see his eyes, still smell his breath as he closed in for the kill. I'd had no choice, and yet . . . I faltered.

'It's all right,' she said. 'I understand. A lot of this is going to take some getting used to. The last thing I can recall is how happy we were. You were safe, in spite of your leg. We had a lot to look forward to. That's the way it's going to be again.'

'I think so too.'

'Well. Now that that's out of the way, what have you been doing? Have you been working?'

'It was hard,' I said. 'You being here and everything. I didn't feel exactly like taking anything on. But then— ' I grinned— 'they made me an offer I couldn't refuse.'

She grinned too. She plumped the pillows behind her and settled in. 'Tell me,' she said.

I filled her in on the Babel job. What I'd been hired for, why I'd taken it, what I'd accomplished so far. It took a while in the telling, but she listened intently. She was hungry to learn about the lost

184

days. She knew where she'd been; but what had the rest of the world been up to?

When I'd brought her to the events of the morning, she said, 'Whew. That's one of the strangest stories I ever heard. Did you just make that up?'

'Nah.' She looked at me suspiciously. 'Honest. You know I'm not imaginative enough for that.'

'Well, what do you think about it all?'

'I think someone out there committed murder. But considering the circumstances, it may have been as close to a perfect crime as you can get. I don't see how I'll ever be able to untangle it enough to separate out the killer.'

'No, you'll do it,' she said.

'Thanks for the vote of confidence, but I'm afraid it's misplaced.'

'Sounds to me like the Indian did it.'

'Yeah, he's a prime suspect, all right. In fact, I'm gonna talk to him this afternoon. He's here in the hospital.'

'And this Sally sounds like a good one. Is she cute?'

'Yup.'

There was a moment of unasked questions left hanging. They were questions to be asked and answered, but at a different time and in a different way.

'You'd like her,' I said. 'She was with me when the doctor called. She was so happy that she cried.'

Patricia smiled. The awkward moment passed as if it had never been.

'Loren,' she said, 'when can I get out of here?'

'Soon. Patrick and I will get the house ready for you. After that, lady, your wish is my command.'

'Then get me out of here today!'

I laughed and we chattered on. Patrick returned. The three of us concocted grand schemes for the great vacations we were going to take with the money I got from Fail-Safe. I think we were somewhere west of the Marquesas when Pastreich came into the room.

'How's everyone doing?' he asked.

We all grinned like idiots. We were doing fine.

'Great,' he said. 'Ah, Mr Swift, could I have a word with you? Privately?'

The Ryans looked immediately concerned.

'Don't worry,' he reassured them. 'It's nothing to do with you.

Just something Mr Swift had me check into.'

'I'll be right back,' I said

Out in the corridor, Pastreich said, 'It's about that patient you wanted to see. Mr Chaudri.'

'Uh-huh.'

'Well, I'm afraid you can't.'

'Why not?' I said, though I had a pretty good idea.

'He's in intensive care. There have been complications.

'Damn! What happened?'

'A blood clot, from the blows to his head. He had a cerebral haemorrhage. It's a moment-to-moment thing now. I'm sorry.'

I thought of Rags the way I'd first seen him, as a gingerbread man. Whether he'd killed Ballard or not, I didn't want the little guy to die.

'Chances?' I asked.

He shook his head. 'Not good.'

'Thanks, Doctor.'

'Sure. Anything I can do?'

'No, I don't think so.'

'Okay. Don't wear Patricia out the first day, please. I'll see you tomorrow.'

He loped off down the corridor, leaving me with my thoughts. First among them was the strong desire never to have anything to do with Babel again. Patricia was okay, and it didn't look like we were going to need the money. Why not just drop the whole thing? Yeah, why not? It'd be easy. Call up Devin Pethco, tell him about Jeff's confession, wash my hands of the whole affair. Nothing to it.

Why wasn't I going to do it, then? I knew that I wasn't. Some quaint notion of justice? No. I no longer believed in that. Life serves up justice in only a few widely scattered and completely random instances. I'd end up finishing the job because it wasn't finished. I'd do it for me, and for those close to me. Because I'd learned something once upon a time. And that is: Quitting when things aren't going well can very quickly develop into a habit. Once it does, you aren't worth much any more. To yourself or to anyone else.

24

The memorial service was held on Saturday afternoon, in the large open field near the housing cluster where he'd lived. The weather had turned sunny and warm again. People were in their shirtsleeves. The setting was spectacular. The field sloped down to the gravel drive, which ran on past the barn and the core house to the river. On the other side of the river there were woods and small farms stretching away to the Blue Ridge. The fall foliage stood out, and after a day of heavy rain, the haze had slightly blue cast to it. The angle created by the slope of the field distorted distances, so that the distant peaks seemed to loom over us, almost close enough to touch. The lightness of the day belied the solemnity of people's feelings. It urged us not to take life, or death, too seriously.

Chaudri had died on Thursday without ever having regained consciousness. His body wasn't here. His parents had come down from Washington to claim it and to take it wherever they thought it should finally rest. The memorial service at Babel wasn't a church-type one. The members of the community had come together, gathering in the field to pay their last respects however they wished. It was a ceremony without Ceremony, simple and dignified. It was somehow more touching than any funeral I'd ever been to.

I had set foot on this land for the first time only the previous Saturday. That seemed odd to me, almost unbelievable. It had been an event-filled week. My past three days had been spent primarily, of course, with Patricia. There was so much that she wanted to know , from the news of the world down to our own small fits and starts. You try to summarize a long month for somebody who's been away, and you quickly realize how much information we're bombarded with on every day of our existence.

And then there was our relationship to attend to. That part turned out to be an unexpected delight. We were like strangers at first. Then, as we began to poke into old, familiar corners, it was as if we were being allowed to fall in love all over again. We both realized that we had been offered a gift of rare value, and we seized it, tentatively at the beginning, and then with an unembarrassed greediness. Our bodies purred when we touched. And, on occasion, we violated a hospital regulation or three.

I'd thought about Babel only once. After Rags had died, Sheriff Jakes had wanted me to come to Lovingston so that they could take a formal statement from me. The charge against Jeff was now murder, of course. I drove down there and put on record everything I thought was relevant to Chaudri's death and Jeff's part in it. I also had a lengthy off-the-record chat with Jakes about the continuing mystery of Temple Ballard. I told him I wasn't ready to close that file yet. He allowed as to how I might have a point and would keep an open mind on the subject. He hadn't been able to get anything further out of Jeff, so the 'confession' was still only hearsay to him. There was a psychiatrist working with the kid now.

Before meeting with Jakes, I'd given some long and hard consideration to how much to tell him of what I'd learned. The real nut was the rearrangement of the death scene. Legally, I was obliged to inform him. But should I? In the long run it might prove important, but at the moment it didn't seem particularly relevant. By bringing it up, all I would do was cause trouble for the people involved. I especially didn't want that to happen to the Evanses. They'd suffered enough.

Once I made the decision not to reveal how Ballard had actually died, the rest was easy. The law can only hang you once. So I decided not to tell any of what I'd heard from the combo of Berlinger and Bender. If there was something there, I wanted to make the connections myself. I did, however, repeat Spock's story. That one couldn't harm any of the living. I said that I was suspicious of Chaudri, and Jakes said it was gonna be hard to prove anything on a dead man. I agreed, but told him I was pursuing it all the same. He shrugged. I also let him know that I still had a gut feeling that Commander Zero had been involved in some way. He shrugged again. My gut feelings were not important news.

In the end, Jakes and I agreed to continue to cooperate as much as possible. He would have to talk to people in the community while he was building his murder case. If he came across anything that appeared to be connected to Ballard, he'd let me know. I was given the green light to pursue my own investigation some more. Naturally, I was to keep him informed. We shook hands and parted on reasonably good terms.

On the return trip to Charlottesville, I'd thought of detouring and dropping in on Babel. But I didn't do it. I was anxious to get back to Patricia. Besides, I hadn't heard from Sally. She might be on to something, and I didn't want to queer it by showing up at an inopportune time.

All of this went through my mind as I stood in the field listening to people eulogize Chaudri. The whole community had turned out, it seemed. There must have been thirty or forty there, men, women and children. Everyone except . . . except Sally. That bothered me. There was no reason why she shouldn't have been there. I reminded myself to check under the carpet in her room for a note to me.

There was someone else missing too. It was more a feeling than a recognition of fact. I couldn't decide who it might possibly be. I looked at all the familiar faces. Some of them I'd gotten to know well, some I'd only seen here and there. A few of the faces in the group belonged to strangers, as well. Two of those were fitted to a middle-aged couple who looked exactly like what they probably were, native central Virginia farmers. Neighbours who'd somehow or other become acquainted with Chaudri and had cared about him.

But who was missing?

It was Anne. I scanned the group again. No, she wasn't there. No Sally, no Anne. It meant something or it meant nothing.

Ike Bender had begun to speak. Though he spoke softly, you could feel the power in his voice. No one had trouble hearing him.

'Raghu Chaudri descended from the most ancient spiritual tradition on the planet,' he said. 'And he was a man entirely worthy of that long and glorious history. If there is such a thing as a sacred heart to every group of people, then he was ours. He provided us inspiration when we needed it; he led by his example. We will never replace him. We will never forget him.' He knelt and picked up a handful of dirt and grass, which he threw high into the air. 'Rags,' he said to the sky, 'I am honoured to have called you my friend. . . .' His cheeks were wet as the debris settled back to the ground.

Mary Beth was more succinct. 'Rags,' she said, 'we didn't always see eye to eye, but I never doubted the purity of your love. I will miss you.'

And so it went. Each took his or her turn, or passed it up.

I said, 'I didn't know Rags very well, but I respected him. I share your sorrow.'

When everyone had had their say, we all joined hands. Slowly,

189

the group opened outward, like a flower, until we had formed a perfect circle of linked human hands. We stood that way in silence, for a long minute, the idea being to help speed Chaudri's spirit on to its next stopping place. It was strange, I thought. Here was Babel, its life solidly rooted in a technology that is widely believed to be godless and soulless. Yet in the face of death the community would gather together like this, around a religious ceremony that has probably changed little since the dawn of man.

As if on cue, two crows flew over, cawing loudly, and the circle broke. The people began to scatter. Ike Bender came over to me.

'A good omen,' he said.

'The crows?'

'Rags, speaking to us. If you care to look at it that way.'

'Do you believe that?'

'Walk with me, Swift,' he said.

We set off down the road that skirted the field, passed below the Ark, and continued along the fields near the river. The road that eventually wound its way to Ike's house.

'Thank you for coming,' he said to me.

'I needed to,' I said. 'I know that I could have been merely tolerated here, yet I have been made to feel welcome. I wanted people to know that.'

He smiled. 'We'll have you yet.'

'You might at that.'

'We shall see. After today, who knows?'

'Why? I thought the funeral service was very touching.'

He shook his head. 'I did not mean after the service. I meant after you hear what I have to tell you.'

I looked at him questioningly.

'You must understand, Swift, how traumatic the past week has been for the community. First you came and opened up the old wound of Temple's death. Then Jeff went crazy and attacked Rags. And then Rags died. It is too much. The dark side looms over us. We need some quiet time now. I am hoping that if I tell you the truth about Temple, you will go away. Not as a person — we would always welcome you in that way. But as an investigator. We need some time to begin to put Babel back on the path of light.'

'You haven't told me the truth?' I said.

'Not entirely. And I never would have. You will understand. Now things are . . . changed.' He stopped and looked me in the eye. 'I'd like to have your word on something. I'd like you to

190

promise me that if I clear up your doubts about what happened to Temple, then you'll leave us be.'

'Of course I will. But that's an awfully big *if*. I'm not sure you can do it. There are so many questions.'

'Yes. And as with many things, the answers are simple. Can you also smooth it all over with the sheriff? People fear him.'

'Well, I can't make you any promises there,' I said, 'except that I'll do my best. If you can explain to me exactly how Temple Ballard died, then my job is finished. I report to my employer and it's over. How much I have to tell the sheriff depends on what happened. If there's no crime, I don't have to tell him anything. But if you've been keeping the truth from me, then I assume there *was* a crime. I'll listen to you, Ike, but I think you understand my position. If Ballard was murdered, I can't cover it up, not unless I want to end up doing time. Which I don't.'

He started walking again, and I followed. There were people in the road ahead of us, others moving toward the core house, still others climbing the ridge behind the Ark. They spoke quietly to one another, or they swam alone with their thoughts. The sun was sinking behind the Blue Ridge. Soon these folks would uncork bottles of wine, slice up loaves of home-baked bread. They would eat, make love, perhaps laugh a little. But tonight, at least tonight, they would know that they shared their world with the dead.

'It is difficult,' Ike said. 'I wouldn't tell you except . . . well, there is no way to put a nice shine on it, is there? You are correct. Temple was murdered.'

'You can prove that?'

'No. There is little that can be truly proven, as you know. But I can tell you what I saw. I think that you will be convinced.'

'All right. Who killed him?'

He took a deep breath. 'Rags did,' he said.

'That's a pretty easy way to go, Ike, since he can't defend himself.'

'Hear me out,' he said. His voice cracked. 'This isn't easy for *me*.'

'I'm sorry. Of course. Go ahead.'

'There isn't much to add. Nearly all of what I told you was the truth. I went to the Ark. Lisa was there. Temple was dead. I walked her up to Mary's house. The only part that wasn't true was what happened next. When I got to the top of the ridge, I saw Rags come out of the woods. I sort of crouched down, instinctively. He

191

didn't see me. He went down around the Ark and into the shed.'

'How do you know that?' I asked. 'You can't see the shed door from there.'

'You're right. But I know he went in there, because a few moments later the alarm went off. And a moment after that he was back in sight. He ran into the woods. I just squatted there. I was stunned. I think I must have known what it all meant, but I suppose I just couldn't face it. Down the drive, Freddie had started toward the Ark. So I stayed where I was. I literally couldn't move. The rest is as I told you. Freddie did what he did. Rags came *back* out of the woods, and I finally decided that I had to go down there. Now you see why I couldn't say anything to you before. And why I . . . can now.'

'No,' I said, 'I don't see. Why did you protect a murderer?'

'Swift, did you get to know Rags?'

'A little.'

'Did he seem like a killer to you?'

'No. But isn't that beside the point?'

'It *is* the point,' he said. 'Rags was a gentle person. He wasn't a murderer, not in any meaningful sense of the word.'

'Except that he killed someone.'

'Temple drove him mad, as he did all of us at one time or another. The difference was that Rags loved him, really loved him. It was more than he could bear. For one terrible moment he became something he was not. Is that so hard to understand? The rest of the time he was, well . . . what I said back at the ceremony I meant. Rags *was* the spiritual heart of this community; that's why we need some peace and quiet to pull together again. He was a very good man. What conceivable purpose could have been served by handing him over to the police? Tell me that.'

I couldn't.

'You see?' he said. 'Temple was dead, and that was bad enough. Anything further that we did would only have compounded the crime. If you're looking for justice, I'm sure that Rags . . . paid for what he did. I'm sure he paid for the rest of his . . . life.'

He began to cry. I put my arm around his shoulders. Though he was considerably wider than me, he wasn't nearly as tall. My arm rested comfortably there. We walked. When his grief subsided, I took my arm away. He wiped his face with his sleeve.

'I'm sorry,' he said. 'It just all seems so damned unfair. Temple.

192

Rags. All of it. Sometimes it's difficult to believe that nothing really matters.'

'Ike,' I said, 'does anyone else know?'

'No. No one.'

'I appreciate your telling me.'

He nodded.

'You were right. That answers all the questions,' I said. 'I can close the case. But I'll have to report to the people who hired me. Now, we can probably arrange something quietly with Mary Beth. She'll have to be told, of course. I promised her. And the sheriff is going to need to know too. I have no idea how he'll react. If you give him a sworn deposition, telling everything, we may be able to get by with that. I'll see what I can do.'

'Thanks.'

I didn't have to believe Ike Bender's story, of course, but I decided that I would. It had the ring of truth to it. It was corroborated by both Spock and Lisa, two additional eyewitnesses. And Spock had been threatened. All three people denied having mentioned Rags to anyone else. The possibility that they had independently fabricated Rags's actions was so remote as to not even merit consideration. The far, far greater likelihood was that Rags had in fact done it.

If I accepted that, the scenario was easy to visualize. Sometime after the gasifier had last been loaded, Rags had gone to the shed, displaced the top of the filter unit, and disabled the alarm. It wouldn't have taken long. Then he may or may not have waited in the woods while Ballard got himself asphyxiated. When he'd been sure enough time had elapsed, Rags had gone back, intending to reactivate the alarm. But the sight of his dead lover had unnerved him and he'd fled from what he'd done. That was when Lisa saw him. Instinctively, he'd headed for home. And he'd run into Spock. He'd gone to his house, paced around wondering what to do, then decided to return to the Ark. That's when Spock saw him the second time. He made it back to the shed — while Ike and Lisa were on the other side of the ridge — and somehow steeled his nerve enough to go inside and set the alarm off. Then he'd run into the woods, unaware that Ike was now watching him from the ridge top.

It fit.

I walked back to the core house. My plan was to find Sally and

193

tell her I thought it was time to break camp.

She wasn't at the core house. There were a number of people milling about aimlessly, the way people will when a funeral is over and no one quite knows what's supposed to happen next. I talked to the ones I knew. None of them had seen Sally in a couple of days.

I went to her room. It was empty. Not just of Sally but of all her belongings as well. I looked under the carpet. No note. I began to get a very bad feeling in the pit of my stomach. I sought out Lisa.

'No,' Lisa said, 'she left.'

'What do you mean, left?'

'I don't know, exactly. One day she was just gone. Didn't even say goodbye to anyone. That happens around here. People come, they decide we're not for them, and they're gone. Why?' She grinned. 'You make a mistake with that one?'

'This isn't a joke, Lisa.' I clamped down on my temper. 'When did you last see her?'

'I don't remember, Swift. Wednesday or Thursday. I wasn't baby-sitting the girl.'

I felt like slapping her, but I didn't. It wasn't her fault Sally was gone. I was looking for an outlet for my anxiety, and she was handy. Besides, there might be a simple explanation.

'Has anyone else seen her?' I asked as calmly as I could.

'I don't think so. She took her clothes, you know. She probably went home.'

'Okay. Thanks, Lisa.'

If there was a simple explanation, the man who might have it was Devin Pethco. I pretended there was no reason to panic yet. I drove to the nearby store, like I was carefully preserving our cover, and called Pethco at home. He hadn't heard from her, either. But now, of course, he wanted to know what was up. I thought fast, then told him I was still in Charlottesville, tending to Patricia. I said I didn't want to risk calling Sally at Babel, but that I wanted to know if anything was happening. I had phoned him on the off chance he might have heard from her. The lie seemed to satisfy him. He reiterated that he hadn't heard a thing, and we hung up.

This was bad. I got into Clementine and started for Babel. And then it hit me, like one final blow to the side of the neck. I realized who else hadn't been at the memorial service. Someone I hadn't even looked for, because I barely thought of him as a member of the community. Commander Zero. Just like that, all of the pieces fell

194

into place. There was a sudden awareness of just how blind I'd been.

This wasn't just bad. It was the worst.

Kicking myself, I wheeled a U-turn and hurried back to the store. The dispatcher at the sheriff's office put me through to Faber Jakes at home. I convinced him that it was a legitimate emergency. Since he lived only fifteen minutes from Babel, he told me to come over there.

25

We sat in Jakes's kitchen, drinking coffee. The kitchen was as austere as he was. I was anxious as hell, in no mood to be doing this, but I needed his help and knew he was slow to take action. So I sat there and drank coffee with him.

'You think this here survivalist has snatched your partner?' he said.

'It's the only thing that makes any sense,' I said. 'He wanted her from the moment he laid eyes on her; even I could see that. She thought she could handle him. She's tough and she's young and she thinks she can handle anything. But Commander Zero is way out of her league. He had real training somewhere. He's smart, he knows weapons, he's learned how to move so you don't see him or hear him. That's how he was able to knock me out so easily.'

'You figured him for that all along, as I recall.'

'Yeah, but for the wrong reason. I kept trying to connect him to Ballard's death, which now I don't think he had anything to do with. It was a very easy mistake to make. Somebody wanted me to drop the investigation. What else was there to think except that it was *because* of the investigation? Hell, he probably even calculated that I'd assume that. He hoped that I'd get scared and pull out. They might send someone else in my place, but he didn't care. It was *me* he wanted to be rid of. He didn't give a shit about the investigation.'

'He wanted you gone so he could have this Sally,' he said.

'Right,' I said. 'He had no way of knowing we were partners. It

195

looked to him like we had just bumped into each other and fallen into one of those romances that come and go in your life. Since Sally and I didn't have a past, he probably thought it wouldn't mean much to me to leave her. Then, when I was gone, he could take her by force one night. He could empty out her room at three in the morning and no one would hear a thing. He's that good. The next day it would look like she just went back to wherever she came from. He'd figure it'd be a long time before anyone missed her, if ever. By then he might be tired of her himself.'

'I don't know about all of this, Swift.'

I put everything I had into my eyes.

'You've got to believe me, Sheriff,' I said. 'I *know* that's what happened. She wouldn't disappear without telling me or her boss or anyone. She isn't that kind of person. She's loyal and she's conscientious and she's an excellent detective. Trust me. You're a good cop. A woman in your county has been kidnapped, probably raped, maybe abused in other ways. You've got to do something about it.'

'It's still just your hunch —'

'For Christ's sake, Jakes!'

He leveled his forefinger at me. 'Don't you raise your voice at me, son,' he said. His eyes were cold behind the rimless spectacles. I was afraid to death of losing him.

'Sheriff,' I said evenly, 'I've been a detective for a lot of years. I'm a good one. I don't do *any*thing on blind hunches. This is *not* a blind hunch. I can recognize the work of a professional when I see it. If he's the only other one around, then he's the one we're after.' I paused, then I pleaded. 'Sally Hatch is a fine person. I need your help, Sheriff. Please.'

He loaded up on his smokeless tobacco, the way he did when he was thinking something over. I could have strangled him on the spot, without the slightest guilt.

'What is it you want I should do?' he said finally.

The feeling of relief was overwhelming. But I wasn't quite there yet, and I knew it.

'I can't take him alone,' I said, holding up the cast on my right arm as if that were the only reason. 'I need you to come with me. It wouldn't hurt to bring as many men as you can spare.'

'You can't ask me to turn my whole staff loose on what might be some wild-goose chase,' he said.

'Whatever you think is best,' I said. 'You're the one I really want. I'll lead you to his bunker. But I warn you again: this guy is dangerous. He's a fighter, and he's crazy, which makes him twice as dangerous. If Sally isn't there, okay, you've wasted some people's time and I'll eat whatever crap you feed me. But if she is, there's going to be serious trouble. A carload of men won't be too many.'

He thought some more. I wasn't nearly so frantic this time. We were going.

'I'll get Deputy Anders,' he said.

It probably represented a fair compromise to him. I'd hoped for more, but I was prepared to accept whatever I got.

'Thanks, Sheriff,' I said.

He nodded coolly. This was no favour to me. He probably only half believed the story. But he was a cop with an ingrained sense of cop duty. He'd weighed the potential seriousness of what I'd told him against the possibility that he might come up looking like a fool. The real cop in him had won out. If there was someone out there who needed help, then he was going to try to give it. I didn't care whether he liked me or not. I was just real happy to have him on my side.

He got hold of Anders, told him what to bring and to meet us in the lower parking lot at Babel. Then he turned his attention to me.

'You armed?' he asked.

I shook my head. I hadn't thought I'd need a gun to attend a funeral. He grunted and went into the next room. When he came back, he tossed me a .38 revolver with a four-inch barrel.

'Good gun,' he said.

I hefted it. It was. I checked the cylinder. Full. He dropped some extra cartridges into my hand, and I put them in my jacket pocket. I tucked the pistol into my belt. Meanwhile, he was strapping a .357 magnum to his hip. A small cannon. You shoot someone with one of those, it doesn't matter where you hit them. They die. Jakes was a man who'd want that kind of edge.

He buttoned his uniform jacket. The badge gleamed brightly, right out front there for everyone to see. For just an instant I wondered if I'd put the facts together correctly. Then the doubt vanished. Even though it meant the eternal enmity of a Faber Jakes, I'd have given anything to be wrong. But I knew that I wasn't.

'Let's go,' he said.

We rode to Babel together, in the sheriff's cruiser. On the way he had me describe Zero's bunker in detail, as well as give him a general idea as to where it lay on the land. He asked a lot of questions and he listened intently. When I'd finished, I was confident that he could handle the situation if anything happened to me.

Anders was waiting for us. He wasn't either of the deputies who had come out the night Jeff had attacked Rags. He was older, in his late thirties, and he was big, maybe six-two and two-thirty. He had a friendly Virginia farmer's face, one that had been weathered by years of living outdoors. I felt instinctively that Jakes had made a good choice.

The sheriff introduced me and then outlined what it was we were up to. His voice was all business. It betrayed none of the doubt that I knew he must feel. I admired the way he handled it. Anders would be going in expecting the worst, which is exactly what you wanted, in case that's what happened. The deputy would be ready. When Jakes had finished, we got in Anders's car and drove up over the ridge, to the end of the road. The cluster where the Evanses lived. It was a cool, clear night with a three-quarter moon. The hollow, with its little knot of houses by the creek, looked like the most peaceful spot in all the world. I felt like part of an invading army that was about to change that forever.

Jakes and Anders went to the trunk of the car and opened it. Anders took the shotgun. It was a sturdy, 12-gauge pump-action riot gun, a match for Zero's if it came to that. He slung it over his shoulder. Jakes's rifle had a sling too. It was an Armalite light assault rifle, a very high-quality weapon that I'm sure wasn't standard-issue in the sheriff's office. It was fitted with what looked to be about a thirty-round magazine. If you need more than that, you're in very deep water. It also sported a nighttime sniperscope that was raised enough so that the iron sights could also be effectively used. That was careful planning. It was tough to hit a moving shadow using a scope.

Whatever Jakes thought of my story, he wasn't skimping on the armaments.

'No heavy artillery for you, Swift,' he said. 'It ain't that I don't trust you, but . . . ' It was that he didn't trust me. I didn't care. What with the wrist cast, I didn't trust myself.

I saw a couple of faces at windows, but only Freddie ventured out to see what was happening. We were showing a lot of hardware;

Jakes and Anders were in uniform. People would take a look and decide right quick to mind their own business. But Freddie wanted to know. He would.

'Police business,' Jakes said curtly. 'Go on back inside, son.'

For a moment I thought old volatile Freddie was going to give the sheriff some lip, but Jakes's expression must have convinced him that that would be unwise. Freddie left without a word.

'Before we go,' I said, 'y'all need to understand one thing. Zero has some sensors out there. I don't know where, what kind, how good, or how many. Now, they can't be everywhere. I'll stop when I think we've reached the perimeter he's protecting. But it'll only be a guess. We'd better assume that he's gonna know we're coming.'

They nodded, and we set off down the trail. I took point, with Jakes behind me and Anders guarding the rear. I didn't like it out there, yet I felt I should lead. It was my show. Early on, my thigh began to throb. Fear is supposed to make you forget, but mine only seemed to intensify the ache.

It was slow going. The moon provided enough illumination to see, but there were still enough leaves on the trees to make it difficult. We didn't want to show any lights. And then, I was being doubly cautious. For all I knew, Zero had laid out some booby traps since I'd last visited. If he had, they'd nail me first. I tried to remember everything I'd ever learned in the army about infiltrating enemy lines.

The temptation to keep the pistol in my hand was strong, but I resisted it. I wanted the safety off. If I stumbled in the dark and I was holding the gun, it was likely to fire. In addition, if I carried it in my right hand, the weight of it would tire my damaged arm; if I carried it in my left, I would be dangerously awkward. I left it snugged behind my belt. From time to time I reassured myself by patting it gently.

We plodded ahead and finally arrived at the last fork in the trail. I pulled up short of it. This was where I figured Zero would have established his perimeter. The three of us conferred as quietly as possible.

'This is it,' I said. 'The clearing is down that fork maybe three hundred yards.'

'Where does this other fork go?' Jakes asked.

'I don't know. I've never been down there. I would imagine it

199

ends at the same rock face that's at the back of the clearing. Or else it'll just start up the mountain.'

Jakes turned to Anders. 'You think you could find it going thataway?' he asked.

'Yeah,' Anders said. He'd probably hunted these mountains all his life. He'd find it.

'Okay. You come up on him from behind.'

'It's probably the first clearing you'll come to,' I told Anders. 'Just in case, there's another way to recognize it. Right behind the bunker there's a cleft in the rock wall. It's big enough for a man to slip into. I think it's Zero's escape route.'

'Got it,' Anders said.

'What do you reckon?' Jakes asked.

'Give me fifteen minutes to get into place,' Anders said.

'Okay. Go.'

Anders slipped down the right fork. He was quiet. He stayed to the side of the trail as much as he could.

Jakes and I waited, not saying anything. When the fifteen minutes was up, he spoke. 'Let me do the talking,' he said.

'Sure.'

This time he took point. He walked to the clearing. No alarms went off, no concealed crossbows impaled us with barbed arrows.

About twenty-five yards from the bunker the floodlights came on. They were mounted back in the cliff somewhere. They were aimed at the area where the trail widened out, and they blinded anyone coming in. I raised my hand above my eyes. Jakes never even flinched.

Commander Zero — I assumed it was he — stood atop the bunker. The way the lighting was set up, he was no more than the most vague outline of a person. We could barely see him, while he had us pinned down like insects in a glass case. I have never felt so nakedly vulnerable in my life. Jakes, however, seemed calm.

'Commander,' he said, the same way he might have said *mister* or *doctor*. 'This is Faber Jakes. I'm the Nelson County Sheriff. I'd like to talk to you.'

'What about?' Zero said.

'A woman named Sally Hatch.'

'Never heard of her.'

'Then we have nothing to talk about, after all. Would you turn out the lights now?'

He took a step toward the bunker.

'Hold it!' Zero shouted. 'I don't talk to no one!'

Jakes stopped.

'Okay, let's put the guns away and talk.' It was a calm, measured voice. Anders, from over by the cliff face.

'You're surrounded, Commander,' Jakes said. 'How about let's do like the man said?'

He took a step toward the bunker, then another. His hand rested on the Armalite. He'd be able to have it firing in an instant, but he didn't want that. No matter how quick he was, he wouldn't be as quick as Zero, not if the Heckler and Koch were pointed at us. Which it undoubtedly was.

'Come on in, Anders,' Jakes said. 'Let's meet with the Commander.'

There was the sound of some scrabbling in the rocks, and then there was an explosion. For a moment the cliff was garishly illuminated, like some sound-and-light show at an archaeological monument. The figure of Commander Zero stood out starkly in the backlighting. The noise was deafening. Anders had stepped on something and he was gone.

Rock and debris came flying out at us. Something hit Zero from behind and he went down hard, but he must have bounced back up on his knee instantaneously, because he fired before Jakes even had a chance to level his rifle. The force of the slugs knocked Jakes back into me, and we fell, he on top of me. He was dead weight, dead meat.

It was a miracle I hadn't been hit. I knew that the bullets from the H&K packed enough punch to go through two bodies if they weren't deflected by bone. Jakes's flesh wasn't any real protection. I wriggled like a snake, trying to get the .38 out. Commander Zero entered the circle lighted by the floods. His face was still in shadow. I heard a faint, muffled thud from the vicinity of the bunker. I had no idea what it might be. Zero appeared not to have noticed. He'd been a lot closer to the explosion, and his ears would still be ringing.

I yanked at the pistol, but even as I did, I realized what a futile gesture it was.

'Forget it, Swift,' he said.

'Wait,' I said. 'There's no point in this. You can't get away.'

Moronic things to say. As long as I was talking, I knew I was still alive.

'I know these mountains,' he said. 'I can hide here for years.'

Moronic thing for him to say too. They'd hunt him down. No matter how good he was, he was no match for the technology of modern warfare. There'd be no long-lived guerrilla in the foothills of the Blue Ridge. From the tone of his voice I think he realized that too.

But he still raised his gun. I looked up at the shadowed instrument of my own extinction. My hand lifted automatically, to ward off the bullets. What filled my mind in that last instant? I can't remember, but I think it was nothing, nothing at all. I may have screamed.

And then his chest blew apart. It was as if I could see each droplet of blood, each individual piece of flesh, each shard of bone as it was flung out into space. I heard the shot as a separate and distinct event. My perceptions were sharpened to the nth degree and my sense of time was slowed to a crawl. Zero's body must have hit the ground in a hurry, but to me it was all slow motion. His fall fragmented into a hundred falls, every one ending in the same way, with his nose buried in the dirt two inches from Faber Jakes's lifeless feet.

The silence was so complete as to be painful. I lay there, stunned. Then I levered Jakes off me. And I heard her voice. It was little more than a croak.

'Swifty,' it said. 'Swifty?'

I ran to the bunker. Sally was lying prone on top of it. She was naked. Her right arm was extended in front of her, the Colt Commander gripped tightly in it. Her left hand still braced the firing arm. One handcuff was clamped around her wrist; the other lay at the end of its short length of chain. It was a mangled mass of metal.

She raised her head. There were deep hollows under her eyes and bruises on her cheeks. Her hair was matted and filthy, more brown than blonde. Her lips were cracked and split. She looked as if she'd lost some weight.

'Sally,' I said. 'Oh, God, Sally.' And I gathered her in my arms. She lay there until she began to shiver. Then I carried her inside the bunker and wrapped a blanket around her. I got her to drink some water. It made her cough at first, but then she consumed it hungrily. She began to get her voice back.

'He cuffed me to the water pipe,' she said.

'Sally, you don't have to talk,' I said.

'No, I want to. He wouldn't let me, because I wouldn't co-

202

operate. He starved me and he beat me and he taped my mouth sometimes. He never left me alone, not since . . . I don't know. When his alarms went off and he knew you were coming, he got the rifle and one of the pistols out of the trunk and he went outside. I was alone. He didn't think I could reach the trunk. I didn't, either, but I stretched myself and I did it.' Her wrist had been flayed bloody by the effort. 'I just got my big toe around the corner of it. It was heavy. I moved it maybe half an inch. Then I moved the other corner half an inch. I thought it took me hours to bring it across the floor. Did it take hours? He left the automatic in there. Then I heard a terrible explosion. What was that? I shot the handcuff away from the water pipe. I didn't know whether to take the pistol or the shotgun. But I realized I was too weak to handle the shotgun. When I pushed open the door to outside, it took almost all my strength. The lights almost blinded me. I wasn't even sure it was night, and I didn't know about the lights. I had to crawl up on top. He was walking toward you. He was going to kill you. I didn't think I'd ever get the gun steady; I was so weak, and the lights had made flashes that bounced around in front of my eyes. I had to lie flat. Even so, the gun wouldn't steady. I didn't know if I could hit him, but I had to shoot, didn't I? He was going to kill you. . . . '

It was an incredible story. Sally had freed herself by firing a .45 in a confined space, with all the risks that entailed, then had come crawling up out of the bunker, naked and vulnerable, without an idea in hell what was waiting for her and had somehow, weak as she was, figured it all out quickly enough to deliver a perfect heart shot at twenty yards with one of the most inaccurate weapons around. She hadn't done something that was amazing for a woman. She'd done something amazing, period.

I hugged ker and kissed her temple.

'Hatch,' I said softly, 'I think you're the most courageous person I've ever known.'

I held her then, for a long while. She was talked out. I think she dozed. There was no hurry to do anything. The dead would get no deader.

Finally she stirred and opened her eyes.

'How are you feeling?' I asked.

'Better. Can I have some more water?'

She drank, and then we were able to discuss what to do next. There was no phone in the bunker, of course. There was a radio, but neither of us knew how to operate it.

'Do you feel up to travelling?' I asked. 'I won't leave you alone here.'

'If I get something to eat,' she said.

I reclaimed some freeze-dried tuna-fish casserole. She thought that was amusing, the tuna-fish casserole, and she smiled for the first time. It was a lovely sight. Less than half the food disappeared before she was full. She pronounced herself ready to go as soon as we got some clothes on her. We had to do the best we could with one of Commander Zero's camouflage outfits. He'd destroyed everything she had.

Before we left, I looked around for Deputy Anders, just to be sure. But I knew damned well what I'd find. Nothing. I also checked the other two bodies on our way out of the clearing. They were as dead as it was possible to be.

The trail back was longer than it had ever been. We stopped whenever she needed to rest. I didn't question her about what happened, but she told me, haltingly at times, sometimes in a rush of heated words.

He'd kidnapped her on Thursday night, after I'd been gone for a day and a half and had seemed truly gone. She'd made it easy by walking up to drop in on Nancy Evans. He was waiting in the woods near the Ark. He had the .38. He told her he would kill her on the spot if she didn't come with him. She looked at his face and she believed him.

He brought her to the bunker and chained her to the water pipe. She lost track of day and night. He only left her once. She had no idea where he'd gone, or for how long, but she still tried to escape. That time he'd pushed the trunk an inch farther under the bed, and she hadn't been able to reach it.

I told her that he'd gone back to the core house at some point and stripped her room. That must have been when he did it. It would have been in the small hours of Friday morning.

The reason he kidnapped her, she said, was in order to mate with her. From the first moment he saw her he'd known that she was the one to bear his children. They'd be a new breed, he told her, trained from the start to survive no matter what happened to the world.

For a long time he tried to convince her that it was their common destiny, but she just told him he was crazy. Finally, he became enraged. He beat her and took her by force. It was the most difficult part for her to tell. I knew then what that ultimate violation was

204

like. She made me feel it. I realized that I would never again react to rape in quite the same way.

It had gone on like that for two days. Starvation, beatings and humiliation, in a savage attempt to bend her to his will. It was clear that she'd never broken. If she had, she wouldn't have been able to do what she'd done.

It was a story I would never have wanted to hear, except that it seemed to make her stronger in the telling. I waited until she was finished before giving her the news. The mystery of Temple Ballard's death had been solved, I said.

26

It took the better part of a day to sort it all out.

The first thing I did was to get the rescue squad to come for Sally. They knew the way.

Before she left, she said, 'Will I see you again?'

'Count on it,' I said.

'Well . . . thanks for coming to get me.'

'Yeah, thanks for that little number you did for my life, kid.'

It was an odd parting, awkward yet touching, heavy with feelings that could never be verbalized. The one thing I wasn't worried about was whether we'd become friends. We had.

Then came the cops. With Jakes and Anders, his senior deputy, both dead, the Nelson County Sheriff's Office was in disarray. They had quickly given up trying to pull it together and called in the state boys. The staties had taken over fairly efficiently. A state chopper had been flown in to evacuate the bodies. Jakes, Commander Zero, and whatever they could find of Anders. The bunker area had been gone over by experts from the bomb squad. No one knew how many booby traps there might be out there, and no one just wanted to leave them in the woods. The squad found one other trip mine. That was it, hopefully. After the area had been declared conditionally safe the evidence gathering crew went in. They were at it for hours.

I told my story, several times. To various cops. To my friend Jonesy from the Charlottesville *Daily Press*, whom I'd tipped. I told it all, including the resolution of the Temple Ballard affair. There was no point in holding anything back now. I'd been prophetic when I'd felt like I was bringing an invading army to Babel. Its citizens were in deep shock. The best that I could do for them was to clear up everything at once and get the invaders the hell off their land as soon as possible.

In the late morning a chartered helicopter from Richmond arrived, bearing Devin Pethco and some other brass from Fail-Safe, as well as a representative of the corporate parent. Pethco was properly solicitous but could barely contain his delight after he learned that I was going to save them their millions. I was glad to see him go when he choppered off to Charlottesville to see Sally at the University Medical Center. She was due for some serious company recognition, and she'd earned it.

The day dragged on. I somehow managed to keep going with the help of numerous cups of coffee. Finally, about mid-afternoon, they let me go. One of the deputies shuttled me to Jakes's house where I picked up Clementine and drove back to Charlottesville. I went directly to the Medical Center. First I checked on Sally, to make sure she hadn't suffered any injuries that weren't immediately apparent. I was still spooked by what had happened to Chaudri. But Sally was doing fine. Considering.

Then I looked in on Patricia. She was itching to be released, but they weren't quite ready to do it yet. Which was fine with me. I was in no condition to administer home care. I hadn't slept in a day and a half and had come within a heartbeat of having my ticket punched. After telling her an abbreviated version of the story, I drove to my apartment, went straight to bed, and slept through to Monday morning.

The dream came shortly before I awakened. I've always paid close attention to my dreams. Quite often I've had dreams that helped me make connections I was unable to make while conscious, like that chemist who made a famous discovery by dreaming of a snake eating its own tail. I've solved cases that way. In addition, I occasionally have premonitory dreams. I had a particularly eerie one during the case that ended with my wrist broken and Patricia in a coma. I don't know how such things happen, but I know they do.

This dream was brief. In it an Indian dressed like Nehru was staggering drunkenly across a barren, rock-strewn plateau. I was

206

chasing after him and wanted to catch him for some reason that wasn't clear. The sun was mercilessly hot. Despite the Indian's uneven gait, I couldn't close the gap between us, no matter how fast I ran. Eventually, he came to a cliff and just kept on going. I pulled up at the cliff's edge. I looked over. There was nothing there, only an empty blackness. The Indian was gone.

I woke up with the dream vivid in my mind. The feeling was strong that it had been a message from my subconscious. I lay there, examining it, searching for its meaning. Assume that the Indian was Chaudri. Assume that I was pursuing him because he had something to tell me. But he vanished before he could. Or did he? Maybe the message was *nonverbal*. Maybe he *was* the message. I began to get that cold, familiar feeling, like something was not quite right.

I tried to remember people's exact words. What had Spock said? That Rags was acting weird. Nervous, yes, but more than that: 'Like his balance was off.' And Lisa. She'd been sure that it was Rags whom she'd seen, because of his shape, but he hadn't moved like Rags. He'd been 'lurching'.

Okay, the guy had just murdered his lover. You'd expect him to be a little disoriented. That was enough of an explanation. Wasn't it? Maybe. It'd been what I assumed. But there was an alternative.

I thought back to a long-ago hunting trip. Myself, my father, a friend of his. I'd been young, but it was my first stay in the woods, and I recalled it like it was yesterday. It had rained hard, and we'd been cooped up in the cabin. We'd run the kerosene heater for too long in a space that wasn't ventilated quite enough. I'd gotten sick. The first symptom had been dizziness.

Carbon monoxide poisoning.

I felt the chill of that rainy weekend reaching out to me. Suppose Chaudri was innocent. Suppose he'd gone to the Ark like the rest of them, simply to talk to Ballard about something or other. And he'd found his lover dead. He wouldn't have known why. Though the shed was filled with carbon monoxide, he'd never have suspected it, because the alarm hadn't sounded yet. Maybe he'd sat there for a while, staring at Ballard's lifeless body. Then he'd freaked out. He'd stumbled from the shed, by that time suffering the first effects of poisoning himself. Dazed and confused, he'd blindly headed for home. Lisa had seen him first, but he hadn't seen her. Then he'd met Spock. After that he'd continued on to his house. As his head cleared, he decided, for reasons forever unknown, to go back to the Ark, and Spock saw him for the second time, headed that way. This scenario covered the facts perfectly up to that point.

What had happened next? That was the key question. Had Chaudri then reconnected the alarm, run from the shed, and hidden? Bender said that he had. It was possible. Rags might have taken action in order to get the body discovered and the night over with. But under the revised scenario that was extremely unlikely. Because if he *was* the killer, then he would have known how it was done, and it would have served no purpose for him to go to the Ark (the first time) and *poison himself*. And it couldn't, of course, have happened inadvertently.

Okay, suppose he wasn't the killer. Might he still have done the things he was supposed to have done? Again, it was possible. He could have figured out what had happened — by his own accidental poisoning — then decided to re-arm the device that someone else had disabled (on his second trip to the Ark), for reasons unknown. He might then have run away so as not to be found at the scene of the crime, since he would have been a likely suspect and he already had Spock to deal with in that regard. Or all of his actions might have constituted a knowing cover for somebody else. Or Bender may have lied to me. And maybe there were other possibilities that I couldn't yet see.

Now, if Rags were completely innocent, could his subsequent actions then be explained? I thought they could. He'd been the one to suggest the rearrangement of the death scene, true; but that might have simply represented a genuine concern for the future of Babel. And then he'd threatened Spock. Or had he? The boy's account of the incident had been a little confused. Perhaps Chaudri had merely asked him to keep quiet about what he'd seen, for obvious reasons, and it had been Spock who'd blown it out of proportion, because of his fear and dislike of the Indian.

There were too many ifs and buts. I'd gone to sleep secure in the belief that I'd set foot on Babel for the last time. I knew now that that had been wishful thinking. Perhaps, subconsciously, I'd known all along and it had just taken the dream to make me face the facts. There was no indication here that Rags *hadn't* done it, of course. But there was just enough doubt that I couldn't let it be.

For a moment, though, I wavered. Rags was dead. Clearing his name didn't matter a whole lot, did it? No, not in the long run. Yet in some way, here and now, it mattered to me.

So, once again, I went back through everything I'd been told about that night, probing for something, anything that would give me a clue to the truth. If only my witnesses had been able to give me the times when things had happened. But they hadn't.

And then it came to me. It was no sure thing, but it was a possibility. Maybe I didn't really need to know *absolute* times. Maybe if I knew some *relative* times, the answer would be clear. There was one person who just might be able to give me what I wanted. If he couldn't, it was hopeless. If he could . . .

After a quick visit with Patricia, I went to see him.

I didn't stop in the lower parking area this time. I drove directly up to the cluster. The Ark loomed over the land, gathering up the morning sun. It was only an indifferent, lifeless building, yet over the course of time it had somehow taken on a dark and sinister cast, like one of those Victorian mansions on the cover of a Gothic novel.

They were packing.

'Going on a trip?' I asked.

'Yes,' Mary Beth said. 'A permanent one, I think. Babel has kind of . . . lost its appeal.'

'I don't wonder. California?'

'Uh-huh. That's really home. And how are you, Loren? How's Sally?'

'Both doing fine.'

'She's nice,' she said. 'Not that it wasn't horrible, but I'm glad that it wasn't any worse. It could have been. The whole thing still gives me the creeps.'

'Yeah, me too. But Sally's young and she's a very tough cookie. She'll bounce back.'

'I believe you're right.'

'How's it going, Spock?' I asked.

'Okay.'

'You excited about going to California?'

'You know it. San Francisco's a good scene. Lots of music. They won't think I'm so weird out there.'

I laughed. 'Everyone's weird in their own way, kid. You're just you. But you're right, the city's a better place for you right now.'

'You told me that a long time ago, didn't you?'

'Yup. People need people their own age. That's not really here for you. Not in stodgy old Virginny.'

He gave his mother a look. She smiled. 'Thanks for being on my side, Swift,' he said.

'Hey, maybe you'll come back someday. I want you to remember me if you do.'

'I will.'

'So is this visit business or pleasure?' Mary Beth asked.

'Is it too schlocky to say that knowing you both has been a pleasure?'

'Way too schlocky.' She grinned. 'That means it's business, of course.'

I spread my arms in defeat. 'Okay. But I meant it. What I told Spock goes for you too. If you're back this way, you're my guests. I cost you a lot of money.'

'It was worth it to find out what happened to my husband.' She gave me a suspicious look. 'We do know, don't we?'

'Ah. Well, I'm just not sure, you see.'

'Oh, God. Loren, you are a trial.' She sat down. 'Tell me.'

'It's not to tell,' I said. 'It's to ask. And Spock's the one who may know.'

'Me?' he said.

'Yeah. I've been doing some thinking, and there's one question I should have asked you. That's the way it happens sometimes. You get wrapped up in something as complicated as this, and the key question might not occur when it should.'

'What is it? I didn't do something wrong, did I?'

'No, no. It's a matter of the timing. I need to be sure of it. Now, I realize you don't know what time it was when you met Rags in the field, but can you tell me this? The second time you saw him, you watched him go back across the field and into the woods, right?'

'Right.'

'How long after that was it that the alarm went off?'

'Gee, I don't know,' he said, shrugging.

'Five minutes? This is important, Spock.'

'No, not that long.'

'Try to think of it like this: how far down the road did you get before you heard it?'

He thought about it. 'Not real far,' he said. 'I was a little past the barn.'

'You know how fast you were walking. So we're talking about what? Two minutes?'

'Not more than that, for sure. Less, I think.'

'Okay. Let's say a minute and a half, give or take a little. That about do it?'

'Close enough.'

'Good. Now, how far up the ridge was Rags when he went into the woods?'

'About halfway.'

I paused. Was there anything else? I didn't think so.

'What does this mean?' Mary Beth asked.

'I don't know yet,' I said. 'Maybe nothing, maybe everything. I've gotta check something else out.'

'Are you going to tell us?'

'Soon. Thanks, Spock.'

I went outside. First I checked Spock's estimate. I started at the point from which he'd seen Chaudri enter the woods, and I walked from there to just past the barn. I knew Spock's normal pace. To be on the safe side, I dawdled a little, though in winter he might well have been walking faster. I clocked it. One minute and fifty-five seconds.

Then I returned to the field. The patch of woods stretched from the ridge top down to the road. If there was a path through it, that was probably the way Rags had gone. I climbed to the top, then came slowly down along the edge of the woods, searching carefully. No path.

From the bottom I took a bearing on the Ark. Then I climbed back up again, until I reckoned I was about opposite it, across the woods. I was at the approximate point where Rags had disappeared from Spock's sight. I took some deep breaths. Then I plunged in. I moved quickly, following the line of least resistance. The trees were thick, and there were fallen, dead ones strewn around. The undergrowth was heavy. It'd be less so in February, and I made allowance for that. But no matter what, I couldn't keep up speed. And I had the distinct advantage of a clear head.

When I emerged from the woods, I was slightly below the Ark. I couldn't have hit it much closer. I went around the gasifier at a trot, hyperventilating, and went through the shed door holding my breath. I crossed the shed, stood under the detector, and made the motions of connecting it up. Then I looked at my watch. Three and a half minutes. Even with all possible adjustments, it was way too much. Chaudri could not have reconnected that alarm.

Ike Bender had lied. It was just the smallest discrepancy, but it

211

was a very big lie. He had been almost unnaturally clever all the way, had calmly prepared for every possibility except the one that he couldn't have known about: that while he was on top of the ridge, watching Rags come across the field, there was someone down on the road, crouched in the shadows, watching too. The rest was evident. When Rags reached the woods, Bender had activated the alarm, then slipped out the other end of the Ark, to wait for things to begin happening.

The door to the Ark opened.

'Swift,' he said. 'I thought I heard someone in here. What a surprise.'

'Hello, Ike,' I said.

'I'm just feeding the fish. Come on in.'

I followed him into the Ark. He was throwing mounds of meal into the tanks. The fish were going nuts.

'What brings you our way?' he asked. 'The charms of Babel get to you?'

'I think you know why I'm here.'

'Why, no, I don't.'

'You lied to me, Bender.'

He set down the bucket of meal. 'Whatever do you mean?' he said.

'I mean that you never saw Chaudri going into the shed to set off the alarm.'

'Swift, I told you the truth.' He looked perplexed.

I glared at him. 'It won't work, Bender. You're one of the best actors I've ever known, I admit it. Those tears after Rags's funeral, they really got to me. They were so genuine. I'd have believed anything you said after that. How'd you manage it?'

'They were real tears.'

'Sure.'

He looked at me for a long time. Even now it seemed like he was carefully weighing his options. He had a complex mind. I'd never be able to read what was going on inside it. Finally, he sighed.

'You have some proof of all this?' he said.

I nodded. 'A witness. Someone you didn't know was there. Rags couldn't have re-armed the detector. He didn't have time. I can prove it.'

'I believe you,' he said. 'I think that you are a man who does not bluff. Will you at least concede that I cried for Rags because he was

212

my friend?'

'No.'

'I'm sorry you feel that way. I am not an evil man, Swift. I'm as capable of love as you are.'

'You're a killer. You murdered a man in as coldly calculating a way as I've ever seen.'

'Well, you can't be sure of that, can you?'

'I'm sure,' I said.

'You'll never convince a jury.'

'I'll find a way. Why'd you do it, Ike?'

Again he stared at me while he pondered. Then he shrugged.

'Temple and I were always rivals,' he said. 'The two finest minds at MIT in our day. I was always the better scientist, technically. But the great ones are never the most technically proficient. They're the ones who can make those leaps where you have to have intuition. Temple Ballard was a great one. We would have gotten to the moon without him, but it would have taken longer.'

'You hated him,' I said.

'No, not personally. You couldn't. I was glad we ended up in different parts of the country, though. I really never expected to see him again. When he wrote and told me about his life after Houston, I felt in some way vindicated. He'd gone down and out. I'd managed to hang on to our ideals and accomplish something of value. I *wanted* him to come here. I was eager to show off what I'd done to one of the few people who could really appreciate it.'

'But it didn't work. Ballard upstaged you again.'

'Babel, as I conceived it,' he said, 'was a great experiment. A minimal-technology approach to self-sufficiency. The applications are boundless. We're talking about eradicating hunger here, Swift. Temple murdered that dream. He was a slave to the gadgetry of our age. Unfortunately, he had the charisma necessary to sell his vision to other people. He carried the day. Rather than destroy democracy at Babel, I went along.'

'While you plotted his death,' I said.

'Without Temple the high-tech people are powerless. He was the only one who truly understood all the details. It's only a matter of time until the original vision is restored. In another year, at most, I will have done it.'

'No, you won't.'

'Swift,' he said, coming over to me, 'does any of this really make

213

a difference to you?'

'Rags was innocent,' I said.

'We're all innocent, in our hearts. And we're all guilty of murder. The condition of the world is our collective responsibility. I'm trying to make it better.'

'No sale, Ike. You use the end to justify the means and you can rationalize anything.'

'They're all leaving me,' he said mechanically. 'All the good ones. It's been too much. Temple, Rags, Jeff, Zero. Too much. My people are packing their bags and leaving me. They shouldn't do that. They should stay, Swift. Babel is the way.'

I had thought he'd surely give it up when he realized the situation was hopeless. He was a man of logic. But I was wrong. It was all there in his eyes. They were flat and lifeless. They looked at me as they must have looked at Temple Ballard in the last days of his existence. They looked at me and saw merely another obstacle in the path.

He sighed. 'Swift,' he said resignedly, and he reached out his arms as if to embrace me.

I shrank back on instinct, but not far enough and not fast enough. He seized both my arms, just above the elbow, and pinned them to my sides. Though he seemed weary beyond words, his blocky body was enormously strong.

'What the *hell*—' I said.

'Swift,' he said softly, 'I like you. I do.'

He lifted me and carried me to one of the tanks.

'Bender!' I yelled. 'For Christ's sake, this is *insane! Bender!*'

He raised me up, ever so gently, and folded me over the top of the tank. I kicked madly, but he wedged himself between my legs.

'Goodbye, Swift,' he said, and he lowered my head into the water.

I fought as hard as I could. I wasn't nearly good enough. The breath I'd taken before going under used itself up. Catfish brushed my face, their whiskers like windblown straw. I began to sink into a bottomless blackness. I stopped struggling. It no longer seemed worth it. Falling, falling. I was free. Far, far away, there was a pinpoint of golden light. It began to grow, as slowly as the opening of a flower. I fell toward the light. It felt like heading for home. . . .

It was a face of such unearthly beauty that I gasped. That made me choke and sputter. The dead still have to breathe, I thought.

214

But dying is not so bad, if there is yet the beauty of women.

And then she spoke.

'Swift,' she said, 'can you hear me?' She slapped my face. Her hand felt like good old flesh and blood.

'Swift, it's Mary Beth. Come on!'

I coughed again. I was lying on the dirt floor of the Ark. The morning light was streaming in. I was alive. Mary Beth was squatting, her hands on my chest. Spock stood looking down at us.

'What?' I croaked. It was the only word I could think of.

'Why didn't you just take us, you idiot?' she said. 'You're lucky Spock convinced me that the way you were acting, we ought to follow you. And you're *damned* lucky I know CPR.'

'Ike?'

'We tried to pull him away, but he was like a madman. Spock had to brain him with that silly nightstick of his. I never thought I'd be glad he carries it. What in the hell was going on here, anyway?'

'You called the cops?'

'Of course.'

I managed myself to a sitting position, propped against one of the tanks. My lungs ached. Terrible pain was gathering in my head. I felt as though the world were on crooked. But I was alive. None of the rest mattered, not at all.

'Thanks, Spock,' I said.

'Oh. Sure.'

'Come on,' Mary Beth said. 'Why was Ike Bender trying to kill you?'

'Well,' I said, 'it's kind of a long story.'

27

It was Saturday afternoon. Patricia had been released from the hospital and we'd spent four days rediscovering the pleasures of a quiet home life. Now I was at my apartment, alone, preparing my final report for Fail-Safe Detection Systems, Inc. I had a tumbler of Jameson over ice, and classic feel-good Frisco rock and roll on the box. Big Brother, the 'Plane, Garcia and Co. Come what may, I was a teenager in the sixties. I loved that music then, and I love it now.

Contentment is an elusive thing. All of the world's good intentions won't get it for you, but then it can even be found doing something as mundane as typing a boring report, if the moment is a good one. And my recent moments had all been good ones. They were those of someone sprung lately from the dead.

The phone rang.

'Hello, Loren,' she said, and here came that special sinking feeling that is brought on only by certain voices from the past.

'Hello, Marilyn.' My ex-wife. I hadn't spoken with her in six years. 'How are you?'

'Not so good. Can I talk to you?'

'Sure, Marilyn.' I settled into the couch with the Jameson next to me.

'I just broke up with Paul,' she said.

'Who's Paul?'

'He's the one who came after Lee.'

'Oh.' Lee I remembered.

'I can't figure men.'

'Me, neither,' I said. 'Or women, for that matter.'

'You remember how I always criticized you for not being able to commit yourself to anything?'

'Uh-huh.' How could I forget? It was what we broke up over.

'Well, Lee was committed. Paul too. They're fighting for the right causes, Loren.' I knew the causes: nuclear disarmament, international peace, the Democratic Party. I even believed in a lot of them. But some people are joiners, some aren't. I'm not. 'Good men,' she went on. 'I've seen them lay their lives on the line. I was sure it was what I wanted. No, I'm still sure. It *is* what I want. I feel too guilty if I'm not *doing* anything.'

'I know that,' I said. 'You don't have to apologize for it.'

'I'm not apologizing. It's just that it's too depressing, the way it always turns out. We believe in the same things. We care for each other. But in the end they can't let go of their conditioning. Lee and Paul, they were both the same. Trying to save the world is *important*, Loren. But maybe it's just as important for one man to treat one woman as his equal. Maybe that's where it all has to begin.'

'Yes. That's what I think too.'

'God, it's taken me a long time to see that,' she said. 'I was